ROSES ARE RED

MIRANDA RIJKS

inkubator

.

1

dam Palmer. He thinks he is so superior, blessed with intellect and good looks. At the top of his game, living in a period English house, surrounded by his loving family. Money is no object for Adam Palmer. Perhaps I should rephrase that. Money allows him to buy whatever objects he desires. You only have to look at the ostentatious Bentley parked outside his front door to know that.

But Adam Palmer is just an animal, as we all are. A creature of habit. He may think he holds all the cards, but he doesn't.

I do.

Because I know him as well as, if not better, than he knows himself.

This evening he arrived home from work. He grabbed a beer from the fridge. He had a screaming match with his wife. Nothing unusual there. It happens most nights. Then he disappeared into the bowels of the house, and now, ten minutes later, here he is, naked except for a pair of garish yellow-and-green tropical-print swimming trunks, striding towards his outdoor swimming pool. A large blue-and-white striped towel is draped over his left shoulder, a designer brand, no doubt. His Rolex watch is strapped to his wrist. It's an Oyster Cosmograph Daytona made from platinum with a blue face. It costs nearly sixty grand. I know because I Googled it. He is fit for his forty-eight years. Broad shoulders, a well-toned stomach, a dark hairy chest and a confident gait. It's his hair that gives away his age, receding at the temples and on the crown of his head, dark brown waves splattered with grey. I'm surprised he hasn't got himself a hair transplant.

He drops his towel on a sun lounger and then lifts his arms up into the air, swinging them in large circles.

My heart is pumping now. The time has come.

He stretches his left leg and then his right leg, and now he takes five paces to the end of the pool. If he looks, he might see it. A tiny wire that runs across the grout line of the pale stones surrounding the turquoise pool. A thin wire that touches the base of the metal steps. Pace one, two, three... His eyes are fixed on the horizon, that sweeping vista of ancient woodland that surrounds the five-acre garden. He has stepped right over it and hasn't noticed.

I let out my breath and for the first time register the burning pain in my legs. I've been crouching behind a bush for too long. And now, here he is. Ready to go. Climbing up onto the diving board at the deep end of the pool, flexing his muscles, and then, with his hands held together high above his head, he makes a little jump and dives neatly into the pool with a modest splash.

A grin edges at the corners of my mouth. I press the button on my phone. The remote control.

Done.

I'm ready to show myself, to execute the next step.

But there is silence.

Where the hell is he?

I expect gasps and spluttering.

I wait. Ten seconds, twenty seconds, a whole minute. I have a good view of the house and the pool. There is no one outside.

Adam Palmer hasn't surfaced. It's worked. Wonderfully well.

And then I have to control my laughter. It's hilarious, really. He's just sunk straight to the bottom. Now I need to get out of here without leaving any evidence behind. I scroll through my mental checklist.

I pull the wire. It's five metres long and easy to pull back. I coil it up and put it in my rucksack. And now I tiptoe along the perimeter of the garden, darting behind large oak trees and rhododendron bushes, keeping in the dark shadows, holding my breath every time I accidentally step on a twig, until I reach the barbed wire fence that edges the public footpath. I crawl underneath it and then walk briskly along the wooded trail. People walk their dogs along here, but I've got that one covered. If I see anyone, I'll call out for my imaginary Buster – an Irish wolfhound perhaps, or a Staffie.

But I don't see a soul.

I'm safe.

Shame about Adam Palmer.

2

There was a summer storm last night. Torrential rain and heavy wind whistling through the hairline cracks in our old, creaking house and pummeling the thick, verdant branches of the English oaks and beeches in the garden. Perhaps it was a pathetic fallacy, a forewarning of what is to come today. But this morning, the sky is a clear pale blue, and everyone except me seems to have a spring in their step.

I turn the car into the industrial estate and drive slowly towards our car park. Most mornings, I'm on autopilot and I don't look. Not properly look, anyway. I'm normally in a hurry, having dropped the kids at school and eager to get behind my desk to come up with some exciting marketing strategy or try out a new piece of crafting kit. But today I'm in no hurry, despite the fact our board meeting should have started five minutes ago. I glance up at our nondescript red-brick building with its white PVC windows and door and notice that the *r* in the company's name has slipped. The result of the storm, no doubt. It reads *Cacking Crafts* rather than *Cracking Crafts*.

Bloody hell. It's exactly how I feel. Shit.

I snigger.

I park my black Porsche Cayenne in my allocated space, in front of the sign that reads 'Sales & Marketing Director', wedged between Ajay's dark red Mercedes on the left and Adam's navy Bentley on the right. A row of ostentatious, ridiculously expensive cars that demonstrates to the world just how far we have come. Adam bought my Cayenne. I returned home one March day two years ago to find it and the Bentley parked at the front of the house. I wanted to send them both back. There was absolutely nothing wrong with my Skoda estate. Adam threw a hissy fit, and back then I was still trying to be the pacifist, so after he reassured me we could afford a fleet of the things, I accepted the car. It would be churlish to say I don't enjoy driving it. I do.

I walk in through the front door, clutching my files, my stilettos clip-clopping on the vinyl floor, past the open-plan office towards the boardroom. Nicky pirouettes before me and I jump. She has flawless ebony skin and large white teeth that have a wide gap between them. She's the organiser of my diary and she keeps me focused.

'They're waiting for you,' she whispers. 'Is everything ok?'

'Other than the fact we're now Cacking Crafts and not Cracking Crafts, it's all hunky-dory!' It's not fair of me to be sarcastic with Nicky, but I can't help it.

'I know. Unfortunate. Rod will fix the sign this morning. Would you like a coffee? Everyone else has got one.'

'I'm fine. Thanks, Nicky. Better get going.'

My lovely assistant nods and lets me go. I tug down my navy linen skirt and straighten my jacket, then open the door. I still can't get used to wearing formal clothes. Another edict from Adam. I dress up for meetings, and the rest of the time I'm in jeans and hand-knitted jumpers.

'Good morning and sorry I'm late,' I say as I walk into the boardroom. I had hoped that Ajay might have shifted the chairs around, but no. We're in our normal places, and Adam and I have to face each other across the table. It's our monthly management meeting, where our eight most senior executives report on the previous month and share their outline plans for the forthcoming month.

'Morning, Lydia,' they reply in their varying pitches and accents. Adam doesn't look up.

'Right. As we're all here, let's get started on the agenda,' Ajay says. 'Number one: last month's sales. Adam, can you talk us through the figures, please?'

I zone out.

Yes, we have come a very long way.

WE SET up Cracking Crafts nineteen years ago. Cassie, my best friend, and I took a Greyhound bus holiday along the west coast of America. I was blown away by all the homespun crafts and the hobbyists attempting to make a living from their passions. With her startling blue hair, everyone thought Cassie was the one into crafts; but it was me. When we returned to England, I declared that I was going to set up a shop selling new crafting gizmos from all over the world. My ambitions were modest, just the desire to indulge in my knitting and card-making hobbies (which were seriously uncool back then) and hopefully meet other like-minded folk. Although I had the idea, with a mediocre degree in textiles from a low-ranking college and parents who had zero business experience, I had no clue how to go about making my shop a reality.

One night, shortly after we got back from our grand tour, Cassie and I were out with friends. Ajay sat down next to me. He had recently got together with Marianne. They seemed like an unlikely couple. He had just turned thirty, a handsome Asian man with a cut-glass accent. She was a year younger than me; a peroxide blonde who had had recently begun an apprenticeship at a small hairdresser in town, a shy girl despite her brassy appearance. Our mums were friends, and we used to hang around together growing up. Despite having little in common, I liked Marianne. She didn't say much, but when she spoke, she was hilarious.

Ajay asked me what I was doing, and when I explained my vision, he told me I should set up a bricks-and-mortar business as well as take the brand online. What brand? I asked.

Three hours later, we had a basic plan, and I had a business partner. Marianne didn't get a say in the matter, not that she seemed to mind. Two months down the line, we were awarded a business loan from The Prince's Trust. We split the shares fifty-fifty, and I opened up our first shop in Worthing. Ajay carried on working as an IT manager for a hardware group, helping me in the evenings and on his rare days off. Marianne supplied us with food. I ran daily courses on knitting and scrapbooking, macramé and pot throwing. The shop was a riot of colour, and it seemed as if I had caught the crest of a wave. Crafting was big and sales were impressive. A year later, we opened a second shop in Brighton, followed by another in Horsham. Ajay quit his day job and joined Cracking Crafts full time. That same year, he married Marianne, and aged twenty-three she gave birth to their son, the first of their three children.

Ajay was, and still is, a tech wizard; it's largely thanks to his business acumen and foresight that Cracking Crafts now has over fifty shops around the UK, one of the most profitable crafting websites in Europe, and a multimillion-pounds turnover. The media describes Cracking Crafts as the number-one go-to brand for people – mainly middle-aged, middle-class women like me who like to do home crafts. Not bad for a first-generation immigrant and a girl from a council estate.

Cracking Crafts was two years old when I met Adam.

I was carrying a bulky, heavy box full of fun new products that had arrived from China, and I was eager to try them out. Dressed in scraggy patchwork jeans and an old white long-sleeve T-shirt, I pushed open the door to our largest meeting room with my bum, edging in backwards. The only time we used the room was for important meetings with the bank manager, and I expected it to be empty.

I jumped and nearly dropped the box.

'Who are you?'

The man looked up from his laptop and hurried over to assist me.

'Adam Palmer. I'm your auditor.'

When his hand brushed mine, I shivered.

If there was one thing that Adam Palmer didn't look like, it was an accountant. He had the face and the physique of a male model, smoldering dark looks, designer stubble and an open-necked shirt. And I couldn't stop staring at him.

Almost a year to the day we met, Adam and I got married. Ten months later, Mia was born, followed three years later by our son Oliver. Two years after our wedding, Adam joined Cracking Crafts as our finance director. Ajay oversaw operations and technology, and I did the marketing, including presenting our products on online shopping channels. We made a good team, Ajay, Adam and I. I say *did*. We are still a team.

Although today, I'm not so sure that the word *good* still stands.

I TRY to focus on the agenda. It's hard. I have a pounding headache and I'm worrying about Adam. *Worry* is too weak a word. I seem to be carrying around a leaden lump in my sternum these days, fearful as to what he's going to do next. How is it possible that the person I thought was the love of my life has turned into my enemy? An enemy that I have to be around twenty-four seven, at work and at home.

'Lydia, what do you think?' Ajay asks.

'Sorry, I was miles away,' I murmur, embarrassed.

Ajay sighs. 'Last month, Adam proposed closing down our five least-profitable stores. We agreed we would make a decision today. Now you've had time to reflect on it, what are your views, Lydia?'

'I still don't think it's right. I have a couple of proposals for growth that may do wonders for our profits and obviate the need to close down any stores,' I say brightly. 'We have several new product ranges coming in that have done really well in America–'

Adam interrupts. 'First rule of business basics. We all know that if something has done well in the States, there is no guarantee that it will succeed here. Not a reason to bring them on board. Have you done your market research?'

Adam speaks in the tone he uses when chastising the children when they have done something silly.

I try to ignore him. 'The ranges would be ideal for BUYIT TV, and I was thinking we could approach some of the other TV channels, such as QVC and Home Shopping Network, as well as social media influencers–'

Adam interrupts me again. 'No. You just don't grasp the fact that we are hemorrhaging cash. Do you want me to explain the spreadsheet to you yet again?' He sighs. 'I did explain it to her a couple of days ago.' He rolls his eyes as he glances around the room, but no one meets his gaze. The wave of embarrassment that envelops our staff is palpable, causing them to shift uneasily on their chairs and tense their shoulders.

Ajay pushes his chair back and stands up, then leans forwards with his palms on the table. 'I don't know about you guys, but I could do with a coffee break. Why don't we take ten minutes out? Adam and Lydia, perhaps I could have a word with you both in my office?'

The other managers bolt from the boardroom.

. . .

Our offices are in a row. Mine is nearest the boardroom, Ajay's is next, and Adam's is closest to the pool of staff who sit in an open-plan office. From the outside, our premises are functional: a warehouse and office block located in a business park in Partridge Green, just outside Horsham. Inside is a riot of colour – in my room at least. My office has turquoise walls, a cerise velvet sofa and a large glass-and-chrome desk. One wall is covered in wooden crates used as shelves. Inside each are brightly coloured yarns, stacks of fabric offcuts and the latest must-have crafting tools. I love the colour, the haphazard collection of crafting delights and particularly my crafting table, where, when I have time, I try out some of the newest products. I'm like a kid in a sweetie shop.

In contrast, Adam's office has white walls, a black roller blind and an old-fashioned wooden pedestal desk, which he keeps clear of clutter. Perhaps the difference in our offices says it all.

Ajay leads us into his office. The walls are lined with beautiful landscape photographs in frames that we sell. The photographs were all taken by Ajay: Tuscan hills, the jagged mountains of the Dolomites and the Amsterdam canals. But mostly, they are vistas of the green, rolling hills of the South Downs throughout the seasons, and the atmospheric lights caught in the woodlands surrounding Horsham. Ajay is an accomplished photographer. On top of his silver filing cabinet are three photographs of Marianne and their kids.

He waves his hand at the two chairs in front of his desk and shuts the door firmly behind him. I feel as if we're the naughty kids being brought in for a dressing-down from the headmaster.

'This has got to stop,' Ajay says as he sinks into his swivel chair with a sigh. 'Your warring is killing off the business. If Lydia gives an instruction, you, Adam, cancel it. If Adam says we need to tighten the purse strings, you, Lydia, opt for expansion. Do you know how many staff we have lost in the past two months?'

Adam is staring out of the window. I shake my head meekly.

'Seven. Two store managers, four from head office here, and this morning, Joe, Adam's deputy, gave us three months' notice. We have lost more people in the past month than we did in the whole of the previous three years. The atmosphere in the office is horrendous, staff morale is at its all-time lowest, and we're about to have our second loss-making quarter in a row. And do you know why that is?'

'Declining economy and political mayhem,' Adam says, with narrowed eyes.

'That doesn't help, but the real reason is your warring. It's killing Cracking Crafts.'

Adam stands up suddenly, knocking his chair backwards. He places the palms of his hands onto Ajay's desk and leans forwards. 'You're being melodramatic. Our relationship is our business and no one else's. Do you understand?'

'Surely you get what–'

But Adam doesn't let Ajay finish his sentence. He storms out of the office, slamming Ajay's door behind him.

Ajay closes his eyes and lets out a long sigh. I right the chair that Adam knocked over.

'I'm sorry,' I say. 'It's an impossible situation.'

Ajay looks at me. I see pity in his dark eyes and a weariness in his sallow face. 'You need to sort it, Lydia. At this rate, one or the other of you will have to go. You need to be civilised to each other; put the interests of the business above your personal quarrels.'

'I know,' I say softly.

I gaze out towards the car park. Adam's Bentley Continental speeds from his parking space, and it's only the impressive power of the car that stops it from screeching and spinning as he turns at high speed onto the exit road.

'He's gone. Let's go back to the boardroom,' I say.

'I think you and I should go out for a drink at lunchtime,' Ajay says, picking up a folder from his desk.

THE WEAVER'S Arms pub is located down a narrow country lane about ten minutes from the office. Ajay and I used to go there often, and many of our most important business decisions were made at a little wobbly table in an alcove surrounded by low oak beams. But about five years ago, Adam had an upset stomach, which he attributed to their food, and we haven't been there since.

Today, Ajay and I are back, seated at our regular table. I assume the place has changed hands during the past few years, because the walls have been painted a rich dark blue, the colour of a summer's night sky, and the tables are no longer rickety.

'Are you getting divorced?'

'At some point,' I say, holding my glass of bitter lemon tightly.

'What does that mean for the business?'

'I don't know. We haven't talked about settlements and stuff.'

'What does your lawyer say?'

I scrunch up my eyes. 'I haven't got a lawyer. Not yet.'

Ajay grabs my hand. 'But he'll screw you, Lydia. Adam's a great accountant; he'll use every loophole in the book to make sure he comes out of this smelling like roses.'

'You've never told me before that you don't like him,' I murmur.

'I do like him.' Ajay releases my hand, but his eyes suggest otherwise. 'Well, I don't like how he's behaving towards you, and I don't agree with his current ideas for Cracking Crafts, but generally he's a good guy, and he's an excellent financial director. But this isn't just about your marriage. Your arguing and his erratic behaviour are in danger of affecting the livelihoods of over a couple of hundred people. You must fix this and get a good solicitor.'

'We've talked about divorce, but haven't started proceedings yet. I think he's having an affair again. And the children don't know anything.' I sigh.

'Children aren't stupid. They'll be picking up on what's going on. Get this sorted, Lydia.'

I let out a groan as I close my eyes. 'Honestly, Ajay, I don't know what to do. Mia has exams coming up, and I don't want to rock the boat right now. I'd rather have the discussion in the school holidays.'

'Ok, love,' Ajay says, leaning over and giving me a kiss on the cheek. 'You know I'm always there for you, don't you?'

Tears come to my eyes as I nod at him.

'And Adam. He's not a bad man.'

'I know that, but he's been acting strangely ever since his father died nine months ago. I suggested that he go to therapy to discuss it. He went ballistic at the idea.'

'It's hard for all of us when we become orphans, whatever our age.'

'He wasn't even close to his dad. After his mother died six years ago, I had to force Adam to visit his dad.'

'Marianne was depressed for months after her mother died. It affects us all in different ways.' Ajay tips back the remainder of his Coca-Cola.

'How is Marianne?' I realise I haven't seen her for ages. The last time we met, she told me how hard she was finding her empty nest.

'She's fine,' Ajay says, crossing his arms and briefly glancing away. 'I suppose we'd better get back to the office.'

As I stand up, I feel exhausted. Ajay is right. Adam and I need to sort things. But how, I really don't know.

3

It is just after 1 p.m. Adam hasn't been in the office all morning. I don't know where he is or what he's doing. Nicky might know, but I can't be bothered to ask. He was at home, swimming lap after rapid lap, when I eventually got back yesterday, having collected the kids from school after my lunch with Ajay. Adam ignored me all evening and walked out of the room when I said we needed to talk.

We are running some big promotions on craft kits to get the kids (or, more appropriately, their parents) through the long summer holidays. Things such as 'make your own wigwam' or 'crochet a bikini'. It's up to me to come up with marketing slogans for our in-store promotions as well as articles for our blog and website. Business is never great in the summer, when people prefer to be outside rather than indoors making things. But I'm acutely aware of our poor sales and am desperate to come up with some bright ideas.

My mobile phone rings. Oliver's name flashes up. My heart sinks. It's never good when one of the kids calls me during the day.

'What's up, love?'

'Mum, I forgot my games kit. We've got cricket this afternoon and I'm going to be in such trouble. Please, Mum, will you drop it into school?' His voice trembles. This is Oliver's first year at senior school and the transition has not been easy. He has moved from a small local primary where he was a big personality, well liked by all, to a big private school with kids from all over, and although my two are day children because we live nearby, half the pupils at the school board. He has two or three close friends, but he has definitely become more reserved over the past year, and I worry about him.

'All right,' I say, knowing that Adam would be livid if he finds out that I have helped Oliver *out of a mess of his own making* again. 'I'll wait outside the main gate in half an hour. Have you had lunch?'

'No, not yet.'

'Don't miss lunch, Ollie. You need to keep up your energy.'

'Yes, Mum,' he says, with a drawl. 'See ya.'

It will take me a good fifteen minutes to get home and then another ten minutes to drive to school, so I haven't got long.

'I'll be back within the hour,' I say to Nicky as I hurry out of the offices.

I DRIVE HOME QUICKLY. There's little traffic at this time of day, but when I turn into the driveway of our beautiful eighteenth-century farmhouse, I'm surprised to see Adam's Bentley parked outside the front door. I wasn't expecting him to be home.

I unlock the front door, kick off my shoes and take the stairs two steps at a time, rushing up towards Oliver's bedroom – the smallest of our six bedrooms. Goodness knows what sort of mess it will be in. Our lovely cleaner, Daria, comes twice a week, but her daughter was sick on Monday, so the house isn't looking it's best. At the top of the stairs, I turn left onto the upstairs corridor, past the modern abstract paintings that

Adam bought three years ago at obscene expense, and then I glance down and notice that my toenails desperately need a new coat of nail polish when I run slap bang into…

'Marianne? What the hell?'

She takes a step backwards, a look of absolute horror on her face. She has one of our large blue towels wrapped around her torso, her sunbed-bronzed legs and arms are bare, and her hair is wet. It is quite obvious that she has stepped straight out of the shower.

I stand stock-still and stare at her. Marianne is meant to be my friend. We have known each other most of our lives. She is married to my business partner.

And she is having an affair with my husband.

'It's not what it seems,' she says pathetically, but the flush on her face, her oscillating eyes and the squirming of her hands betray her words.

'You! You're having an affair with my husband! How could you do that! How could you betray me?'

I know I'm shouting, stabbing my finger at her, but I don't care. How dare she stand here, in my house, with my towel wrapped around her surgically enhanced bust!

'Adam,' I spit.

'He's in the shower. Please, Lydia. Please don't create a fuss. I'm sorry that we hurt you, but Adam said you're getting divorced and–'

'Because he's been cheating on me with *you*! That's why we're getting divorced. I thought he'd have better taste than…' I change tack. 'Ajay! Does your husband know? Does Ajay know that you're a lying, scheming, unfaithful bitch?'

Tears spill down her cheeks. I don't care.

'I'm sorry, Lydia. We didn't mean to fall in love.'

'Get out of my house!' I spit the words out.

'Please, Lydia. Please don't tell Ajay. I'll tell him soon. Don't break his heart.'

'You might have thought of that before you banged my husband,' I say, pushing her against the wall as I walk past. I stride into Oliver's room, trying to control the shock, the pain, the humiliation. Fortunately, his cricket whites are still in his games kit bag, so I grab the bag and rush out of his room. Marianne has disappeared.

'Fuck you, Adam!' I shout at the top of my voice as I career back down the stairs. I shove my feet into my pumps and slam the front door behind me. As I pass his Bentley, I kick his front tyre. 'Fuck you, Adam,' I say, more quietly this time.

I get into my car and burst into tears.

I suspected that Adam had been having an affair. Or, if I'm honest with myself, I knew. It's not the first time. It's not even the second time. It got to the point where I didn't want to know. We've been sleeping in different rooms for months. And now I just want him out of my life.

But sleeping with *Marianne*. That's such a betrayal. She is my friend. Did they not stop to think how much pain they would be causing Ajay and me? And it's not even as if she's a younger, prettier version of me. One year my junior, she's a self-absorbed stay-at-home mother, whose children have fled the nest. I have no idea what she does all day. Ajay doesn't often talk about her, but I had no reason to think their marriage was also in trouble.

'I hate you, Adam Palmer!' I scream as I let the tears flow.

Shit. How am I meant to get through this? I wipe my eyes and glance at the clock. I've got to get a move on; otherwise Oliver will get into trouble.

I don't know how I drive to school without crashing the car. I can barely see out of my tear-clogged eyes. I suppose I'm on autopilot. My mobile phone rings. Adam's name flashes up on the dashboard. I kill the call. A minute later, it rings again. I switch the phone onto silent.

I pull up just before the zebra crossing and turn on the car's warning lights. I wipe my nose and eyes and take a deep breath. Oliver is waiting on the other side of the gate, peering at the car. I rush out, his sports bag over my shoulder.

'Here you go, love,' I say, shoving the bag through the railings.

'Are you okay, Mummy?' he asks, frowning.

'Yes, sweetheart. Not sure if I'm coming down with a cold or am allergic to something in the office. Off you go. You don't want to be late.' I shock myself how good I am at lying.

'Thanks, Mum!' He turns around and runs at full pelt towards the school. I stand watching for a moment and then I hear a teacher's strident voice.

'Oliver Palmer, it is forbidden to run!'

I sigh. I hope he doesn't get an order mark. He takes school punishments so seriously. I turn around and walk slowly back to the car.

When I've climbed in, I pick up my phone. I have four missed calls from Adam and three text messages.

'I'm sorry you had to find out like that, Lyd. Please don't tell Ajay.'

'Please answer the phone.'

'I know you're hurting but we need to talk.'

'Fuck off!' I say out loud, and chuck the phone onto the passenger seat. It bounces off and lands on my craft bag. I've always got a knitting or crocheting project on the go that I leave in the car to fill up the time I spend waiting for the kids.

I drive. Around and around town, out onto country roads. I consider calling Cassie or Fiona, my two closest friends, but they will both be at work, and I don't think I can handle sympathy right now. But it's hard to think straight when I imagine Adam having sex with Marianne in our home. I pull up on a lay-by and sob. After ten minutes or so, the anger takes hold once again. I grab my mobile phone and scroll through my messages.

'Please come home. We need to speak before the kids return from school.'

Adam is right about that at least, and I know exactly what I'm going to say to him.

I slam the front door closed behind me as I stride through the house to our massive state-of- the-art kitchen. All I can hear is the blood pumping around my head and my heartbeat drumming on my eardrums. I clench my fingers, and my jaw aches from tension.

Adam is sitting at the kitchen table in his normal place, a mug of coffee in front of him. He leaps up when I enter the room.

'I'm–'

'Shut up,' I say. 'You will listen to me for once. I'm not stupid. I knew you were having an affair, but with Marianne! You disgust me.'

'Lyd–'

'I said shut the fuck up. You have lied and cheated, and I've had enough. I want you out of the house. I don't care where you go.' I point to the front door.

'No, Lydia. I'm not going anywhere.' He takes a step towards me. I take a step backwards.

'Yes, you are. You forfeited the right to stay in this house. I'm going to divorce you on grounds of adultery.'

'We have already agreed to get divorced, but if you state I'm an adulterer, I will–'

'You will do what? You see, the thing is, Adam, you *are* an adulterer, and I'll prove it to the courts. I'll show what a shit father you are and get sole custody of the children.'

'Do not bring the children into this!' His square jaw juts forwards and a large vein throbs on his neck.

'You might have thought about that before you screwed Marianne and the countless women who came before her.'

'Look, I'm sorry, Lydia. I shouldn't have brought Marianne here.'

'So it's all right to shag the bitch, but it was a step too far to bring her here?'

'I'm just saying let's be reasonable. Marianne will tell Ajay in her own time. Let's be grown up. We can share custody of the children.'

'No. You are a liar, and I don't want you anywhere near Mia and Oliver.'

'You're being unreasonable.'

'And you are the epitome of reason? You've lied and lied and lied.'

He flinches. I know my voice is getting louder and higher pitched. Adam hates it when I scream.

'Don't push me, Lydia; otherwise I will prove you're an unworthy mother.'

'What!' I am speechless. Where the hell did that come from? How dare he! What has he ever done for the children other than spoil them with excessively expensive gifts in a futile attempt to buy their love?

I shake my head, astounded. Now he is talking a load of utter bullshit. I have been Mia and Oliver's principal carer since the day they were born. I have been the person who has juggled parenting, home and work. I am the one who makes sure they do their homework, and it is me they come to when they are sad or confused or scared. And he has the audacity to suggest he should get sole custody!

I can't listen to this anymore. I shake my head in disbelief.

'Oh, fuck off!' Adam says. He storms out of the kitchen and slams the front door behind him.

'Fuck off yourself,' I say quietly. Then I let the tears come and I sink to the kitchen floor.

4

After Adam leaves, I tear the sheets off his bed and grab the still-wet towels from the spare bathroom and shove them in the washing machine on a 90-degrees wash. I want to boil away all traces of Marianne. I wonder if I should get the locks changed so he can't come back into the house, but I suppose I should take legal advice before doing that.

With tears dripping down my cheeks, I pace around the house and then walk past the swimming pool and down through our five acres of mature garden to my favourite spot. It's where I meditate (on the handful of times I've actually done that), and it's where I found a four-leaf clover the first summer we moved here. We have a small brook that runs along the bottom of our garden, away from the manicured lawns and shrub-filled beds. This is the wild place, a copse packed with beech and oak trees heavy with leaves and fallen branches that make perfect seats. Adam told the gardener not to bother with tending to this area. It can't be seen from the house. So I've claimed it as my special spot, not that I've told anyone.

I sit on a log underneath an ancient oak tree and sob loudly and indulgently. No one can hear me down here. My marriage is over. I have known that for a long time, but to be confronted by Adam's lover in my house is breaking me. How dare he! How dare she? Can he really be in love with Marianne? It seems like such a terrible betrayal. I can get my head around an affair where sex is the key motivation, but love. That hurts. Just because I no longer love Adam doesn't mean I'm ok with him loving someone else.

Did he ever think of the children when he slept with those other women? Does he think of me or Ajay when he's in bed with Marianne? I wonder if Ajay knows, but I doubt it. He would have said something to me, and he would have been angrier with Adam. Should I tell him? I want to hurt Adam and Marianne, but Ajay is the innocent party in this. Just because I'm hurting doesn't mean Ajay has to be, too.

Eventually I pull myself together and wander back into the house, patching my blotchy face with foundation and concealer. I have to collect the kids from school.

Quite how I manage to get through the next three hours, I really don't know. I'm proud of myself. I have perfectly normal conversations with Oliver, whilst Mia ignores my questions and answers with her normal monosyllables. I make supper. I call them downstairs when it's ready.

'Why's Dad not eating with us?' Mia says as she slumps into her chair.

'He's at a meeting.' I busy myself with serving the quiche and salad. I have no idea where he is, and I pretend to myself that I don't care. Let *her* make supper for him.

'How did your French oral go?' I ask Mia.

'*Assez-bon,*' she replies.

'What's that mean?' Oliver speaks with his mouth full.

'Oliver got an order mark for running through the school corridor,' Mia says.

'No I didn't!' Oliver exclaims. 'Why are you such a snitch, bitch?'

'Hey, you two,' I say. But my tone is lax and does nothing to halt their bickering.

We have just finished eating and I am fishing some ice cream out of the freezer when Adam walks in, his shirtsleeves rolled up. To anyone else, it looks just like he's come home after a long day in the office.

'Hello, kids. You've already eaten?' I hear the surprise in his voice.

'Mum said you had a meeting,' Oliver says.

'Did she.' His voice is flat.

He disappears to his study. The kids finish their food and hide themselves away in their rooms. I hope they are completing their homework, but I don't have the energy to double-check. I clean the kitchen and go to the living room to watch television.

I don't look up when I hear Adam's heavy footsteps.

'I'm meeting with my solicitor tomorrow and you'll be hearing from him.' Adam stands in the doorway with his hands on his hips.

'Look, Adam,' I say, sighing as I switch off the television. 'You've lied and cheated on me, but I don't want the kids to be hurt. We need to do this amicably for their sakes.'

'And what is your definition of amicable?'

'I want to stay in the house, and you can have the children every other weekend and for a few weeks during the holidays. I want their lives to remain as stable as possible.'

'No can do.'

'What do you mean, no can do?' I have to bite my lip to stop myself from raising my voice.

'You'll see, Lydia. You'll be hearing from my solicitor.' He turns to leave the room.

'Adam!'

He ignores me.

I get up and follow him through the kitchen into the utility room.

'Adam, we need to finish the conversation.'

'Oh no we don't, Lydia. I'm going swimming now.' He takes his tropical-print swimming trunks and a large blue-and-white striped towel from the airing cupboard, flinging both over his shoulder.

He pads right past me and out of the back door. I watch him as he checks the temperature and the pH and chlorine levels, as he does every evening. He then disappears inside the oak-framed changing room and barbecue area.

I want to scream.

I WALK BACK through the house to the living room, switch the television on, and watch a dreadful film. I can't concentrate.

An hour and a half later, I've had my bath. Lights are out in both of the children's rooms. One of the parenting advantages of living in a period house is that the doors don't fit as neatly as in modern houses, so I can see whether the rooms are in darkness. All is silent.

I am about to return to my bedroom when I realise I've forgotten to bring a glass of water upstairs, so with my thin silk dressing gown wrapped around me, I pad downstairs and into the kitchen. I'm surprised that the lights are still on. Adam is a stickler for switching off lights to conserve electricity, and it's nearly always his job to switch everything off and lock up before going to bed.

As I'm pouring myself a glass of water from the filter tap, I feel a wisp of cool air despite the warm evening. Frowning, I carry my glass through to the utility room, where it is cooler still. To my surprise, the back door is wide open.

'Adam,' I say, standing on the doorstep, wondering if he's

outside. There's no answer. I shut the door. I'm tempted to lock it, amused at the thought of him being locked out of the house for the night, but deciding that is childish, I leave it unlocked and return upstairs. I wonder if he's having a secret tryst with Marianne at the bottom of the garden, and then dismiss the thought. I can't see Marianne, with her delicate kitten heels and coiffured hair, coming around for a quick bonk in the bushes.

I can't settle. The house is too quiet. It's strange that I haven't heard his footsteps or even the normal creaks and groans that our home makes. It's gone 11.30 p.m., so I decide to check on Adam. I don't want to have another argument, but I do want to make sure the house is locked up for the night. He could have driven off after his swim, for all I know. With the television on, I may not have heard his car leave.

I tiptoe back downstairs and wander through the darkened living room, expecting to see the light on in his study. It's in darkness. I turn on the lights, but Adam isn't there. I open the garage door that connects from the utility room. His Bentley is parked inside.

Perhaps he's upstairs in the bathroom? I hurry up to the spare bedroom with its en-suite, but both rooms are dark and empty, and his bed is made. It's me and me alone who has use of the master en-suite and the luxury bathroom with his and hers sinks, a deep bath for me and a walk-in rain shower for Adam, that he hasn't used for the past four months.

'Adam!' I speak quietly so as not to wake the kids.

I then grab the big torch that we keep on the hat stand in the utility room and walk outside. It's cool and the stars are out. A beautiful night. The floodlights come on as I walk onto the patio, but he's not out here.

I carry on towards the pool. There are outside lights around the swimming pool, but they have to be switched on inside the pool changing room. We've probably only used them three or four times. I'm not keen on swimming. Adam swims most nights during the summer months, so I leave all of the pool maintenance to him.

I shine the torch backwards and forwards across the garden.

'Adam!' I say again.

My heart is pumping quite hard. I'm not scared of the dark, but having been brought up in the city, such pitch blackness has taken a lot of getting used to. I freeze when I hear a distant screech. A fox chasing a rabbit, no doubt. Taking a deep breath, I walk to the edge of the pool, still swinging the light backwards and forwards.

There is a scream.

It goes on and on.

Long seconds or perhaps it's minutes later, I realise where the scream is coming from.

Me.

There is a human body at the bottom of the swimming pool.

Those ghastly green-and-yellow tropical-print swimming shorts are billowing around the slim backside of the man I married nineteen years ago.

Adam.

5

I tug off my dressing gown and I jump in. It's instinctual. But the light is so low I can't see him. I dive and dive again, and then I touch him with my foot. In that instant, I know.

It's too late.

Coughing and spluttering, the chlorine burning the back of my throat, I haul myself out of the pool, and, sobbing, I run across the patio and in through the open utility room door, dripping water across the floor. I rush into the kitchen and grab the phone from its stand. It slips out of my freezing and shaking hand and clatters onto the floor.

I pick it up again and eventually manage to dial 999. I am shaking so violently I can't stop my teeth from chattering.

'Emergency services, which service do you require?'

'Ambulance. Now. Hurry. Please hurry!'

'I'll connect you now.'

'Mum, what's happened?'

I jump.

Mia is standing in the kitchen, wearing a short T-shirt, her skinny legs and arms bare.

'Go back to your room now!' I say, much too harshly. 'Please, darling, go upstairs. Now.'

She scowls at me but turns and leaves the room.

'Ambulance service. What's the address of the emergency?'

I speak in a hushed whisper. My voice sounds as if it's coming from someone else. 'The Oaks, Bracken Road, Horsham. My husband. He's lying at the bottom of the swimming pool. I think he's dead!' My voice catches.

'Where are you?'

'At home. In the kitchen. I tried to pull him out, but I couldn't. I'm sorry.'

'Is he conscious?'

'No! I've just told you! He's dead. Not breathing, sunk to the bottom of the pool.'

I hear a gasp. Mia is standing in the doorway, her eyes wide, a look of absolute terror on her pretty face.

'Help is on its way. I want you to stay on the phone until the emergency services arrive. Is there anyone with you?'

'My children. Please come quickly.'

Mia rushes into my arms and we are both sodden, crying, rocking each other. It seems like forever, but it probably isn't more than five minutes before I hear the sirens. They get louder and louder, and then the hallway is filled with blue flashing lights.

Ambulance men and women, and police.

'Where is he?'

'In the pool at the back of the house.'

They swarm through the house. Someone wraps me up in a silver foil blanket. Another one is put around Mia's shoulders. I am shaking so much my teeth are rattling in my skull.

A young female policewoman leads Mia into the living room. I go to the swimming pool.

There are lights there now, and someone has lifted Adam out of the pool. He is lying on the side. I think how hard the stones must be; how his last moments should be on a feather-filled mattress. His eyes are glazed and open; his lips are blue.

My husband is dead.

Someone pulls a white sheet over him.

'Mummy, what's happened?'

Oliver's hair is standing up on end and he is wearing his too-big navy pyjamas.

'Darling,' I say, rushing towards him and enveloping him in my arms. 'I'm so sorry, Ollie, something terrible has happened.'

I don't know whether to tell him, how to tell him. But it's going to have to be me. He is glancing around, a frown on his forehead as he takes in all of these strangers in uniform bustling around our home. There is no way of sugarcoating it. 'Daddy is dead.'

THE NEXT HOUR or so is a total confusion. There are lots of people talking to me, taking the children into other rooms, making us all cups of tea. At some point I get dressed. Strangers seem to appear in every crevice of our home. They set up lights outside. Adam is put on a stretcher and zipped into a bag. And that's when I realise that my husband is never coming back. We may have been planning a divorce, but this is still the man I loved for so many years, the man I shared everything with, my hopes and dreams, disappointments, failures and successes. My children have lost their father. I have lost a partner in life and in business. And I sob.

'Lydia, is there anyone we can call who can be with you? Siblings, parents?'

I shake my head. My father lives in Australia now. It was such a shock when he and my mum left for the other side of the world. When Mum died, I thought he'd want to come home to be nearer to me and my older sister, Bea, but he explained that he likes it out there. The weather suits him better, and he's got plenty of friends.

Adam's parents are both dead. At least they've been spared the death of their only son. There's only Bea, and she's in London busy with her life. I don't want to call her, not yet. She doesn't even know that Adam and I were going to divorce.

'Cassie,' I say eventually. 'She's my oldest friend. You can call Cassie. Or Fiona. No, call Cassie.'

Another policeman arrives and seems to take over. 'Lydia, my name is Detective Constable Jack White. I'm going to need to take a statement from you.' Young and chubby, he has a mop of yellow hair, a flabby face and thick lips. He is wearing a white short-sleeved shirt with sweat stains under his arms.

'Why? Haven't I already told your colleagues everything?'

'Let's go and sit somewhere comfortable away from everyone. Your living room, perhaps?'

'Ok,' I say. 'But Mia and Ollie.' I look around frantically for them. I need my babies. I need to hold them in my arms.

'They're being looked after by one of my colleagues.'

And there they are, sitting at the kitchen table, both of their young faces as white as snow, eyes red and raw. A woman dressed in sensible grey trousers and a grey-and-white striped blouse is sitting between them, talking softly.

I lead DC White into the living room. The lights are on in every room. How Adam would hate that. I sit on the sofa, and he sits on what is normally Adam's chair. I swallow a sob. He leans forwards, his hands on his knees.

'Whenever we have an unexplained death, we need to ask lots of questions, find out what happened this evening and in the days leading up to Mr Palmer's death. I know it's very distressing and difficult for you, so take your time.' He throws me a kindly glance. 'Your husband's body has been taken to the hospital mortuary for a post-mortem.'

'What?'

'Because we don't yet know the circumstances in which Mr Palmer died, there will be a post-mortem, and the coroner will investigate. It is likely that there will be an inquest. Did your husband have any health issues?'

'No. He's healthy. Forty-eight. He swims most evenings and goes running. It doesn't make any sense.'

'Did your husband drink or take recreational drugs?'

'No, no. He hated smoking or drugs. He drank, but who doesn't? Not to excess, just the occasional wine and beer. I don't think he drank anything this evening, although he was home later than usual.' It sounds as if I'm wittering, but there is a disconnect between my brain and my mouth. None of this makes sense.

'Other than him coming home late, was there anything else unusual about this evening?'

I shake my head. I can't tell this stranger about discovering Marianne here in our house. I can't tell him about my argument with Adam, which was more ferocious than normal. Because what will he think? Besides, we are always arguing these days. We are, aren't we?

'And you didn't see anyone or hear anything?'

'No. What are you suggesting? Wasn't it an accident? Did he take his own life? He wouldn't. Adam would never do something like that!' My hand covers my mouth.

'We don't know at this stage.'

'Did he hit his head? Did Adam have a heart attack?'

It's my fault. If I had looked out at the pool earlier in the evening, perhaps I could have saved him.

I whimper.

'We won't know until after the autopsy. At the moment, it looks like a tragic accident or a sudden heart attack. There were no obvious markings on his body.'

Could he have slipped when he got into the pool? Or did his heart just give out on him? 'He only had a medical three months ago. He was pleased with the results.'

DC White scribbles in a little black notebook.

'Lydia!' Cassie comes dashing into the room and throws her arms around me. 'I'm so sorry,' she whispers, stroking my hair repeatedly. 'I know you were getting divorced, but this is horrendous.'

'Divorce, did you say?' DC White is standing up now and frowning at me. His lips have thinned out.

I swallow my sobs. 'Adam and I were planning on divorcing.'

He nods at me. Surely he doesn't think that I would have done something to Adam, that he died because of me?

That's absurd.

6

I honestly don't know how I get through the next couple of days. If it wasn't for Cassie... I hate to think. She takes charge. She cooks and cleans and answers the phone. She hugs the children and me and produces box after box of tissues. She fields intruding questions from the local paper. She lets the police in and talks to them in hushed whispers. She gets hold of a sleeping pill prescription from the surgery and nips into the chemist to collect them for me. When I'm in a heavy, drug-induced sleep, she's awake and on guard.

Cassie is my best friend. We were besties at school, but then she moved away, and for most of our twenties and thirties we lost touch. A few months before Adam and I bought the luxurious house we currently live in, Cassie got in touch. I was excited to rekindle my friendship with her, even though our lives couldn't be more different. She's still the person I rely on the most. Especially now.

It is Detective Constable White who is our main liaison and the person who updates me on the post-mortem. Initial thoughts are that Adam had a massive heart attack, that there was nothing I, or anyone else, could have done to save him. It doesn't make sense, though. Adam was fit and extremely health conscious. He had an annual check-up, which he paid for privately, and every year he would return home and tell me smugly that he had the heart function of someone half his age. These things happen, apparently. Sudden unexplained death.

It doesn't seem right that the weather should be so glorious, that the sun shines brightly all day, and that the one place we should be is outside, enjoying our glorious garden. I wonder if I will ever sit in it again. I can't look at the swimming pool, and the thought of ever swimming in it makes me shudder. I think I'll drain the pool and get it covered over.

On the third morning after Adam's death, Mia arrives at breakfast dressed in her school uniform.

'Isn't it too soon to go to school?' I ask, rubbing my eyes, which feel heavy after my sleeping-pill-induced sleep. I thought she might be relieved to miss her end-of-year exams.

'I can't sit around here all day. I'm taking my GCSEs next summer. Dad would want me to do well.' She sniffs and lifts her head in the air. I wonder how she can be so brave when all I want to do is crumble into little pieces and awaken from this nightmare in several months' time.

'I'll take her to school,' Cassie says as she fills up the dish-washer with our dirty plates.

'I don't want to go,' Oliver says. I'm not sure that he has changed out of his pyjamas during the past three days.

'You don't have to.' I loop my arm around him and pull him towards me. 'If you don't return until next term, that's fine, too.' There is less than a fortnight until the end of the summer term.

I HAVE SENT CASSIE HOME. She has taken three days off work to be with me, and as she's a primary school teacher, she hates taking time off and letting down her pupils. Although I wish she would stay permanently, it's not fair on her. She has been the most incredible friend. Without Cassie, it means that I have to answer the doorbell when it rings.

I hesitate. I don't want further bad news or to have to explain my grief to a well-meaning neighbour. But when the doorbell rings for the second time, I take a deep breath and open it.

'Oh, thank goodness it's you,' I say, relieved that it's only Ajay. We spoke briefly on the phone two days ago, but this is the first time I've seen him since Adam died.

'Lydia, I'm so sorry.' He flings his arms around me. 'Marianne and I are deeply shocked and upset. How are you doing?'

I freeze, rigid in his arms. Marianne. Of course she's distraught; she's lost her lover. I wonder if she's told Ajay, but I suppose not. Why would she? There's no need to upset the apple cart now, because she won't be leaving her husband for Adam.

Ajay releases his grip on me, and I step backwards, still blocking the doorway. For a moment, I think about how I want to hurt Marianne, to destroy her life in the way she destroyed mine. But then I change my mind. At least I can grieve openly. She will have to keep her pain under wraps.

Then I change my mind yet again. Marianne is not deserving of my pity. She is a liar and a cheat.

'Lydia?' Ajay peers at me.

'Sorry, sorry. Come in.' I step back to let him in through the front door.

As Ajay stands in the hallway, waiting for me to close the door, I notice that he is holding a box full of papers. I have given work barely a second's thought.

'I hope you don't mind me turning up unannounced, but I assumed you wouldn't be answering the phone.'

I frown. That's a strange assumption. I am answering the phone, or at least Cassie was. Ajay and I spoke on the phone the day after Adam's death, but I have no recollection as to what was said.

'There are a few urgent things we need to discuss, not least insurance.' He follows me through the house and into the kitchen. Oliver is sitting at the table, playing on his iPad.

'I'm sorry, little man,' Ajay says, ruffling Oliver's hair. 'If you need someone to play footie with, just give me a shout.'

'Not 'til the autumn,' Oliver says. 'I'm playing cricket now. I'm reserve for the under thirteens first cricket XI at school.'

'Are you indeed! That's impressive. You'll have to give me a lesson in bowling one of these days. Despite my Indian heritage, I never quite mastered it.' He grins at Ollie, and I realise what a gaping hole Adam has left in my son's life.

I swallow a sob and turn to Ajay. 'Would you like a cup of tea?'

'A glass of water would be good. It's baking out there.'

I haven't noticed. It's cool in our old house. We're most of the way through yet another blue-sky day, and I haven't stepped outside. Under normal circumstances, if the kids weren't at school, they would be in the pool, and Oliver would be practicing his bowling on the lawn.

'Can we have a chat?' Ajay slants his head towards the living room as he mouths, 'Alone.'

'Sure. Ollie, Ajay and I just need to talk about some work stuff. Are you ok in here by yourself for a little while?'

Oliver nods, but not before I notice tears welling up in his eyes. He has been alternatively mine and Cassie's shadow non-stop since Adam died. At night, he's sleeping with the light on, and this morning, in the early hours, he slipped into my bed. He hasn't done that in years.

I lead the way into the living room, carrying two glasses of water. It is a large room with a low-beamed ceiling, but despite the height of the room, it is light and airy due to the patio doors and windows looking out onto the garden. Ajay sits down on the cream sofa, adjusts the cushions, and pulls out a pile of papers, which he places on the glass coffee table. I hand him his water and sit in my favourite armchair. It belonged to Mum. I had the cushions refilled with goose feathers and the chair re-covered in pale blue linen. Something about its sturdiness and the memories of her give me reassurance.

'I'm not sure if you remember, Lydia, but we all have life insurance and key man insurance through the company.'

'Oh.' I hadn't remembered. I shiver at the thought of putting a monetary value on a life.

'I don't mean to be insensitive, but it's something we need to think about, and action. Adam's death will result in a very large payout. These are the forms.' He pushes over some papers towards me.

My bottom lip quivers. Ajay notices.

'I'm sorry, Lydia. I know it might seem insensitive to discuss this so soon, but the company could do with an injection of cash, and we'll need to recruit someone to take over Adam's position.'

I read the first page and then flick to the second page. 'But the sums are so high. One and a half million pounds for the key man insurance. Is that right?'

'Yes, it's a lot of money, but Adam was valuable to the business. All three of us are covered for the same sum. Key man insurance protects the company from the financial impact of losing key personnel through death or illness.'

'So the payout will be made to Cracking Crafts?'

'Yes, although the life insurance policy will be paid to you as his beneficiary. That's two hundred and fifty thousand pounds,' Ajay points to the sum on the relevant page.

'Are these amounts normal?' I have no experience of this.

Ajay shrugs. 'I'm not sure. I've completed all the forms, so we just need a signature from you. I've already signed.' He points to the blank box at the bottom of the sheet and holds out a biro for me to use. I sign as instructed.

'There are also a few payments that need authorising. I've signed off the payroll, but could you go through these quickly?'

I nod. These are all par for the course; things that I do on a weekly basis without even thinking about it.

'Finally, we're going to need to find a new financial director. With Joe having left, we've only got Suraya who knows what she's doing in account. She can manage the basics, but I was wondering whether the auditors might be able to step in until we can recruit someone else. Are you ok with that?'

I nod. We may have been getting divorced, and he was a lousy husband, but even so it is hard to be thinking about someone filling in the gap Adam has left.

Ajay leans forwards and squeezes my hand. 'I'm sorry, Lydia.'

It's the first time I have to go and collect Mia from school since Adam died. Oliver doesn't want to come with me.

'Sweetheart, I can't leave you here by yourself. You'll have to come.'

'I don't want anyone to see me,' he says, trembling.

I know how he feels. I am dreading the pitying looks from some and the crossing the road to avoid us by others.

'We'll park a couple of streets away. You can stay in the car and I'll message Mia to meet us.'

We both put on our sunglasses in the forlorn hope that they are going to protect us from the world. As I park the car on a quiet residential street, I pull my mobile out of my bag to message Mia. I have twenty-seven new messages, in addition to all the ones I've received over the past couple of days. It's extraordinary how bad news travels so quickly. Many are from work colleagues, a few from friends. I don't have the energy to read them.

I walk to the end of the street to meet Mia. She emerges with two of her besties. They have their arms around her. I am glad that Mia is getting support. But when they see me, they let Mia go and hurry off in the opposite direction.

'How was your day, darling?' I ask.

Mia turns her head away from me, her chin in the air, as if she hasn't heard.

'You know I'm here if you want to talk.'

'I don't.' She throws her rucksack into the boot and flings open the rear passenger door.

'You can sit in the front,' she tells Oliver. 'I'm going in the back.'

Oliver doesn't hesitate. It's rare that he gets to sit in the front seat.

As I pull the car into the drive, I see there is an unfamiliar silver saloon car parked in front of the house, a BMW, I think. Even before I see DC White, I know they're police officers, not from the way they're dressed, but the way they hold themselves. The two men climb out of their car at the same time as I get out of my car.

'Mrs Palmer, could we have a private word, please? My name is Detective Inspector Cornish.' The tall, older man has a long, heavily lined face.

I chivvy the kids inside and tell Mia to help herself to drinks and biscuits. I lead the policemen into the living room and shut the door behind us. My palms are sweaty and I try to keep my knees from trembling. I indicate for them to sit on the sofas. I sit on Adam's armchair. It seems appropriate when I'm about to receive news of him.

'We have had the results of the post-mortem. Unfortunately, Mr Palmer's death doesn't seem to have been as straightforward as we initially assumed.'

'What do you mean?' I ask, leaning forwards, my damp palms smoothing down the cotton fabric of my maxi dress.

'We think your husband's death was suspicious,' DI Cornish says. I notice now how all of his features are severe. That long aquiline nose, the angular jawbone and deep-set eyes; his coarse black hair and the black trousers paired with a black long-sleeved shirt, despite the summery day.

I try to focus on what they're saying. 'Suspicious?'

'According to the post-mortem report, he suffered a sudden cardiac death by ventricular fibrillation, but the pathologist found evidence of heart muscle damage and fibromuscular dysplasia.'

'I don't understand.' I feel myself trembling again and sit on my shaking hands.

'We believe Mr Palmer was electrocuted.'

'What!'

'The symptoms are indicative of electrocution.'

'But I dived in and I wasn't electrocuted! That doesn't make sense.'

'No, on the face of it, it does seem strange; however, the pathologist is positive that your husband died from electrocution.'

I shake my head. It's not possible. How could I be unaffected, but Adam was killed?

'It is a very rare form of death, and due to the considerable improvement in electrics, no one has been killed through electrocution in a swimming pool in the United Kingdom during the past ten years.'

'So why do you think it happened to Adam?'

'We got lucky,' DC White chips in. His senior colleague glares at him.

'What DC White means is that our pathologist recently returned from a secondment in the United States and saw a similar case over there.'

'So he might be wrong,' I say, my eyes bouncing from DC White to DI Cornish.

'It's a she,' DI Cornish says, 'and no, she is adamant that she has reached the correct conclusion.'

'But we could have another pathologist double-check, couldn't we?'

'That has already happened, Mrs Palmer. It's why it's taken us over three days to get the report and to notify you of the findings.'

I sink back into the pale leather armchair. How is it possible that Adam was electrocuted?

'Could you tell us again the exact order of events on the night that Mr Palmer died?'

So I do. I admit that we had an argument earlier in the evening prior to his death, but I don't tell them what it was about. I say that I dived into the pool the moment I saw his body. I tell them everything I have already told them.

'Could a mouse have eaten through some wiring?' I ask.

DC White shakes his head. 'Appliances and sockets in the areas around water and swimming pools are separated by extra-low voltage, not more than 12 volts. Our colleagues are talking to the company that maintains your pool, and they have confirmed that their last visit was two months ago.'

'Adam swam most nights.' I can't stop shaking my head. It makes no sense.

'Do you know anyone who might want to harm Mr Palmer?' DI Cornish asks.

It feels as if someone has clasped their hands around my throat. 'No. He was a good man.'

And it's true. Most people liked Adam; he was charming; it was only me who found him intolerable, fed up with his cheating. He *was* a good man, wasn't he? Of course he had his flaws. He had a tendency towards ostentation and was frequently intolerant. He wasn't a hands-on father, but he certainly loved our kids. And I loved him. I mustn't let the memories of the last few years cloud what was, for at least eight years, a happy marriage. I can't imagine anyone wanting to kill him.

I miss their next question. 'Sorry, what did you say?'

'I was asking if you could explain the structure of your company.'

'Yes. Ajay and I each own fifty percent of the shares.'

'That's Mr Arya?'

'Yes.'

'And Mr Palmer?'

'He didn't own any shares, but he was our finance director.'

'And how is the company doing?' Cornish glances at his notebook and adds, 'Cracking Crafts. They call you the queen of crafts, don't they?'

I grimace. 'The last six months have been difficult. It's the same for all retail businesses. But what has that got to do with Adam's death?'

'What was Mr Palmer's relationship like with Mr Arya?'

'It was okay.'

I stare out of the window. I can't tell them that Adam was having an affair with Ajay's wife. Ajay is the injured party here, as am I, and he deserves my support. I try to imagine how I would feel if the police had told me my husband was having an affair. Too awful to countenance. So much better to find it out myself or to be told by someone I know. But Adam and Ajay's relationship has been strained the last few months. I thought it was due to Adam's father's death and the disintegration of our marriage. With hindsight, I suppose Adam must have felt guilty about what he was doing to his old friend and business partner.

'Mrs Palmer?' DI Cornish says, startling me.

'Sorry.'

'You were telling us about the relationship between your husband and Mr Arya.'

'Yes, well...'

'We understand that you are still in shock and grieving, but it's vitally important that you are totally transparent with us regarding any strained relationships your husband had with friends, colleagues or acquaintances.'

'Things were not great between Ajay and Adam, but that was probably due to our crumbling marriage.'

'Are you in a relationship with Mr Arya?'

'No!' I exclaim. 'No! You've got that totally wrong. It was Adam who was having the affair. Ajay knows nothing about it.'

DC White leans forwards.

'And who was your husband having an affair with?' DI Cornish asks, his eyes narrowed.

'Marianne,' I say, in a whisper. 'Please don't tell Ajay. He doesn't know, and there's no need to tell him now that Adam is dead.'

'And Marianne is who exactly?' DI Cornish frowns.

'Marianne Arya. Ajay's wife.'

'So Mrs Arya was having a relationship with your husband?'

'Yes.' I rub my eyes. 'I only found out last week.'

And then I sit as still as a statue. Don't they say that nine times out of ten, it's the spouse who is responsible for the suspicious death? Have I just given the police a reason for suspecting me?

I spring back to life.

'I didn't hurt him. I never would. I was angry, and we had already decided to get divorced.' My fingers are gripping the seat of the chair, my fingernails digging into the soft leather.

'Thank you, Mrs Palmer. We will be back in touch very soon. We will need you to make a formal statement at the police station. Expect to hear from us tomorrow morning.'

Have I just thrown Ajay to the wolves?

What the hell have I done?

7

DC White rings me the next day as promised. 'Mrs Palmer, we would be grateful if you could attend the police station for a formal interview. Can you get to Crawley for 2 p.m.?'

'Y-yes,' I stutter. 'Do I need a solicitor?'

'You have the right to free and independent legal advice.'

'Ok, yes. Thank you.'

He hangs up and I have no idea why I'm saying thank you. If Adam has died an unnatural death, or if he's been murdered, I want to know who did it. But most of all, I need to clear my name. I am trembling. What if they arrest me? Mia and Oliver will lose both of their parents. And what about a solicitor? My mind draws a blank. I don't know anyone who specialises in criminal law, and I can hardly ring around my friends, saying that the police suspect me of murdering Adam, and do they know any lawyer who might represent me?

Or *do* they suspect me? Why would they be asking for a formal statement if they didn't?

And then I think of Fiona. She's a solicitor, and she knows what's been going on in my life. She's exactly the sort of friend I need right now: sensible, understanding and unflappable. The first time we met was in the coffee shop adjacent to the gym. Cassie was carrying a large glass of orange juice and walked straight into Fiona, spilling her juice all over Fiona's white T-shirt, orange bits dripping onto her brand-new trainers. According to Cassie, Fiona was totally charming about it. By way of apology, Cassie invited Fiona to join her for a coffee, and a few minutes later, I turned up.

Fiona plays down her success as a solicitor, but I get the impression she's much more high-flying than she suggests. Hers was one of the numerous text messages I received and still haven't responded to. If anyone can help me, surely Fiona can. Not only is she a lawyer and my friend, she's widowed herself.

I call her.

'I'm so sorry for your loss, Lydia,' she says.

She sounds genuinely shocked when I tell her that Adam died through electrocution in our swimming pool. But then again, who wouldn't be?

'The thing is, I can't help you myself, because I don't do criminal law, but leave it with me and I'll find someone for you. And don't panic. The police are just doing their job, investigating every avenue.'

'Thanks, Fiona.'

Half an hour later, I receive a text message from her. *'Clive Seaham will meet you at the entrance to the police station at 1.30 p.m. Good luck! Fiona x'*

CLIVE SEAHAM CAN'T BE MORE than five feet five inches tall. He is diminutive and insignificant looking, with grey hair, a grey suit and skin also strangely grey. His shoes are caked with mud, and the moment we sit down in the carpeted room at the police station, he starts biting his nails, from time to time startling me as his teeth make an unpleasant cracking sound.

I tell him briefly about Adam's death; about how the police think he might have been electrocuted, murdered even. I lean forwards, speaking in a strained whisper and hoping that there are no listening devices in this featureless room.

When Clive Seaham frowns, his eyes seem to sink further into his skull. He is frowning a lot, and it's making me more nervous than I already am.

'I suggest you say as little as possible. You have every right to remain silent.'

'Have you represented people like me before?' I ask.

'Like you?'

'Being charged with murder, but innocent.'

He stares at me for a few long, drawn-out seconds, one eyebrow raised. 'You haven't been charged with anything, Mrs Palmer. If, however, there is something I need to know, now might be a good time to tell me.'

I am horrified. Does he think I'm guilty?

'No, there's nothing. I've done nothing wrong!'

'In which case, I suggest we get this interview over and done with.'

He stands up. 'Stay here, please. I'll tell the police officers we're ready.'

I had assumed I'd be taken to another part of the police station, so I'm rather relieved that we're staying here in this small room with a window that looks out onto the car park, and a table with chairs positioned either side. It feels like I'm at a meeting in an office, not being questioned at the local nick. As one minute passes, then three, and Clive Seaham doesn't return, I feel increasingly nervous. I don't belong here. I have never done anything wrong. Ever. Well, nothing seriously wrong, that hurt another person. Not fatally, anyway.

And then the door swings open.

'Mrs Palmer.' DI Cornish enters first, followed by DC White and Clive Seaham. I stand up and my handbag falls to the floor.

Instead of shaking their hands, I find myself scrabbling on the ground to pick my belongings off the carpet.

The police officers sit on the opposite side of the desk. I sink back into my chair and rub my arms. The air conditioning is set to high, making it artificially cold in here.

'Thank you for coming in to see us, Mrs Palmer, and I'm sorry for your loss,' DI Cornish says. 'You are not under arrest and you are free to leave anytime. You have agreed to be here to give a voluntary interview, and you are entitled to legal advice.' He nods at Clive Seaham. 'Please let us know if you require refreshments or need to use the facilities. Mrs Palmer, please talk us through the events of the evening Mr Palmer died.'

'Again?' I ask and then look at Clive. He nods at me. So I tell them exactly what happened, repeating myself for at least the fourth time.

'What did you do when you discovered your husband was having an affair?'

'I shouted; I cried; I left the house. It didn't come as a surprise. We had already decided to divorce.'

'Nevertheless, it must have been a shock.'

'Of course.'

'What are the terms of your husband's will?'

'I'm not sure.' Do they think I've done this to get my hands on Adam's assets? That's ridiculous. But I do know the contents of Adam's will. We only changed our wills five years ago. 'Actually, I think I inherit most of it, but I don't see how that–'

'We just need to establish all the facts,' DI Cornish says. 'We understand that your husband was a very wealthy man, so you are set to inherit considerable sums. Am I right in thinking that the inherited wealth after his father's death last year made him a multimillionaire?'

'Yes, but that money is nothing to do with me. I had no intention of asking for any of that money when we divorced. It's

Adam's money, and if he wants to leave it to our children, I'm fine with that.'

'Maybe, but you have just said that under the terms of his will, it all goes to you.'

I pale and sit on my hands to keep them still.

'I earn a good salary from the business, and I didn't know anything about the insurance payouts.'

'Insurance payouts?' DI Cornish's eyes crease. Both Cornish and White lean forwards. Clive sits upright, then whispers in my ear, 'You don't need to say anything.'

But I do. I need to make them all understand I had nothing to do with Adam's death.

'Adam organised the insurance. He was our financial director. Ajay Arya came to see me a couple of days ago and told me about them. There is a life insurance policy and key man insurance.' Should I have volunteered this information? Will they think I have another motive now?

'Insurance policies for how much?'

'One and a half million goes to the company; a quarter of a million is Adam's life insurance.'

DC White whistles under his breath. DI Cornish throws him a filthy look.

'You are set to gain one-point-seven-five million pounds in insurance payouts. That's a lot of money by anyone's standards, isn't it?' Cornish says.

'Yes, but the one and a half million goes to our business, Cracking Crafts.'

'Which I understand has not been doing well for the past few months. I have no doubt that a sum like that would be very useful.'

I wonder how the police have obtained information on Cracking Crafts. Our financials are not made public until our year-end accounts are published, so they don't have access to our current financial status.

'Yes, but–'

'You can see why we're struggling here, Mrs Palmer. You had just found out your husband was cheating on you. If you had gone through the divorce, at best you would have lost half of your wealth, and quite possibly you would have had to sell your beautiful family home. On the other hand, if your husband dies, you stand to inherit the whole lot, and thanks to very generous insurance policies, you gain a further 1.75 million pounds. You also freely admit that you were at home all evening, yet you didn't see or hear anything suspicious. Indeed, your husband had probably been dead for at least three hours before you contacted the authorities. It doesn't look good, does it?'

'No, no! You have it all wrong. I'm not bothered by the money; in fact, I didn't know anything about it, at least not the insurance policies. And I wanted my kids to grow up with a father. Besides, I couldn't hurt a spider, let alone the man I used to love.'

'How did you learn about electrical wiring and SELV?'

'I'm sorry, I don't know what you're talking about?' Why are they asking me about electrical wiring? It doesn't make any sense. Surely they can't think that I did something to the wiring of the pool in order to electrocute Adam? That's ridiculous.

'Separated extra-low voltage systems. The electrical systems used in swimming pool installations.'

'You don't need to answer that,' Clive Seaham interrupts.

I ignore him. 'I don't know anything about wiring. Adam did everything regarding the pool. He organised the maintenance, the cleaning, the heating. I don't like swimming, so I wasn't interested.'

'Tell us about your relationship with Ajay Arya.'

'I've known him for twenty years. We set up the business together. I met him through Marianne.'

'And what does Mr Arya think about the affair between your husband and his wife?'

'You don't need to answer that, Lydia.' Again, I ignore Clive.

'I don't think he knows. Or at least, if he does know, he hasn't let on to me. Marianne asked me not to tell him. I think he would be incandescent with rage if he knew. He keeps Marianne on a tight leash as it is.'

DI Cornish raises his eyebrows. He writes something down on a small notepad and holds it under the table so that only DI White can read it.

'Mrs Palmer, we would like to search your house. As you know, there was a forensic examination of your garden shortly after your husband was deceased, but now this is a potential murder investigation, we wish to look inside the house.'

Clive Seaham inhales as if he's about to speak. DI Cornish cuts him off.

'And before you object, yes, we have a warrant.' He places a formal-looking document on the table.

'That's fine,' I say, thinking, *No, it isn't.* How horrible that strangers will be rifling through our things. And the children, it's horrendous for them. I'll have to take them away for a couple of days.

'Thank you for your assistance. We would be grateful if you could remain in Sussex for the foreseeable future. We will be back in touch should we require any further information or if we need to question you further.'

Cornish brings the interview to a close and switches off the recording equipment. We are dismissed.

'What does that all mean?' I ask Clive as we step outside the police station.

'Clearly, they have insufficient information to charge you, and they're still on a fishing trip.'

'So what's going to happen next?'

'I'm afraid I don't know, Mrs Palmer; however, I will stay in close contact with DI Cornish. As soon as I find out any more, I will contact you.'

'Thank you. I am very grateful for your support.'

MIA AND OLIVER mustn't know that the police are going to search through our house. They are disturbed enough as it is. I need them to go away for a couple of days, and hopefully by the time they return, everything will be back to normal. As normal as it can be without their father.

I ring Bea. Oliver, in particular, loves his cousin Finlay. Mia is in awe of Bea's eldest, Louis. At eighteen, he is – according to Mia – coolness personified.

'Of course they can come and stay,' Bea says. 'As he's finished his exams, Louis is lounging around the house doing sweet FA. Fin is at school, but he hasn't got anything on this weekend. How about I collect your two in the morning?'

'Thanks, Bea.'

'And how about you, Lydia? How are you coping?'

'I don't know if I am.' I swallow a sob. I don't want to tell my older sister that I have just come out of an interview at the police station, and that the real reason I want her to have my children to stay is because our house is going to be searched so as to establish who killed my husband. I suppose I should be grateful that I have been warned in advance. At least they haven't ram-raided our home at some ungodly hour.

'I'm here for you,' Bea says.

But she isn't. Not really. She lives in London, and although we care for each other, we've never been close. I can't share the intimate intricacies of my life with her in the way I can with some of my friends, like Cassie and Fiona. She doesn't even know that Adam and I were planning on divorcing. I love Bea, but sometimes I don't like her. She can be holier than thou and the uber-efficient, judgemental older sister. For that reason, I've learned to keep my distance.

Mia is delighted at the prospect of staying in London for a couple of days. Oliver, less so. Nevertheless, I am relieved when Bea comes striding into the house at 9 a.m. the next morning, dressed in navy chinos and a blue-and-white striped boat top. Goodness knows what time she got up to get here so early.

WITH THE CHILDREN GONE, I decide to go to work. I need a distraction. On the drive, I stop off at the garage to fill up with petrol, and to my dismay see the headlines in the local paper.

Sussex owner of Cracking Crafts murdered in family swimming pool

I gasp. Who has told the papers that Adam was murdered? They don't even know for sure if he was murdered. It's horrible, and I have to blink repeatedly to stop the tears from over-flowing.

The moment I walk through the door at Cracking Crafts, I can sense something is wrong. The staff are neither rushing over to express their dismay about Adam's death nor avoiding me. They just sit glued to their computer screens, faces pale. I know that expression. It's shock.

Nicky glances up and sees me. She hurries over.

'What's happened?' I ask.

'Can we talk in your office?'

'Sure.'

I glance into Ajay's office as we walk past, but it's empty. 'Is Ajay in a meeting?'

'Um, no.'

She holds my office door open and I enter my happy, colourful den.

'He got arrested an hour ago.'

'What?'

'The police came here and arrested Ajay. At least they didn't put handcuffs on him, but they did take him away in a squad car.'

'Shit,' I say, sinking into my chair.

'Do they think he murdered Adam?' Nicky asks.

'I don't know what they think. It's a nightmare. I feel like I'm living through a real-life hell.'

'I'm sorry, Lydia. You really are. Can I get you a cup of tea or anything?'

'No, thanks.'

I try to think straight. I suppose it's obvious that both Ajay and I must be the key suspects. We both have a motive to kill Adam. But the thought of either of us actually doing it is laughable. I have known Ajay for nearly two decades, and he is level-headed and exactly the sort of person you want around you in a disaster.

I try to recall when I have seen him lose his temper. There was one occasion, back in the early days, when we discovered an employee had been stealing from us. Ajay went mental. He threw a mug at the lad. Fortunately, it missed and splintered on the office floor.

I try to recall any other time. He and Adam had a shouting match about six months ago. Ajay stormed out and Adam refused to tell me what it was about. It happened shortly before I told Adam our marriage was over, and with the fallout over that, I never discovered what they fought about. But those occasions were rare. Normally, Ajay is the voice of reason.

And then I wonder: If Ajay found out that Marianne and Adam were having an affair, could he have murdered Adam? He's a practical sort of man. I have little doubt he could work out how to mess with wiring to create an electrical current, but would he? It seems so unlikely. Then I remember how he calls Marianne at least once, sometimes more often, every day. I used to think it was because they were still in love, but now I wonder if he is just a controlling husband. I remember how Marianne used to say I was so lucky having a job. I thought it was strange. There she was free to be a lady who lunched, filling her days with shopping and beauty treatments. But perhaps Ajay was an overbearing husband. Perhaps Adam was a wonderful husband in comparison. None of us really knows what is going on behind marital closed doors.

Then there's the insurance money. Ajay knew all about it. He knew that if Adam died, then the company's financial woes would be sorted. But it's not like Cracking Crafts is on the brink of financial ruin. The thought of Ajay murdering Adam seems totally outlandish.

My head is spinning, and if I thought I could get any work done, I was naive. Instead, I take out a crochet project: a cushion pattern in a rainbow of pastels, an easy, meditative pattern. The staff know that I try out all our new products, so if anyone glances into my office they won't be in the least bit surprised to see me busy making something. The repetitive motion calms me down, and I'm left alone for an hour or so.

But then my office door swings open. Most people knock, so I look up in surprise.

'How dare you!' Ajay strides towards my desk. The door slams closed behind him. 'You knew all of this time and you didn't tell me!'

He leans his hands on my desk and stares at me. His eyes are red and he has blackened circles surrounding them.

'Can you imagine how humiliating it was to find out from the police that my wife was having an affair with your husband, and you knew. How could you not tell me, Lydia?'

I lean backwards. His breath smells sour. 'I'm sorry, really I am. Marianne asked me not to tell you, that she would tell you in her own time, and then Adam died, and it all seemed a bit irrelevant. I asked the police not to say anything.'

'How long have you known?' He steps away from me. Some of the fury seems to have dissipated.

'A matter of days. I've known Adam was having an affair – I told you – I just didn't know who with.'

'It's a fucking mess.' Ajay slumps into the chair opposite my desk. 'They think I'm a suspect because of what you told them.' He points his finger at me. 'I thought you were my friend, Lydia. I know your husband has died, but how could you imply to the police that you think it's me?'

'But I don't. I never implied that, Ajay. I promise.'

He stands up again. 'I don't believe you, Lydia. I think when you are hurting, you want to bring other people down too, so you're not all alone in your bubble of misery.'

'No, Ajay! It's not like that!'

But he ignores me and storms out of my office.

8

I suppose I've watched too many police procedurals over the years and read too many crime novels, because my expectations of a murder investigation are not met. It seems to me as if nothing is happening. DC White calls every other day to update me that they have nothing to update me with. I ask if Ajay is still a suspect or is likely to be charged, but he refuses to answer the question. So today, I lose the plot.

'You must have some information for me.'

'I'm sorry, but–'

'You've got to tell me what's going on.' And then I burst into tears. Loud, sniveling sobs down the phone line.

'Mrs Palmer, I can confirm that Mr Arya is still a person of interest,' he says quietly.

I sense that he is speaking out of line. Do they really think Ajay is a suspect? I've played around with the notion repeatedly during the past few days, and at first it seemed totally outlandish, but the police wouldn't be investigating Ajay unless they had a good reason to. Have I got him totally wrong? I suppose he could have killed Adam if he had found out about the affair. Even so, I find it hard to believe. I can't even look at

Ajay now that the police have planted these suspicions in my head, but I've got to work with the man. The situation is untenable.

'So why isn't he locked up?' I ask, sniffing.

'As I said, he is a person of interest. We don't have enough evidence to – look, I'm speaking out of turn here. Just rest assured you will be the first to know as soon as we have any more information.'

I think of Ajay sitting in his office, running our business. Could he really have killed Adam? We all need some closure, and fast.

'When can I organise Adam's funeral?'

'As soon as the coroner releases his body.'

I DON'T GO into the office much. Nicky emails me every few hours, so I work at home, pottering alongside Oliver, who seems to be surgically attached to his iPad. I haven't got the energy to suggest he do something else. I spend hours mulling over Ajay's relationship with Adam. Would he really have electrocuted Adam? Has Ajay got it in him? And I try to avoid any direct contact with Ajay. I'm worried that if I see him, I might ask him outright if he killed Adam, and I suspect that isn't a good approach. On the odd occasion when I go into work and I have to speak to him, I call him, even though he is in the next-door office. The trouble is, now that the police have planted that enormous seed of doubt, my trust in Ajay evaporates further every day. He had the motive, I suppose he had the means, but is he a murderer? I guess it's possible.

It's my girlfriends who get me through, particularly Cassie and Fiona.

Fiona sent me a text a week or so after Adam's death to say that having experienced the sudden death of her own husband (although he died in a car accident, so no questions of it being a suspicious death), she knows what it's like to organise a funeral, and is happy to help in any way she can. I take her up on the offer.

Just over two weeks after Adam's death, DI Cornish rings to say that Adam's body is being released and we can organise the funeral. At this stage, the coroner's report states death by electrocution and an open verdict, although the police still think Adam's death was suspicious. There will be a full inquest, and the police investigation will continue.

TODAY IS the day we lay Adam to rest. Time doesn't seem to flow in a linear way when you're navigating grief. Sometimes it feels as if I last saw Adam weeks ago; other times, it feels like last night. And my grief is confused. I no longer loved Adam in the way I used to, but I didn't want him dead. Of course I didn't. I simply didn't want to be married to him anymore, and the feeling was mutual. But today, I need to focus on the man he was: husband, father, friend and colleague. I need to play a part. Our wider circle of friends and family have no idea we were planning on separating, and they will expect me to be devastated. I suppose I am, but in a different way.

'You don't need to come,' I say to Oliver as I straighten his black school blazer. 'Dad wouldn't mind.'

'I want to come.'

I nod, and holding his hand, we walk together to Mia's room. She's wearing a short black skirt and a black blouse that I have loaned her. It makes her look pale and very young. Bea, her husband, Craig, and their two boys, Finlay and Louis, are hovering in the hallway downstairs. Even Louis, her favourite cousin and all-time idol, can't muster more than a watery smile from Mia.

'The cars are here,' Bea says. Fiona suggested that we organise limousines to take us to the crematorium. They are parked up outside, long, dark, foreboding. Too big for our diminished family.

I sit on the back seat between the two children, clasping both their hands. I think it's the first time we've clutched hands like this since they were both in primary school. We are the last to arrive. Perversely, it's a bit like a wedding. The most important guests turn up last. What surprises me is that there are quite so many people here. Every pew is full, and people are standing at the back of the room. All eyes swivel to look at us, me specifically. I can't tell if their expressions are of pity or suspicion. I suspect a mixture of both. I clutch Mia's and Oliver's hands tighter. Mia whispers, 'You're hurting me, Mum.' I let go.

As we ease into our front-row seats, Cassie leans forwards from the row behind us and squeezes my shoulder. Fiona is sitting next to her, her blonde hair tied back in a ponytail, looking smart in a dark grey, lightweight trouser suit. Cassie is wearing a long, shapeless, drab cotton dress that I haven't seen her in before. Funereal garments are not her thing.

As both the kids sob quietly, I wonder if I should have insisted they stay at home. It was Bea who said they should come; that it might give them the closure they'll need. She forgets that they were both there when the ambulance men took away their father's body.

Last week, when Fiona and I were at the funeral parlour, the funeral director turned to me and asked what my budget was for the coffin. For a brief moment, I thought of putting Adam in the cheapest pine box. It would be sweet revenge. But then I thought again. He was my husband. I used to love him. He didn't choose to die. He should have had decades left to live, so I pondered what he would have wanted. I chose the most expensive coffin in their catalogue. I think he would be pleased with the cherry-red coffin with gold handles and the sumptuous flower arrangements draped on and around it.

I don't know how we get through the service, but we do. Perhaps it helps that the non-denominational celebrant didn't know Adam, so the service is depersonalised. All three of us squeeze our eyes together as the curtain comes down and Adam's coffin disappears.

When the service is over and everyone is milling out in the hallway, I notice DI Cornish and DC White standing in the corner, observing us all. I am quite sure they're not here to pay their respects. Bea and Cassie marshal us through the crowd of well-wishers, and the limousine whisks us away to a local hotel.

'You never know how many people are going to come to the wake,' Fiona had said. 'Best have too much food and drink rather than too little.' The hotel concurred. But then they would. They'll be in the money.

The hotel is large, and the building is squat and rather ugly, with a white rendered finish that looks odd in its rural settings in woodland at the foot of the Sussex Downs. I'm not sure how, but quite a few people have arrived before us and are already milling around in the sterile conference room. There are a lot of faces I don't recognise, and for a moment I wonder if I've got the right funeral. But then I spot Ajay; Marianne is clinging onto her husband's arm for dear life. I turn away from them. What cheek for them to attend Adam's funeral.

Cassie hands me a glass of white wine, and I take several large gulps. I look outside through the large patio windows, towards the well-tended gardens. The kids are with their older cousins, sitting outside on a bench. Louis says something that makes them laugh. I'm relieved. Now I have to play the grieving hostess.

How come there are so many strangers here? How did Adam know all of these people? Are they all from the golf club, or are they people from other parts of his life that I knew nothing about? Adam had so little family. An only child, with both parents dead and no cousins that I am aware of. He never talked much about his childhood, although I know that he was sent off to boarding school, where he was desperately unhappy. It was very obvious that neither of his parents thought that I was good enough for their only son. But they misjudged us: their constant criticism of me and everything Adam did only served to make us closer. I wondered whether they thought they were displaying a weird form of tough love. It didn't work. Adam didn't cry at either of his parents' funerals, just as I'm not crying at his.

'Are you all right?' Bea asks as she brings me over a small plate filled with sausage rolls and open sandwiches. I place it on the windowsill. I'm not hungry.

'I don't know half these people.'

She places a kiss on my cheek. Bea never kisses me. I finish my glass of wine and another appears immediately.

After shaking hands with queues of sombre mourners, I slip out of the room to go to the ladies'. I feel slightly tipsy, having drunk two glasses of wine and eaten nothing all day. When I come out of the cubicle to wash my hands, Marianne is standing with her back to the sinks. She is wearing a black silk dress and lots of heavy gold jewelry. Her Prada sunglasses cover most of her face.

I ignore her and step to the furthest sink.

'Lydia, I'm so sorry,' she says.

I turn the tap on full blast.

'Please. Please forgive me. I didn't mean to cause such pain. I miss him so much.'

I turn with a snarl. 'And you think that is going to give me any comfort? I don't care what you think, what you feel.'

She takes her sunglasses off. Her eyes are red, and mascara has smudged underneath her eyes.

'Please, Lydia. Please forgive me and forgive Adam. We didn't want to hurt you or Ajay.'

'Too little, too late,' I say, drying my hands on a little facecloth and dropping it into a wicker basket under the sinks. She puts a manicured hand on my arm, but I shrug her off and storm out of the ladies. How dare Marianne and Ajay turn up here? How dare Marianne ask for forgiveness? And what about Ajay? What does she think about him being a murder suspect, or does she even know?

I find Bea. 'I want to go home now.' She nods. Five minutes later, we're wedged into a taxi. Mia, Oliver, Bea and I sit in silence all the way home. Craig and the boys will follow. My heart bleeds for my babies, fatherless now. How will I cope being both mother and father? Will their childhoods be ruined? I need to talk to someone, find out what support I should be giving them; making sure that they understand that life is fragile, but at the same time, not being scared to live theirs.

When I open the door to our silent home, the sadness and confusion is replaced with a sense of lightness and relief. Such a significant chapter has closed in my life, but I feel a sense of liberation, a little frisson of excitement for what the future may hold. I know it's wrong of me to feel that, today of all days. Of course I didn't want Adam to die, but in a perverse way, it's easier that he is dead. If we had gone through the divorce, we would have fought over the children, the house and the business. I realise it makes me sound like a bad person. And really, I'm not.

9

THREE MONTHS LATER

I slip the black dress off the white satin padded hanger. Goodness. I have forgotten how very flimsy it is. Such an expensive dress for so little fabric. As I'm applying my make-up, I run through my usual mental checklist. There's a lasagna in the oven, bubbling away nicely, ready for Cassie to eat with the kids. I've put a freshly made salad on the table, covered in cling film, and homemade salad dressing in a little cut-glass bottle.

'Mum, where's the sellotape?' Oliver stomps into the bathroom without knocking. It will be a matter of months before my little boy transforms into a lanky teenager. He's at that precarious stage where he still needs me, but doesn't want to admit it. I watch him swagger with his newly formed friends, trying so very hard to be in with the cool crowd, but still on the periphery. Thank goodness we had the summer for him to steel himself before having to return to school. When I drop him off at the school gates in the mornings, he braces himself before walking through the gate. A deep breath, shoulders tensed, a purposeful walk. I see so much of Adam in him, but unlike his father, Oliver has a soft centre, and I worry for my gentle boy.

'The sellotape should be in the second drawer down in the utility room.'

'Are you going out?' he asks.

I pull my dressing gown tighter around my waist.

'Yes, I told you. Cassie is coming to babysit.'

'Where are you going?'

'Just out for a bite to eat with an old friend,' I say, wishing I didn't have to lie to my boy.

He grunts and leaves the room.

'Have you finished your homework?'

I don't get an answer.

I apply my make-up carefully. More foundation than usual, and mascara. I have naturally dark lashes and don't normally bother, but tonight I'm hopeful. I slip on the black dress. It is silk, with little spaghetti straps and a cowl neckline that makes my bust look more substantial than it is. I do a twirl in the full-length mirror in the bedroom. The saleslady told me I looked twenty-five in the dress, that I was stunning. Oh, how easy it is to flatter. I didn't believe her, I'm not that stupid. But I do look all right. My legs are shapely and slender, my waist slim. I've lost nearly a stone over the past four months. As I glance at my watch, the doorbell rings. Cassie is always on time.

I grab my black patent leather clutch bag, double-checking that my wallet, phone and keys are inside, and hurry downstairs, pulling on my trench coat as I go.

'You look stunning!' Cassie exclaims as I open our heavy oak front door.

She gives me a kiss and walks past me, down the hallway towards the kitchen, her trainers squeaking on our supersized dark grey flagstone floor.

'Something smells scrumptious!'

'Just a ready-made lasagna, I'm afraid.' I hold on to the thick carved oak post at the bottom of the stairs.

'Mia, Oliver, Auntie Cassie is here!'

Silence. I remember the days, not so long ago, when the children would speed downstairs, careering into Cassie's legs, desperate to share their latest news or demonstrate the toy of the moment. These days Mia refuses to call Cassie Auntie. 'She's not my aunt,' Mia hissed last month. But old habits die hard.

'There's white wine in the fridge. Help yourself. You're in the normal room.'

'Are you expecting to be back late?' Cassie grins and then winks.

'No. Just in case you're tired.'

'I'll wait up for you. Right, off you go.' She flaps her hands at me. 'Go meet Rory, the solicitor. The one with the smoldering dark eyes and pecs that show through his tightly fitting white shirt. The one who looks like a sex god.'

'Ha ha,' I say, biting my lip. I still feel bad about it. It's too soon to be internet dating, just four months after my husband died. But as Cassie has told me on numerous occasions, (a) we were planning on divorcing anyway, and (b) Adam is dead, so it's not like I'm doing anything wrong, and (c) I'm not trying to replace their father, just seeking a bit of happiness for myself, and surely the children will understand that.

I'm still not sure that Cassie is right. It seems that I'm looking for a new relationship with indecent haste, and I am riddled with guilt. Perhaps I shouldn't go? It's not too late. But Cassie will be furious. She set up the account on 4everlove.com, she has chosen my date, and she insists that I deserve happiness. I know she means well, but still I wonder. There is no way that I'm going to broadcast that I'm already on the lookout for love.

'How was your date?' I ask Cassie as I check my bag for car keys and house keys a second time.

'Crap. His profile said he was in haulage. He's a lorry driver with a red, bulbous nose and a stomach that looks like one of those big pink Pilates balls. Needless to say, we won't be meeting again.'

I sigh. Cassie doesn't give up. She is looking for love and is determined to find it, but she's not prepared to compromise. In some ways she's lucky. Pete and Cassie got divorced years ago, when Dale was just three or four years old. They've stayed friends and have managed the co-parenting thing remarkably well. Cassie has had a couple of long-term relationships over the past fifteen years, but she's been single for a while now. She's hot on internet dating. And although Mia and Oliver are probably old enough to stay home alone, she babysits too.

'Fingers crossed you'll have an amazing date,' Cassie says, blowing me a kiss.

'Thanks, hon. I'll try.'

THIS IS my first internet date ever, and frankly, I'm terrified. Rory Morrison is a solicitor. I checked him out before we started talking on the phone. He works for a medium-sized firm in Leatherhead, specialising in property law. Annoyingly, there is no photo attached to his bio on the firm's website. If he's on Facebook, I haven't found him.

He seems a nice enough guy, and during our short conversations on the phone, he made me laugh a couple of times. I would have preferred to meet for a drink, but Rory insisted on us going out for dinner at Barney's, one of the smartest restaurants in the area. His treat, he said. Hence why I'm dressed up. One thing is for sure, Rory will not be getting any action tonight.

The restaurant is in a side street in Horsham, tucked away on a narrow alley. I park the car several roads over. I don't want him to see my fancy motor.

I tie my trench coat tightly around my waist and walk quickly towards the restaurant, glad that I chose the kitten-heeled shoes rather than the stilettos. It's a warm, balmy evening and there are plenty of people milling around, enjoying the unseasonably fine weather. I check my watch. It's 7.20 p.m. and I'm five minutes late. Perfect timing. Nevertheless, my heart is beating too fast and I glance at myself self-consciously as I see my reflection in shop windows.

For a moment, I stand outside the restaurant. It's not too late. I can turn around and go home. But the maître d' sees me and flings the door open. 'Madam,' he says in a pretentious manner as he takes my coat. I smooth down my dress and ease a gold-and-black throw around my shoulders.

'Mr Morrison is already here.'

I glance around the small restaurant. There is no one even faintly resembling the swarthy good looks of Rory Morrison's profile picture. My heart sinks as I follow the maître d'. A man jumps up and extends his hand.

'Lydia, it is so wonderful to meet you. And you look absolutely stunning!' he gushes as he pumps my hand up and down. 'Please, please take a seat.'

Alas, he doesn't look so stunning. I suppose with a large dollop of artistic license or some serious photoshopping, his profile picture could have been him, but it must have been taken a decade earlier when he was fit with a full head of hair and wasn't approaching twenty stone. His eyes are kindly, but his jowls are flabby, and he has a large cold sore on his upper lip. There is a shiny tinge to his pale grey suit. I focus on his eyes. Yes, they are nice. Bright, the colour of conkers on a sparkling autumn day.

'How are you, Lydia? I've been so looking forward to meeting you in the flesh!'

I wish I wasn't wearing the new, revealing dress. I should have trusted my gut. It's too much. Even though it is warm in the restaurant, I will keep my throw around my shoulders.

'I've taken the liberty of ordering you a glass of champagne, and then I thought we could have a nice bottle of red, or if you prefer, white is fine too...'

'Thank you, but I'll just stick to one glass of something. I'm driving.'

The disappointment makes his double chin wobble.

'Cheers!' he says, lifting his glass towards me. I watch as he takes a large gulp. Could I find this man attractive? If I could just look at his eyes. He would have to sweep me off my feet with his charisma and humour, and even so, I can't imagine myself wanting to kiss those lips.

'Tell me about yourself,' Rory urges. 'What do you do?'

'I have my own business.'

'You're an entrepreneur!' he exclaims.

'Well, not exactly. I have co-directors.' I wonder how he would react if I said that one is dead and the other is a suspected murderer; that the police still haven't closed the investigation into my deceased husband.

'In what sector?'

'We're in craft supplies.'

He puts his glass down on the white tablecloth and claps his hands. 'I knew I recognised your photograph from somewhere. You own Cracking Crafts! You won businesswoman of the year. Good heavens, I never thought I would be having dinner with you!'

I squirm. Cracking Crafts makes me a target for gold-diggers, which was another of the reasons I didn't want to do internet dating. I wish I hadn't been persuaded by Cassie. She told me it would be fine. If I use my maiden name, then any searches wouldn't link me to the business.

'Why is a beautiful, successful woman such as yourself going out on dates?'

I have steeled myself for this question, but it isn't phrased how I assumed it would be. Evidently, this man doesn't read the local papers. A relief.

'I want to meet someone, I suppose.' *But not you*, I think uncharitably. I give myself a mental kick. *Give this man a chance.* I take a swig of champagne as the waiter arrives with the menus.

'Are you divorced?' Rory asks, leaning forwards.

'Um, no. I'm widowed,' I stutter. I find it hard to say that word.

He frowns. 'I'm sorry to hear that.'

'And you?' I ask.

'Divorced for six glorious years. She left me. I thought it was the end of the world at the time, but now I realise it wasn't. I get to meet beautiful, intelligent women such as yourself.'

I stare at the menu and we sit in silence for a moment until the waiter comes over to take our order.

'I'll have the smoked salmon mousse and the chicken, please,' I say. 'And I'm extremely allergic to peanuts.'

'I will ensure the kitchen are aware of that,' the waiter says, underlining the word allergy on his notepad.

Rory selects mussels followed by lamb.

'My ex was allergic to everything. I think it was just an excuse not to have to eat with me. So it's a real thing, then, this peanut allergy?'

'Yes. I have an EpiPen. My daughter used to have a peanut allergy, too. Anyway, tell me about you. I gather you're a solicitor.'

'Yes, a boring, old solicitor. I go skydiving at the weekends to try to shed the aura of being a grey dullard.'

'Really?' I ask, my eyes widening at the thought of his bulk hurtling through the sky.

He guffaws. 'No, of course not! Can't stand heights. I'd leave a crater in the ground when I landed. What about you? Do you have any hobbies?'

'I don't have much time to myself, what with working and looking after the children.'

'I don't have children,' he says as he tears off a large chunk from the white bread roll on his side plate.

'Oh,' I say lamely. 'Mine are twelve and fifteen. Tricky ages, especially Mia, who is fifteen going on twenty-one.'

'When did your husband die?' he asks.

'Quite recently.'

When I glance up at him, he is staring at me, no doubt wondering why I've started dating already.

I fill the silence.

'We were going to get divorced, but then he died.'

'His loss, my gain.'

I have no answer to that statement. Fortunately, the starters arrive quickly, and Rory breaks a mussel and pops it in his mouth. After a few moments, his chin is smeared with buttery slime.

'Jane had an affair with her boss. Broke my heart, it did. They're married with kids now. Anyway, where would you like to go on holiday? I'm planning a trip to Florida next year.'

I nearly choke on my mousse. Is he suggesting that I go with him? 'I'm sure it'll be lovely. We haven't got any holidays planned.'

He shoves his empty plate to one side and lunges for my right hand. I pull it away just in time, but Rory doesn't seem to mind. He smiles at me while I try not to look at the little smudge of butter on his wobbly double chin.

We both start talking at the same time and then conversation dries up for a bit. It's a relief when the main courses arrive.

We're only a few mouthfuls in when he says, 'I've got a bottle of champagne in the fridge and some fancy ice cream in the freezer. Thought we could have dessert back at mine.'

Oh, good heavens. Surely not! Is this normal behaviour for a first date? I scramble around for a suitable response and feel my cheeks reddening. His eyebrows are raised as he looks at me expectantly.

'I'm sorry. I don't...'

'Too soon? Next time, hey? How are you set for next Friday?'

'I'm sorry, Rory. You're a lovely man, but the chemistry isn't there for me. I don't think–'

'Just because I'm a few stone overweight doesn't mean I'm not a considerate lover, Lydia.'

I cringe. I have got to get out of here. Now.

'I'm sorry, I didn't mean to cause offence. It's probably just a bit too soon for me to get involved with anyone.'

He turns a shade of deep cherry as he finishes off the last morsels on his plate.

'It's not fair, Lydia. You can't lead people on.'

'I'm very sorry. I didn't mean to. Please let me get the bill.'

'Absolutely not. Tonight is my treat. Perhaps next time–'

'It's been a pleasure meeting you, but there won't be a next time.' I feel like a total heel now. Rory looks crestfallen. I feel sorry for this man. He is gentle and humourous, and he does have lovely eyes. I wonder for a moment. Could I be with someone who I don't find sexually attractive? If we got on well, we could be travel companions and share a laugh.

And then I kick myself. These thoughts are ridiculous. I have only just started dating and I am far from desperate. Besides, the very last thing the kids need right now is a stepfather.

I stand up. 'Thank you for a lovely meal.' He waddles around to my side of the table and I just manage to dodge his flabby lips so he kisses the air. 'It was a pleasure to meet you. And I wish you the best of luck with your dating,' I say.

'You too,' he says quietly. I collect my bag and walk away.

As I slide into my car, I let out a yell. If that's what dating is all about these days, I'm not interested. Thank goodness Cassie is at our place and I can drown my sorrows with her.

Ten minutes later, I am pulling into our driveway, the gravel crunching underneath my tyres.

In contrast to our grandiose home, Cassie lives in a one-bedroom flat in a red-brick block in Southwater. She moved there the year before Dale, then aged seventeen, left home and joined the army. On the rare occasion he returns to his mum's, he sleeps on the sofa.

Sometimes I feel embarrassed that our circumstances are so different, but Cassie doesn't seem to mind. Neither of us have said anything. We just focus on what we have in common, which is a lot. Laughter, failed marriages, kids and our shared childhoods.

'Didn't go well, then?' Cassie says as I walk into the living room. She switches the television off.

'Nope. He doesn't look anything like his profile picture, and we didn't really have anything in common.'

'Oh.'

I peel back my trench coat and let it drop onto the sofa.

'That dress is a stunner, Lydia. Where did you get it?'

I evade the question. I don't need Cassie to know that I spent close to her monthly wage on this one dress. 'I'm through with internet dating,' I say, taking the full glass of wine she proffers me.

'You can't give up after one date. You deserve happiness.'

'I'm going to get us some more wine and let the kids know I'm home,' I say.

'Sure.'

They are both in their rooms. Mia is talking to someone on her phone. She glares at me when I walk in.

'Did you knock?' she hisses, throwing a contemptuous snarl. My girl is hurting, so I let it go.

'I'll be downstairs with Cassie.'

'Whatever,' she says, turning her back to me.

Oliver is playing on his laptop. Some computer game that I don't understand.

'I'll come and switch your light off at 10 p.m.' I get no response.

Back downstairs, Cassie sits with her bare feet curled under her on my cream designer sofa. She's wearing cropped leggings and a bright blue oversized shirt, which matches the colour of her eyes. Her short spikey hair is currently dyed the hue of redcurrants. It's not my favourite of hair colours. I preferred the silvery white she sported last month. I top up her wine glass and pour myself a large one. I sit on the armchair opposite her.

'Perhaps I just need to be by myself for a couple of years,' I muse.

'Bollocks to that!'

10

The problem with internet dating is it becomes a bit addictive, that draw to find the perfect one. I may have told Cassie that I'm not interested in having a new relationship, but it's hard to ignore the likes that pop up on my phone with great regularity. So here I am, at my desk, idly browsing through 4everlove.com when I should be checking through our PR agency's monthly report. A notification pings through and I pause to study his profile. He has messy dark brown hair, blue eyes and a rakish grin. But best of all, we are a 100% match.

I read his profile. He's a management consultant, lives in Sussex but travels a lot. He's been single for four years, looking to commit, and loves travelling. I can't believe he hasn't already been swept up.

I click the like button, and a few moments later, he messages me. My heart is thumping. Is this guy for real?

How could I not say hello when we've got a 100% match! I'm Patrick, on the train to Manchester for a boring business trip. If you could choose to be stuck on the train with some famous people, who would you choose?

Hi Patrick. I'm Lydia.

He messages again before I can reply.

PS - I'd choose Oprah, Michelle Obama, the Dalai Lama (clichéd but I do want to meet him), James Redfield and Scarlett Johansson! You look like her :)

My stomach does a little leap. I am sure that none of the men I know would have even heard of James Redfield. His book, *The Celestine Prophecy*, was a game changer for me. Obviously, I wouldn't choose Scarlett Johansson, but I'd probably choose the others.

Great choices but sadly I don't look like Johansson! I'd choose Martha Stewart (I'm into crafting!) Michelle Obama, the Dalai Lama and James Redfield too. And Pierce Brosnan for some eye candy!

Damn, can't compete with Brosnan.

What do you do?

I'm a management consultant – systems etc. Not glamorous, and frustratingly requires a fair bit of UK travel. And you?

I run a crafting business.

That's interesting. Both my parents had their own businesses. I'm fine going in and telling companies what to do but would make a lousy employee!

Me too! Unemployable...

What do you do when you're not running your craft emporium?

Two kids keep me busy, but otherwise I like long country walks, good food, knitting complex jumpers. What about you?

Sadly no kids, but I also like long country walks. Have you been up to Chanctonbury Ring recently?

No. Where do you live?

Between Horsham and Crawley. And you?

Horsham!

I'd love to meet you, Lydia. Perhaps you can teach me how to knit!

I'm a lousy teacher but would happily go for a walk.

My finger hovers. I shouldn't have pressed return. That's much too forward! Going for a walk... I don't know anything about this guy, and what if he attacks me on a secluded footpath up on the South Downs? My phone pings again.

If the weather is nice, are you free to go for a walk at the weekend? I'm doing nothing on both days. We could have lunch at the Three Cygnets.

I hesitate. I'd like to do that, but is it safe? Surely it'll be fine if I leave Find Friends on my phone so that Cassie can track me.

Just need to see if I can get a friend to keep an eye on the kids, but if so, yes, that would be great!

I've got to go now, Lydia. Nearly at Piccadilly Station. Let me know about the w/e. Can't wait to meet you!

Oh my goodness! He didn't use any juvenile text speak. He didn't suggest a fancy dinner. He must be into spirituality in some form, if he wants to meet the Dalai Lama and James Redfield. And we're a one hundred percent match. I jump up from my office chair and do a little jig of joy. Fortunately, no one is passing by my office. For the first time in months, even years, I feel a knot of happy excitement in my sternum.

Both kids have after-school activities this afternoon, so I have plenty of time before I need to collect them from school. Enough time to go to the gym and perhaps meet up with the girls. I send Cassie a message, collect my bag and stride out of my office. I put my head around the corner of the open-plan office.

Nicky looks up and smiles. Five years ago, at our office party, she got hopelessly drunk. Wearing a ridiculously tight black bandage dress, she weaved across the room towards me and flung her arms around me. 'I love you, Lydia,' she gabbled. 'This woman here!' she shouted at the top of her voice, pointing both her index fingers at me. 'Believed in me. She's the only person who ever trusted me. I love you, Lydia!' She placed a big red lipstick kiss on my cheek. Her colleagues clapped and cheered. Ajay stood up, put his arm around her and gently led her back to her table. Adam was furious.

Needless to say, Nicky was mortified the next day. She sent me an email apologising for her behaviour and offered to resign. I refused her offer, but nevertheless, it took her a good two weeks to be able to look me in the eye again. Whether I have been the only person who trusted her is debatable, but I was certainly one of the first. When I told Adam I was offering her the job, he was livid.

'She's been in prison! She's got a record, and what skills has she got? You're out of your mind, Lydia. You'll regret this!'

But I didn't. Aged seventeen, Nicky served her time for pushing drugs. She's been clean ever since, and her work ethic is ridiculous. She went to night school to pass her GCSEs, then studied for two A Levels and finally got a BTEC in business. Even now, I have to force her to take her holidays and remind her it's not necessary for her to be the last person to leave the office. She has a live-in boyfriend these days, so her life is more balanced. I no longer feel a sense of responsibility for her. As for me, I simply couldn't do without her.

'I'm leaving now, Nicky. Call me if anything urgent crops up.'

'Will do, Lydia. Have a good evening.'

'LYDIA, OVER HERE!' Cassie is waving at me from the far side of the coffee shop. I've just done a yoga class and am feeling totally chilled and zen. It's one of the rare occasions I can empty my mind of worries about home and work. If I could, I'd take a yoga class every day of the week. Cassie uses the gym. She's much more self-disciplined than me, and she enjoys all of those classes, particularly spinning. I think she's crazy.

We try to coincide our visits as much as possible, grabbing a quick juice or a coffee after our workouts. Even so, we probably only manage it once a week, and these days, as I'm a single parent, even less. I weave my way through the tables. I bend down to give Cassie a quick peck on the cheek.

'You look chirpy.' She raises her eyebrows at me.

'Any chance you could be with the kids on either Saturday or Sunday?' I feel bad about asking, as Cassie has been helping out so much recently. Initially, she refused to accept payment, insisting that she was only doing what friends do. But now we've come to an agreement. I do an online payment so that no actual cash is exchanging hands between friends. Cassie's proud, and I get it. She glances at the calendar on her phone. 'Sunday is good.'

'I've got a date, and I have a really good feeling about this one!'

'That's so exciting! Show me his profile.'

As I'm digging my phone out of my bag, Cassie waves at someone.

'Fiona's over there.' I look up and beckon Fiona over.

'Hey, girls, how are you both doing? Lydia, you haven't got a drink. What would you like? I'll get you one.'

'A mint tea would be great. Thanks, Fiona.'

She strides back towards the counter. Her hair is tied back harshly from her wide forehead, her well-toned muscles rippling through her Lycra leggings and fitted top. I wouldn't describe Fiona as pretty; she's more statuesque, tall and imposing. A strong woman with an indescribable magnetic quality. Perhaps she has an inner self-confidence that Cassie and I both lack.

And now she's back, dragging a chair over to sit between Cassie and me. Although she's several years younger than us, she doesn't seem it. Maybe it's because she wears heavy foundation, or perhaps it's because she holds herself with that self-contained gravitas. There is something strangely compelling about her; it strikes me every time we get together. Or perhaps it's because she doesn't have kids, and her sole focus is work.

'How was the date with the solicitor?' Fiona asks.

'Dreadful. Well, not totally dreadful,' I say, feeling guilty. 'He was nice enough, just not my type.'

'I'm sorry,' she says, patting my hand.

The three of us have spent hours sharing our dreams of the perfect man. More often than not, I feel as if we're acting like teenagers rather than mature women. Tragic.

'Show us his profile,' Cassie urges.

I hand my phone to her. Fiona leans over to take a look.

They both screech. A couple of women at the adjacent table look up and frown at us.

'He's gorgeous!' Cassie says. 'How come you got to see him first?'

'Lydia deserves it. She's had such an awful year,' Fiona says. 'When are you meeting him?'

I blink repeatedly and swallow a sip of too-hot tea.

'Sunday.' I grin.

WHEN I PULL BACK the heavy cream curtains in my bedroom, I smile. It's a beautiful autumnal day, and rays of sun bathe me in light, little motes dancing and glistening in the air. For the first time in years, I feel hopeful. I pull on a pair of smart jeans, a white shirt and a baggy, pale grey cashmere jumper.

I try to read the Sunday papers whilst drinking my morning coffee, but I can't concentrate on the words. I switch on the television and watch BBC News 24, but I can't even concentrate on that. The next two hours pass painfully slowly.

When Cassie arrives at 10.30 a.m., I am togged up and ready to go.

'The kids are still asleep,' I say as she gives me a quick kiss on the cheek. 'I've left food for you in the fridge. Wake them if they're not up by midday.'

'Go,' she says, giving me a little push. 'Have a fab time and message me. Don't do anything I wouldn't!'

I laugh. That allows me free rein to do things I would never dream of.

I plug Patrick's instructions into my satnav and, with my sunglasses on, drive south. There are plenty of cars in the car park, unsurprising on this glorious day. I pull into a space at the far end, check my face in the sun visor mirror, running my fingers through my shoulder-length dark blonde hair and wiping my tongue over my front teeth. Taking a deep breath, I get out of the car. I glance around, wondering if he's already here and which his car might be. Not seeing any sign of life, I open the tailgate and take out my wellington boots.

'Lydia?'

'Yes!' I jump. I turn around and it's him. Patrick looks exactly like his photograph. Better, in fact. He is tall, slender, clean-shaven and he has a dimple in his right cheek. Wearing a dark blue waxed jacket over an open-necked checkered blue-and-white shirt and faded jeans, he leans towards me and gives me a kiss on the cheek. The scent of his aftershave is sublime. For a moment, I am dumbstruck, so I turn away quickly, fiddle with my wellington boots, then stand up straight and lock the car. If he wonders about my expensive motor, it doesn't show on his face.

My eyes are drawn to his face, but I don't want to stare. His eyes are a clear pale blue outlined with long dark eyelashes. His hair is somewhat unruly, thick and curly. With features that are not exactly symmetrical, craggy almost, I can't put my finger on why he is so gorgeous.

'You chose a beautiful day for a walk on the Downs.' He grins. 'Are you ready?'

I nod.

We walk for a while in silence, our feet crunching on the chalky gravel.

'I haven't been here in years,' he says. 'I used to come up to Chanctonbury Ring when I was a kid. There were more trees in those days. How about you? Have you always lived in Sussex?'

'No. I was brought up in Cheshire. Mum moved to Worthing after Dad died. I went to college in Brighton. My hus... Adam was from here. How about you?'

'I'm from all over. A bit of a nomad. But I like Sussex. Look, forgive me, but I did a Google search on you, Lydia, and I know what happened. I'm really sorry. Just wanted to get that out of the way.'

'Oh.' I stop walking. He also comes to a halt. Should I admit I did a search on him too and I found nothing? Or, at least, I couldn't discern which of the four hundred Patrick Grants on LinkedIn he might be. And obviously he isn't the famous fashionwear designer of the same name.

'You must have had a dreadful year.'

'Yes. Not the best. What the papers won't tell you is that Adam and I had decided to divorce. Our marriage had been over for a few years.'

'Nevertheless.' He gazes towards the sea.

'The kids are devastated, obviously. Do you have any children?'

He shakes his head and I sense a hint of regret. 'Nope. Divorced a number of years ago. My wife cheated on me and turned me into a sworn monogamist.'

I don't want to talk about Adam or Patrick's ex-wife, so I change the subject and ask about his hobbies, but I don't get a straight answer. Instead, he asks me lots of questions. I tell him about my crafting addiction and, out of habit, wince as I'm explaining it, remembering how Adam used to tease me and tell me I was old before my time. But Patrick's smile doesn't falter. He simply says how he's looking forward to seeing what I make, and that knitting and crocheting remind him of his beloved grandmother.

When we arrive up on Chanctonbury Ring, the views are breathtaking. To the south, the sea glistens alluringly in the distance; to the north, the vistas are even more extensive, across the Weald, with its green fields and hedgerows, patches of woodlands and the silvery river Arun snaking through fields to the faraway North Downs.

'This was a small Bronze Age hill fort,' Patrick says, indicating the ridge we are standing on. 'In the Roman days it was a temple, and in 1760, beech trees were planted in a circle. Sadly, many were knocked down in the big storm in 1987, although some have been replanted. Local legend has it that if you walk around the ring seven times in an anticlockwise direction, the devil will appear and offer you a bowl of soup in return for your soul.'

Despite the warmth, I shiver. 'It's a legend, Lydia.' Patrick smiles, briefly touching my arm.

I laugh, unsure why the place makes me feel uneasy.

'Anyway, if we hurry, we'll catch last orders for lunch at the pub. I don't know about you, but I'm starving.'

As we walk briskly back down to the car park, we don't stop talking. He tells me about his work, how he goes from company to company, helping sort out IT and systems problems. I tell him about Cracking Crafts. He tells me that he has had one serious relationship since his divorce and that he wants some stability in his life. I tell him I haven't dated in twenty years. And then I trip over a piece of rock. He reaches for me and stops me from falling. Breathless, I look up at him, at those magnetic clear blue eyes, his slightly wonky teeth and his square jaw, and my heart does a tumble. We are both totally still for a moment, and I desperately want him to take me in his arms, but he hesitates. A woman walks past, a springer spaniel at her heels. She wishes us good morning and breaks the spell. Then Patrick smiles at me, as if he can read my thoughts, and I know that now is not the time and the place. But it will come.

11

There is a cragginess to Patrick. His features are not perfectly symmetrical. His nose is too big and the lines around his eyes are like deep canyons. He is not conventionally handsome as Adam was, but he carries himself with a deep confidence, as if he has an innate knowledge about his place in the world and what he wants. I find him magnetically attractive. There is a similarity to Adam, but it's not obvious and I can't put my finger on it. Besides, it's not important. Adam was the past. Patrick just might be the future.

We have had three dates since our walk on the Downs, and each time he has given me a single red rose. The first time, I cringed a little, thinking it was a cliché. Now I rather like it. The crimson rose appears to be Patrick's calling card.

He has invited me to go away with him for the weekend. I know we're moving forwards at breakneck speed, but I simply can't help it. Cassie, with her big heart, is thrilled for me. Fiona sends me texts asking when she can meet my new man. At this rate, I'm going to have to tell the children.

Pack an overnight bag. Casual clothes. I'm taking you away for a surprise weekend, his text said. *I'll pick you up at 5 p.m.*

. . .

IT IS NOW one minute to five, and I am hovering by the front door. I have changed clothes at least five times this afternoon and eventually settled on a pair of beige woolen trousers, a cream silk blouse and a brown leather jacket that I bought years ago in Italy, accessorised with a burnished orange pashmina. I'm wearing a long thin gold chain necklace that has a gold coin pendant with a lotus flower engraved on it. I bought it for myself from a market stall in Brighton years before I met Adam. It reminds me of happier times.

'Message me,' Cassie says as she steps out of the kitchen.

'And any problems here, you promise to call me?' I say. Despite being ridiculously excited about this date, I am also reluctant to leave the security of home.

'Just go, Lydia.' She flaps her hands at me. 'Have a fantastic time. The kids and I will be fine. FaceTime Fiona and me in the morning, and don't do anything I wouldn't do!' She winks.

I hesitate. I am a cauldron of emotions: excited but scared, guilty but resolute. Is it too soon to be dating properly? And what will he think of me? I haven't slept with anyone except Adam for nineteen years. I try but fail not to think about it.

I haven't told Mia and Oliver where I'm really going this weekend. I hate lying to them, but Cassie agreed that it is better if I say I am going on a spa weekend with a girl friend. She has some diversion tactic in place that involves watching a film and eating popcorn and sweets, so that right now, they are securely ensconced in the living room, eyes firmly on the television screen.

'Go!' she repeats, opening the front door and giving me a gentle shove. She picks up my small overnight bag and hands it to me. 'Stand outside so he doesn't ring the doorbell.'

So here I am, standing on the doorstep to my beautiful home, listening to the crunch of tyres as a car comes slowly down the drive. My heart is racing. Patrick's car is a silver Volkswagen Golf, eleven years old according to the number plate. He leaves the car idling and jumps out of the driver's seat.

'Hello.' He smiles coyly, kissing me on the cheek and picking up my suitcase. He is wearing dark jeans and a pale blue button-down shirt, open at the neckline. 'This is a beautiful house.' He whistles as he looks up at our historic home, with its long sloping roof of reddish tiles and the unique double chimney giving way to the glass hallway that connects the old house to the newer converted barn with its exposed ancient oak beams. It is impressive from the outside, and even more so on the inside, laden with history and centuries of laughter and pain, births and deaths. I am very conscious of what our house portrays. Money. Privilege. From the outside, no one can know what heartache has lain within.

I smile. 'Yes, it's been a labour of love.' I don't add that we bought it as seen. It was the previous owners who had the vision to restore the house and merge the unused barn with the smaller, fifteenth-century farmhouse.

Patrick puts my overnight bag in the boot of the car, alongside a small rucksack. He then holds open the passenger door for me. I slide inside. The car is spotless and smells as if it has just been valeted.

'I've booked us into a boutique hotel in Brighton. I hope it'll be ok. I haven't been there before.'

'I'm sure it will be lovely.'

Unlike our previous dates, there is an awkward silence between us as he drives. I suppose it's because we're both anticipating what is to come. I wish I'd had a strong drink before leaving home. From time to time, I throw furtive glances at his profile, but Patrick's eyes are firmly on the road ahead. He drives quickly but confidently.

Eventually, we check into a hotel set a couple of roads back from the seafront, near the Lanes. There is a small reception area with a black granite counter, two high-backed red velvet chairs and black-and-white prints hanging on the walls, seascapes of Brighton.

'Good evening, Mr and Mrs Grant. Please can you complete this form for us?' The receptionist speaks with a heavy Italian accent as she hands Patrick the booking form.

I turn away, keen to hide the flush I feel blooming on my cheeks as a result of being called Mrs Grant. The fingers of my right hand move to the ring finger on my left hand, where for the past sixteen years, whenever I have felt nervous, I have twirled my wedding band around. I can't get used to my ring-less finger.

Our room is small, with a queen-sized bed piled high with red-and-grey cushions. I stand awkwardly near the door, wondering what the etiquette is. I hope Patrick isn't going to make a move now, in full daylight.

'Shall we have a stroll along the seafront and get some drinks before dinner?' He tucks a strand of my hair behind my ear.

'Sure,' I say, a little too eagerly.

We meander along the promenade, away from the pier. There is a strong breeze and my hair whips around my face. Patrick stops suddenly and turns towards me.

'Can I kiss you?' He doesn't wait for an answer, pulling me into his arms. My heart is beating wildly and I feel like a teenager out for an illicit meeting with her older boyfriend.

When we pull apart, he takes my hand and leads me to a pub. It's busy inside, but he finds us a little table in a corner. He hands me a glass of wine and a packet of peanuts.

'I'm afraid I can't eat those. I'm allergic to peanuts.'

'Oh. I'm sorry. I didn't know.'

He smiles at me, but then gazes off into the distance. I can tell something isn't right. My heart sinks. Didn't he like our kiss? Is it because of my peanut allergy? Am I about to be dumped before we've even started?

'Is everything all right?' I ask, holding my breath.

'Yes, yes. Just a few issues. I don't want to bore you with them or ruin our evening. I'm sure a couple of drinks will do the trick.'

I lean towards him. 'You can tell me. A problem shared is a problem halved and all that,' I say, taking his hand. He doesn't pull away, so perhaps I'm not about to get jilted.

'It's my sister.'

'What about her?' I ask. I didn't even know he had a sister. 'But you don't need to tell me, obviously.'

He throws me a half smile. 'My sister, Sandra. She's battling a rare cancer. It's breaking my heart. They have three young kids, and Ned is doing everything he can. He's a good guy, her husband, but he's had to cut down on his hours to look after her and the children. They barely had enough to make ends meet before, but now it's desperate. I give them whatever I can. Anyway, last night Ned rang me to say that the new drug, MPQ-202, they've been trialing her on, is working.'

'That's fantastic. Is it immunotherapy?'

'Yes.'

'What's the prognosis?'

'They're hoping Sandra will make a full recovery if she continues being treated with MPQ-202.'

I don't understand why Patrick is looking so sad if the outlook is good.

'What's troubling you?' I ask, squeezing his hand.

'I don't want to bother you with my problems. Tell me more about your children.'

'You're not bothering me, Patrick,' I say, twirling the stem of my glass in my fingers. 'What's really going on?'

He looks away from me, grimacing slightly, as if he's embarrassed. I wonder if I'm being too insistent; after all, it is early days in our relationship. He takes a sip of lager and then throws me a weak smile.

'The problem is we can't afford the drug. MPQ-202 costs twenty-five thousand pounds a month and there's no way of getting it on the NHS. I paid for the first two months, and now the docs are saying she needs another six months of treatment. We've got to pay for the next two months up front. It's all or nothing. If she doesn't take this medicine, she'll die.' He swallows hard and glances away. 'Sorry,' he murmurs. Sitting up straighter, he continues, 'Anyway, I should be able to pay for most of it.' He pulls his hand out of mine and rubs his knuckles into his eye sockets. 'I'll have to sell the flat. I earn good money, but because I'm a freelancer, I often have to wait for months for my clients to pay. I've got some hefty outstanding invoices that should cover it, but the dosh won't arrive in time.'

'That's awful,' I whisper, stroking the back of his hand with my fingers. 'I'm so sorry your sister is having to go through all of this. How old is she?'

'Forty-three. She's my little sister. The kids are all under ten. Here.' He opens his wallet and pulls out a creased photograph of a woman cuddling two boys and a little girl; the latter can't be more than two years old. The woman's head is bald; her skin has a yellowish tinge and her eyes are sunken.

'That's Sandra. I took the photo last month.'

'I'm so sorry,' I murmur. I can't tell if there is any familial likeness between Patrick and Sandra because she looks so waif-like, so close to death.

'Your parents?' He doesn't talk about his family and I haven't pressed him. It suits me because I'm not yet ready to share my story about Adam.

'They're dead. It would have broken their hearts to see her like this.'

I hand the photograph back to him. He strokes it and then carefully places it back into his wallet.

'Come on. Let's go and eat.'

THAT NIGHT he makes love to me, and it is unlike anything I have ever experienced before. This is a man who is in control, who knows what he is doing, and who wants to pleasure me. And my goodness, he does. I feel as if I am going to combust. This spectacular man plays my body as if it were an instrument, taking me to exquisite heights of desire that I had never known were possible, always ensuring that I am satisfied first. I have no idea how many times he makes love to me, or what hour it is when I eventually fall into a deep sleep. When I awake, the sun is streaming through the muslin curtains and Patrick is sitting up in bed, watching me, his fingers gently running over my neck and breastbone.

'You're beautiful,' he whispers.

I am sore and tired, but heavy with an intoxicating happiness. And when he makes love to me again, I lose all my inhibitions. Adam and I never made love like this. Never.

As we're lying together, limbs intertwined, I tell him about Adam, the details surrounding his death and the horrendous aftermath.

'Surely the investigation isn't still ongoing?' he asks.

'It is. They think Adam was murdered, but they haven't charged anyone yet. There seems to be no progress.'

'That's terrible,' Patrick says, his eyes closed, his fingers trailing across my stomach. 'How awful for you that you haven't got closure. What are the police doing?'

'I don't know. They don't tell me much these days. I don't think they've got any more leads, and thankfully, it seems that they've discounted Ajay, my business partner.'

We lie in silence for long minutes until Patrick sighs and rolls out of bed.

'Time to get up,' he murmurs.

.   .   .

AFTER BREAKFAST, Patrick settles the hotel bill and he carries our cases back to the car.

'When can I see you next?' he asks.

'Oh,' I say. I had thought we would be spending the rest of the day together; have a hearty Sunday lunch somewhere followed by a long walk. 'I can do next weekend or possibly Thursday evening, depending if one of my friends can look in on the kids.'

'I'm sorry I have to cut today short,' he says, holding my hand as he gazes into my eyes. 'I am inundated with work at the moment. But I had the most amazing time, Lydia. Really, the best ever.'

'Me too,' I say, trying to dispel the disappointment and focus on this beautiful man, my new lover.

Just before he turns the car into our lane, he pulls over onto a grassy verge. I look at him and raise my eyebrows.

'I know you don't want your children to see you doing this, so–' He pulls me towards him and kisses me.

'Do you have to leave?' I ask eventually.

'I don't want to go either,' he says, his fingers creeping up my thigh. He groans and sits back in his car seat. 'But I have to. Too much work. Let me know when you're next free, and please don't leave it too long.' He smiles, that little dimple in his right cheek sending waves of lust through my stomach. Goodness, I have regressed into my teenage self.

'WHY ARE you back so early? Didn't it go well?' Cassie looks up at me, her make-up-free forehead creased with concern. She has a pile of school exercise books laid out on our kitchen table.

'The kids?' I mouth.

'Still asleep.' She rolls her eyes.

I take a Nespresso capsule out of the larder and pop it into the machine. I am so exhausted, I need caffeine urgently.

'It went brilliantly. Better than brilliant, actually. He has to work today and was apologetic that he couldn't be with me. He wants to see me this coming week.'

'That's fantastic, Lydia. I'm so happy for you. Come on, then. Spill the beans!'

I carry my coffee to the table and sit next to her.

'Well, we walked along the promenade–'

'Wait! Let's FaceTime Fiona. She'll want to know what happened, and then you won't need to tell the story twice.'

'Ok,' I say wearily. Sometimes I feel a little pang of jealousy towards Fiona. It used to just be Cassie and me against the world, but recently we've morphed into a trio. It's not that I don't like Fiona. I do; she's amusing and we have plenty in common, and I couldn't have done without her in organising Adam's funeral. It's just this new dynamic is slightly odd.

A moment later Fiona's face fills Cassie's phone.

'How was it?' she asks eagerly.

I fill them in on all of the details – well, not all of it. The most they get out of me is that he is a wonderful lover.

'So it was perfect?' Fiona says. I note an edge to her voice. Envy perhaps? I don't blame her. It doesn't seem fair that I have found a new lover so quickly whilst she and Cassie have been single for ages and are still on the lookout.

'Yes, it was perfect. I can't quite believe it!'

LATER ON, when Cassie has left, I lounge around, doing very little. I can't stop thinking about Patrick, how he made love to me, how perfect he is. And I also can't stop thinking about his sister, that haunting photograph of her looking so desperately sick. To think that her life depends on whether or not they can raise the money is heartbreaking.

Fifty grand. It's a hell of a lot of money, but we have it. I wouldn't even need to sell stocks and shares. In fact, a lot more than that is sitting in cash in my bank account, earning next to no interest. I could give it to Patrick or lend it to him. It seems so wrong that I have all of that money and they have nothing.

And then I wonder. I've read all those stories about scammers and dating. What if he's just with me because he knows I'm wealthy? Only last month, I read about a poor woman being scammed out of a million pounds by her supposed lover, who turned out to be a young man working in an online dating fraud business in Ghana. But no. Patrick isn't like that. He's loving towards me. We are in a physical relationship.

I grab my laptop and open up Google. What was it? MPQ something. The drug comes up. MPQ-202. It's a brand new treatment, being hailed as a miracle cure for inoperable cancers, but because it hasn't yet completed all of the rigorous testing required by the NHS, patients have to pay for it privately. And Patrick is correct. It does cost around twenty-five thousand pounds a month.

I lean back in my chair. There can't be a better way to spend our money than saving someone's life.

I send Patrick a text.

Thanks so much for a fantastic time. Can you send me your bank account details, please?

I have to wait for over an hour until I get a response.

Can't stop thinking about you. Why do you want my bank acc info? Px

I want to send you something for your sister.

No way!

I gulp. I hope I haven't offended him. *Please don't take this the wrong way. I just want to help. It can be a loan. Let me pay for the next two months of her treatment. Pay me back when you can.*

I can see that he has read the text, but he doesn't answer. I wait, holding the phone in my hand as if it is combustible, silently praying that I haven't overstepped the mark. I stand up to go to the kitchen, to switch on the kettle, and then the phone beeps with an incoming text.

Don't know what to say except thank you. Blown away. I'll be able to repay you in three months. Thank you. You're an angel. x

12

It's Saturday evening, and Patrick parks in front of a newly built block of flats. The entrance hall is plush, with a royal blue, thick-piled carpet and two lifts encased in a wall of marble. He presses a gold button to call the lift, and when we're inside, he presses the button to the third floor. The back wall is mirrored. I wonder if he will kiss me in here, but he doesn't. He catches my eye and we smile at each other. We exit the lift onto an equally plush corridor with walls lined with abstract paintings, large splashes of reds and oranges.

'I'm here on the left,' he says as he inserts a key into the door of flat number 308. He holds the door open for me. 'Welcome to my humble abode.'

I'm not sure what I expected, but it wasn't this. There is a small entrance hall and a door straight ahead that opens onto a large living room. The floors are a pale wood, possibly a good quality laminate. The walls are all painted white and the room is so big, the black leather sofa and two armchairs seem almost lost in it. A wide window looks out onto a park, and it lets in plenty of light. On the wall above the sofa is an impressive oil painting; a seascape in dusty blues and greys about four feet long. The kitchen is open plan to the living room: sleek, shiny black granite countertops and a wall of shiny white cupboards. With the exception of one wooden bowl holding a couple of apples and a banana, and a single red rose still wrapped in plastic, there are no things out on the countertops. Not even a kettle or a toaster. The stainless-steel hob sparkles, and it looks as if there is still a sticker on the front of the oven. It has the feel of a hotel combined with a show flat.

He must notice my frown because he laughs. 'I'm away for business so often, I'm rarely here. If the kitchen doesn't look used, it's because it isn't. It helps that I've got a great cleaner who swoops in after me and cleans away any mess. I'm afraid I'm lazy and often call for a takeaway.' He picks up the rose and hands it to me. 'This is for you.'

Then he turns around and starts walking down a corridor to the left. I follow.

'This is my bedroom,' he says, holding the door open. A super king-size bed is covered with a dark grey throw; orange-and-grey cushions sit proudly plumped up leaning against the grey velour headboard, just as one would find in a luxury hotel. Built-in cupboards line the wall.

'The en-suite is through here,' he says. 'And there is the second bedroom.' He opens the door to a smaller room, with shutter blinds across the window and a bed with a tall, navy blue padded headboard. 'And there's another bathroom through there.'

'It's very tidy,' I say, noting the lack of photographs and knickknacks and books. It's also very masculine – the polar opposite to our house.

'I'm a bit of a control freak. I like all my mess to be hidden behind cupboard doors. Anyway, what can I get you to drink? Red, white, gin?'

We walk back to the living room. I place the rose on the countertop.

'A small glass of white, please.'

He takes a bottle out of a largely empty fridge. I note a box of six eggs, a quarter pint of milk, a couple of lemons and a tray of some ready-made meal. I wonder what he intends to give me for supper.

'Where do you keep all of your stuff?' I ask as I accept a glass of wine.

'My work is on my laptop and in my briefcase, and to be honest, I don't have much stuff. My ex kept most of our belongings. I was quite happy to start again. Come here.' He tugs my hand.

I place my wine glass on the marble coffee table as he pulls me into his arms and then bends down and gently places his lips over mine. As his kissing becomes more insistent and his fingers undo my buttons, I think of my bank account. I can't help it. The fifty thousand pounds left my account on Tuesday morning. He must have paid the cheque in first thing on Monday morning. I didn't think cheques went through that fast. As his clothes drop to the floor, I press my body to his. We seem to fit so perfectly. But then I feel terrible. My husband died less than four months ago and here I am with another man. And worse still, I think I'm falling in love.

He must sense my confusing melee of thoughts because he pulls back and holds my face between the palms of his hands, so confident in his own body, he barely seems to notice that he is standing totally naked whilst I am almost fully clothed.

'By the way, I wanted to say thank you. Sandra cried tears of joy. I can't begin to tell you how grateful we are for the loan of your money. She's starting the next month of immunotherapy tomorrow.'

'I'm so pleased,' I say, my shoulders easing downwards.

'And I'll be able to pay you back soon. I promise, Lydia.'

. . .

PATRICK DROPS me back home shortly before 11 p.m. Most of the evening was spent in his bed, with a short interlude for a Chinese takeaway.

I don't want him to go. He leans over the gear shift to kiss me again, and once more I get lost in his arms. Eventually I pull away, grab the rose off the back seat, and step out of the car into the cold night.

'I'll see you to the door,' he says as he swings his long legs out of the car.

'It's fine. It's three steps to the door.' I laugh.

'And three steps I want to take with you.'

I walk towards the house, but he grasps my hand.

'Don't go!'

'I have to. The children. Cassie is waiting for me.'

'One last kiss, then.' He grabs me on the doorstep, his kiss deep and passionate, and I feel like swooning, so lost I am in his arms. And then I hear a click and a gasp.

I pull away.

'Mia, wait!'

My fifteen-year-old daughter darts back along the corridor and runs up the stairs, taking two at a time. Muttering, 'Sorry,' I push Patrick away and sprint after her.

'Wait!'

But she doesn't. She rushes into her bedroom and slams the door behind her.

I hesitate at the top of the stairs, but then I hear a car engine start up and fade away.

'What's going on?' Cassie emerges from the living room and stands at the bottom of the stairs, rubbing her eyes and yawning. 'Sorry, fell asleep in front of the telly. Is everything all right?'

'No,' I whisper. 'Mia just saw me snogging Patrick.'

'Oh shit,' she says. 'Think I'll leave you to it, if you don't mind. I need to get home.'

'Thanks, Cassie,' I say, blowing her a kiss. 'I'll call you tomorrow.'

I knock on Mia's door. There is no answer. I try again.

'Go away!' she says. Her voice sounds choked.

I turn the door handle, but she has wedged a chair up against it and I have to push hard to get it to open. Mia's bedroom is in darkness, the only light coming from her mobile phone, which is lying on her bed.

'Darling, we need to talk.' I squeeze through the doorway and walk to the side of her bed. I kneel down next to her.

'I said go away. Which bit of that don't you understand?' Her clipped tone of voice sounds like mine when I'm chastising her. It makes me want to weep.

'I need to tell you what's going on. To explain.'

'It's pretty bloody obvious. My mother is a whore who couldn't wait for my dad to die so she can bonk someone else.'

I grit my teeth. 'Mia, do not talk to me like that! It's not what it seems.'

She turns then and sits up. I can just make out her pale features, her long, dark hair framing her face, the wetness running down her cheeks. I want to hug her, to make things better for my little girl. But I know I can't.

'You treat me like I'm a kid, but I'm not. I'm more mature than you are.' She stifles a sob.

'Darling, I know you're angry and you feel betrayed, but I need to tell you about Dad and me. You must have noticed that things weren't good between us, that we were arguing loads. We had decided to divorce. We were about to instruct solicitors when he... died.' I still find it so hard to say that.

'Oh, for God's sake, Mother. Don't fucking well lie to me! Just because Daddy isn't here to defend himself. You disgust me.'

I stand up. 'Do not swear at me.'

She slides down the bed again, turning her back to me. She

does nothing to hide the desperate sobs that engulf her body. I bend over her, stroking her forehead like I used to do when she found it difficult to fall asleep. She shoves my hand away.

'Go. Just leave me alone.'

So I do. I back out of her room and gently close the door behind me. I lean against the wall in the hall and let out a sigh.

I feel like the worst mother on earth, as if I have totally betrayed my own children, putting my needs before theirs. Should I dump Patrick and focus on them for the next couple of years, park my own happiness for a while? Or could there be some sort of compromise? I simply don't know.

I SLEEP TERRIBLY, worrying about Mia. Now I'm pacing up and down the kitchen, my coffee cup in my hand, and I decide honesty is the best policy. I will invite Patrick over for supper and introduce him properly. I send him a text and then try to do some work. It's so difficult to concentrate.

It is nearly midday when both the children are up, slurping from bowls of cereal at the kitchen table. Mia refuses to look at me.

'Kids, I want to tell you something.'

Oliver looks up, his spoon held in midair. Mia ignores me.

'Before Dad died, he and I had decided to get a divorce. We were going to tell you when it was a bit more sorted. We wanted to minimise the impact on you. But then... Anyway, we both love you so much, and the three of us would have stayed living here. The thing is, Dad fell in love with someone else, so I started looking for someone else too.'

'Whore,' Mia whispers under her breath.

'Mia!'

A curtain of tangled dark hair obscures her face.

'I've met someone I like a great deal, and I'd like to introduce him to you.'

Oliver looks dumbfounded. He drops his spoon and it clatters into his cereal bowl, splattering milk on the table.

'I'm sorry this is such a shock for you both. I know you've been through so much. Too much. But please know I love you both with all my heart and that will never, ever change. His name is Patrick, and I've invited him for supper so you can both meet him.'

Mia scrapes her chair back and flees the room.

Oliver bursts into tears.

I throw my arms around him. It's obvious I've done this all wrong. But how should I have told them? Surely it's better that they know the truth? Oliver lets me hug him and soothe him until his tears dry up, and all of a sudden, he pulls away from me, as if he's remembered that he's too old for his mother's arms.

'Are you very upset?' I ask him.

He shrugs. 'Are we getting a new dad, then?'

'No!' I exclaim. 'Not at all. He's my... boyfriend.' Such a silly word for a woman of my age. 'I like him very much, and I'd like you to meet him too.'

'Ok,' Oliver says, standing up. He also leaves the room.

I don't know what to do about Mia's reaction. Oliver has always been more straightforward, his feelings showing on his face. He is the sort of child who expresses his emotions and gets rid of them, quickly moving on. Mia is the opposite. It scares me how much of a cauldron is bubbling inside her, when it might rise to the surface and explode. I have offered for her to talk to someone, explaining that a counsellor is just an objective listener, a person who understands the process of grief and shock, but she insists there's nothing wrong with her, that lots of kids lose their parents, that she's got plenty of friends she can talk to. And I haven't pushed it.

I spend the day trying to speak to Mia, but she's either rude to me or refuses to talk. I call Cassie.

'I'm a crap mother.'

'You're not. You're trying to do your best in a crap situation. Mia is hurting and it's understandable.'

'Is it too soon to introduce them to Patrick?'

'Possibly.'

I groan, wondering if I have been too impulsive, whether I should uninvite him.

'But I want to be honest with the kids. No more pretense.'

'Well, then, you're doing the right thing. Tell Mia she can always talk to me if she wants to.'

'Thanks, Cass. I don't know what I'd do without you.'

PATRICK ARRIVES on the dot of 7 p.m. I have made Mia's favourite roast chicken and Oliver's favourite pancakes for pudding. I don't suppose it will make any difference. I'm not sure whether to warn Patrick about the kids' reactions, but decide not to. I don't want to make him any more uncomfortable. He is wearing suit trousers and a white shirt with rolled-up sleeves – strange for a Sunday. He gives me a kiss on the cheek and proffers another rose.

'Do you mind if we don't touch at all whilst you're here?' I whisper, feeling myself flush.

'Of course.'

He follows me into the kitchen, and I try to imagine seeing it through his eyes. It is a fabulous room, part of the converted barn, with the complex oak beams and rafters on display. The handmade kitchen is painted in cream, with a navy-blue island unit, and the work surfaces are a seamless white Corian, beautiful, if somewhat impractical. I hate having to scour the sink with bleach to get rid of tea bag stains. We have a black Aga as well as two conventional ovens. I never use the steam oven. At the far end of the room is a massive oak table large enough to seat fourteen people.

'Wow!' Patrick whistles gently. He isn't the first and he won't be the last to be impressed. Ours is the sort of kitchen you see laid out on the pages of glossy magazines. I know how lucky I am.

'Would you like a drink?'

'A beer would be great.'

'Food is nearly ready,' I say as I hand him a glass. 'I'm just going to call the kids.'

I walk to the bottom of the stairs and shout, 'Supper's ready!'

Oliver comes clattering down and careers into the kitchen. I wonder if he's forgotten that Patrick was going to be here, because he freezes.

'Hello,' Patrick says. 'You must be Oliver?'

Oliver gawps at him.

My boy is well brought up, because he snaps out of the moment quickly and shakes Patrick's hand.

'Are you into *Minecraft*?' Patrick asks. 'Because my nephew is the same age as you and he's obsessed. I could do with a few lessons if you're up to it at any time?'

'Sure,' Oliver says.

'Darling, could you go and get your sister for me, please?'

He sighs, but thumps back upstairs. A few seconds later he re-emerges. 'Mia says she's not hungry.'

'What!' I turn to Patrick. 'I'm sorry. Mia has been struggling of late.'

'That's totally understandable.'

'Why don't you two start, and I'll go and have a word with her.'

'How about I carve and you can go and chat to Mia. I'm sure Oliver and I can manage the serving. Hey, Oliver?'

I find a carving knife and some serving bowls and leave them on the side for Patrick.

.   .   .

UPSTAIRS, Mia is on her bed with her headphones clamped to her ears. She doesn't look up when I stand next to her bed.

'Darling, you need to eat.'

She ignores me and I wonder if she can even hear what I'm saying, as the music is thumping so loudly. I reach over and try to pull her headphones off.

'Don't!'

But one earphone is off now.

'I know you don't want to meet Patrick, but I'd rather you did. It's polite and I don't want to be hiding things from you.'

'You're gross, Mother. I don't want to know who you're shagging. I'll eat later.'

'No, you will come downstairs now. You don't need to make conversation, but you will join us.'

'And if I don't? What can you do?'

'Don't push me, Mia.' I try to withhold my tears. I remember when Mia was a toddler and she threw herself down on the floor in Tesco, screaming and wailing because I wouldn't let her have a packet of jelly babies. I was mortified at the time, but now I think how much easier those days were. I didn't have to walk on eggshells. People are forgiving of parents with temper-tantrum toddlers.

She sighs melodramatically. 'If it means so much to you, I'll come and see lover boy, but don't expect me to talk.'

She follows me downstairs and into the kitchen. She's wearing shorts that barely cover her backside and a shapeless baggy T-shirt with the name of a band I've never heard of. As she sits at the table, she clamps her headphones back over her ears and keeps her eyes on her bitten fingernails.

'Hello, Mia.' Patrick tries to engage with her. She doesn't look up.

'I'm so sorry,' I say quietly, carrying two plates piled with food back to the table. Patrick carries the remaining two and places one in front of Mia and the other at the head of the table.

'You can't sit there. It's Dad's place.' Mia scowls at him.

'Um, do you mind sitting next to me instead?' I suggest, trying to quell the redness I can feel creeping up my neck.

'Of course. No problem. I totally understand.'

Mia eats with her headphones on, totally ignoring the rest of us and refusing to engage in conversation. I am mortified. But what can I do? Fortunately, Patrick and Oliver seem to hit it off. Patrick knows all of the 'in' computer games, and Oliver is suitably impressed. I am relieved and also curious as to how childless Patrick knows so much.

After dinner, when both Mia and Oliver have left the room, Patrick strides over to me and takes my hand.

'I understand, Lydia. Really I do.'

And I burst into tears, thinking how incredibly lucky I am to have met such a gorgeous, compassionate man.

13

A s the autumnal days merge into winter, Mia starts communicating with me again. It's slow, but I've decided not to push her. Yes, she's angry with me for dating Patrick, and as a result, he hasn't been back to our house. Yes, she's angry with her father for dying. My heart bleeds for her. Life isn't fair. But so long as I avoid any mention of Patrick, we seem to be on safe territory.

Now, we're facing the dreaded winter holidays. Our first Christmas without Adam. I think back to the happy times, when year after year Adam insisted on dressing up as Father Christmas, and how he used to creep into the children's bedrooms to lay their filled Christmas stockings at the end of their beds. I think back to last Christmas when we tried so hard to be civil to each other for the sake of Mia and Oliver. I think we succeeded. I hope we did.

My sister, Bea, has suggested that we join them in Switzerland. The kids jumped at the idea; I wasn't so keen. The compromise was that she would whisk Mia and Oliver away at the beginning of the school holidays for ten days in an alpine chalet with her and the boys, for daily ski lessons and fondues with fries. Her husband, Craig, and I are due to join them for a short break over Christmas and Boxing Day. They regularly rent the same chalet in a small resort in the French part of Switzerland. I've seen the photos of wooden walls and fleece-covered chairs, a log-burning stove and breathtaking views of jagged mountains and snow-laden fir trees. They've been so many times, I assume Bea is a pro skier by now.

She has changed since she married Craig. I think she tries a little too hard to fit in with the privileged South Kensington set that she mixes with. Prestigious boarding schools for the boys, organizing charitable events to keep herself busy in their absence, and holidays in Switzerland and the Caribbean. Craig does something in the City I've never understood, and their lifestyle is equally lavish to ours, more so, actually, because they seem to have the time to spend and enjoy their money. Two sisters growing up with nothing, now living with unimaginable wealth. I often wonder how happy Bea is, but I never dare ask. She's one of those closed-up, stiff-upper-lip types who would never admit anything was less than perfect, not least to herself. I think Mum saw through it. She said on several occasions to both of us that money was a great insurance policy, but it didn't secure happiness.

I used to welcome school holidays and half-terms, special times to share with my children, but now I have to juggle child-care and work alone, things are different. Thank goodness for Bea. I wave them off, happy in the knowledge they'll be well looked after, get plenty of cold fresh air and sunshine, and a break from the grief and the memories. In the kids' absence, I intend to concentrate on work.

Things are definitely better with Ajay. He told me that he and Marianne have decided to make their marriage work. I'm surprised. And I have to assume that the police are no longer interested in him, because nothing further has been said or done. As the weeks and months have passed, I have resigned myself to not knowing how Adam died. DC White has confirmed that the case is still open, but I doubt they're working very hard on it. Knife crime has surged; there are other major crimes to solve.

I try not to think about how dismayed Adam would be that his case wasn't at the top of their list. I imagine what he would have done if it had been me who had died. I am sure he would be contacting the police every day to demand answers; turning up at the station, his arms on his hips, his jaw jutting forwards, telling them that not knowing isn't good enough. I often think that I am failing his memory by not doing the same.

Although the business is still suffering from the retail downtrend, the atmosphere is vastly improved in the office, probably because I don't eye Ajay with suspicion. He is cordial with me, we are agreeing on most major business decisions, and I try not to think about Marianne. In fact, it's a bit like the old days, before Adam joined us.

PATRICK HAS BEEN in Manchester for the past three days. He has invited me out for dinner tonight and I'm hoping that he will stay over; the first time sleeping at my house, taking advantage of the kids' absence.

I am fastening the clasp on my rose gold necklace when I hear the crunching of tyres on the drive. I glance out of my dressing room window and am surprised to see a taxi pulling up.

Patrick climbs out of the back seat. His jacket is over his shoulder, a briefcase in his hand, and he looks thoroughly flustered. Barefoot, I rush downstairs and fling the front door open just as he's putting his finger on the buzzer.

'What's happened?' I ask, standing back to let him in.

'I'm lucky I'm not dead,' he says as he strides inside.

I wince and he places a hand on my arm. 'Sorry, that was insensitive. It's been a shit day. My car was nearly written off.'

'What!'

'I need a drink. Is that ok?'

'Of course.'

He follows me along the hallway and into the kitchen. I grab a beer from the fridge.

'Something stronger, Lydia. Do you mind? A whisky, maybe?'

'Of course.' I hurry into the living room and open the door to Adam's bespoke walnut wood drinks cupboard. I find a bottle of whisky. I've no idea if it's a good one or not, but I pour a large measure into a cut-glass tumbler. I carry it back into the kitchen, where Patrick is slumped on a chair.

'What happened?' I hand him the glass.

'I was on my way back from a client meeting when the car started juddering. I pulled up onto the hard shoulder of the M23 and quickly realised I had a flat tyre. I was going to change it myself, but then thought twice about it, what with all of the heavy lorries thundering past. So I called the AA and got myself up onto the bank. Five minutes later, a lorry caught the corner of the car. It flipped over and was bedlam.'

'Bloody hell. Was anyone hurt?'

'Miraculously, no. And now I've got no car for work and it's a total nightmare.' He runs his fingers through his hair, making it stand up on end.

'Have you spoken to your insurance company?'

'Yup, and they won't pay up.'

'What do you mean they won't pay? You've got full insur-ance, right?'

'Of course. They will stump up eventually, but my cover

doesn't pay for a rental car and it's like-for-like cover, so I'll get bugger all for my old banger. What with spending every last penny on Sandra's medication, I've got no spare dosh.'

I don't mention that the last two months of her treatment have been paid with my money, not his.

'What a nightmare,' I say. 'Would you like a hug?'

'Sure.' He stands up and throws his arms around me, but I can feel all the tension in him, the knots in his back, the frown still on his forehead.

'Sorry, Lydia,' he says as he pulls away from me and sits back down again. 'I just don't know what I'm going to do without a car. I need to drive to Maidstone tomorrow, and the trains are so unreliable.'

'You can borrow Adam's car. It's a Bentley, though.' I pull a face to express my embarrassment of owning such a beast.

He laughs and reaches for my hand. 'It's kind of you, darling, but I just need to rent a car for a few weeks. I can't really turn up to my client meetings in a Bentley. It wouldn't give the right impression.'

'Perhaps not,' I say, thinking I should sell it. I won't be driving such an ostentatious vehicle.

'I'm owed so much bloody money.' Patrick tips back his whisky in one go. 'One hundred grand from various clients. You're lucky to have regular cash flow in your business.'

'How much will it cost to rent a car for a few weeks?' I ask.

He raises his shoulders. 'A couple of grand, I guess.'

'I'll write you a cheque.'

'No, not again, Lydia. I haven't paid you back for Sandra's treatment yet.'

'Honestly, it's no problem. I know you'll pay me back as soon as you can.'

'That I will,' he says, kissing me again. 'I don't know what I'd do without you. You're my life saviour.'

'How was Manchester?'

'Cold, rainy, grey and thoroughly uneventful. I went to work, sorted out their systems, was late back to the hotel, had a tasteless omelette via room service and then straight to sleep. The same both nights. Dreaming of you, as always.'

'How long have we got?' I ask, glancing at my watch.

'Forty minutes. I booked the table for 7.30 p.m. Could I have a quick shower?'

'Of course.'

He follows me upstairs, making a grab for my backside. I show him into the bathroom that Adam was using and find him some fresh towels.

Half an hour later we're both ready.

'You are so beautiful,' he says as his gaze travels slowly over me from head to toe.

'I'm not,' I say. I get flustered with compliments like that, not that I have received many. I am a realist. I might be described as attractive, with my thick, dark blonde hair and expensive high-lights and wide hazel eyes, but I am no great beauty. If anything, it is I who is out of my league with Patrick, just as I always thought I had been with Adam.

Patrick couldn't be more loving and attentive throughout dinner, gazing at me as if there were no one else in the restaurant, holding my hand across the table, playing footsie underneath it. He asks me about the business, how the children are doing, and whether Mia has forgiven him for blustering into our lives. And when our coffees arrive, he whispers across the table, 'I don't think I have ever wanted anyone as badly as I want you, Lydia.'

I blush.

He summons the waiter and asks for the bill. He reaches into his jacket pocket, but his hand comes out empty. Frowning, he searches in his other pockets and then looks at me, his face a picture of dismay.

'I am so sorry, Lydia. I'm a fool. I think I must have left my wallet in the bathroom when I took a shower. That's so embarrassing, darling, especially when you are doing so much for me.'

I try to shrug it off, plastering my face with a tight smile. In the scheme of things it doesn't matter. I can afford to pay, and Patrick appears genuinely upset. But there is a little trickle of concern that pings at the back of my throat like an annoying tickle. Did he leave his wallet behind on purpose? Is the difference in our financial status an issue, if not for him, for me?

I try to dismiss the concern. When we're home and I'm downstairs locking up, Patrick bounds up the stairs and then reappears with his wallet in his hand. He starts counting twenty- and ten-pound notes.

'What are you doing?' I ask.

'Paying you back for dinner.'

'Don't be silly,' I say, kissing him on the nose. 'Put your money away.'

He grabs me then and tugs me upstairs. We shed our clothes as we go.

I THOUGHT it would be weird sleeping with Patrick in the bed I shared with Adam. In fact, it feels perfectly ok. I suppose Adam and I had been distant for such a long time, this room seems more like my own rather than our marital bedroom. I awake from a deep sleep, Patrick snoring gently next to me, his face line-free and beguiling in sleep. I glance at my alarm clock.

It's 6.35 a.m., and last night Patrick said he had a taxi coming to collect him at 7 a.m. so he could get to the car rental depot as soon as they opened.

'Patrick,' I say, gently shaking him, 'wake up!'

He mumbles something incomprehensible and throws an arm over my stomach.

'It's time to get up.' I speak louder this time. He startles me by sitting bolt upright in bed.

'Shit, I was in a dream,' he says, rubbing his eyes.

'You haven't got long.'

'Bloody hell.' He jumps out of bed and rushes towards the bathroom. 'I'll have a quick shower, if that's ok?'

'Sure.'

I put on my dressing gown and start collecting the clothes that we cast off in the heat of passion last night. Patrick's crumpled shirt is on the bedroom floor along with his boxer shorts and socks. I have to walk along the corridor and halfway down the stairs to retrieve his trousers and tie. I chuckle as I bend down to pick them up. As I lift up his trousers, a receipt flutters from his pocket. I pick it up and can't help but look at it. It's for dinner for two in at La Belle Gras Restaurant in Mayfair, London. £167. An expensive dinner. And then I note the date and frown. It is dated the night before yesterday. That doesn't make sense. Patrick told me he was in Manchester, not London. He told me what a boring time he had.

The shower is still running when I shuffle slowly back into the bedroom. I put the receipt back into his trouser pocket. He has lied to me. And he has just asked me to lend him money for a rental car, plus I paid for dinner, not forgetting the huge fifty thousand pounds on loan for his sister's treatment. I have a reason to be suspicious, don't I? I sit perched on the end of the bed, listening to the roar of the power shower. I wait until eventually the sound of crashing water stops. Patrick emerges, a white towel around his waist; he's using another one to rub his hair dry.

'I wish I didn't have to go,' he says, pouting. 'I want to ravish you all over again.'

I attempt a smile. He is too busy getting dressed to notice my discomfort. Should I say something to him? I am sure there is a reasonable explanation. Perhaps it's not even Patrick's receipt. Maybe it's for a colleague or something he picked off the ground? But how likely is that?

When he is dressed, he leans down to give me a kiss. He smells of mint toothpaste and my almond shower gel, and then there's that intoxicating scent that I can't quite define but is so authentically Patrick.

'Can I see you tonight?' He slips his hand down inside my dressing gown.

'I'm sorry, I can't do tonight. I'll call you,' I say.

He stands up and stares at me.

'Lydia, I am in love with you.'

'Oh,' I say, unable to articulate any other words. I think I'm in love with him too, but the receipt and the money I have loaned him have thrown me a curve ball, and I need time to think.

Fortunately, we are interrupted by the loud beeping of a car horn.

He throws me another quick kiss and then bounds for the front door.

'Hold on,' I say. 'You'll need the keys to open it.'

I HAVE an unproductive day pottering around at home, mainly because I'm overtired and my mind is in turmoil about Patrick. He says he loves me, and I think I love him too, but is he being really honest with me? I just don't know. Those little niggling doubts at the back of my mind make concentrating so difficult. I chastise myself for not asking him about the receipt there and then, because at least I would have had clarity. I'm just glad that I'm seeing Cassie and Fiona for a drink tonight. They'll help me make sense of my doubts.

We meet at a little wine bar in Horsham. It's a cosy room with low ceilings, dark beams and glass tables. Fiona is already there when I arrive. She stands to greet me, planting a kiss on both my cheeks. She is dressed immaculately as always in one of her ubiquitous trouser suits. It's navy blue today, accessorized by a turquoise blouse. It suits her.

'You look tired,' she says.

I sink into the chair. 'I am. I suppose I didn't put enough concealer under my eyes!'

She pours me a glass of white wine from the bottle already on the table.

'What's up?'

'Just stuff with Patrick.' We are interrupted by Cassie's arrival. She has transformed her hair once again. It's now jet black and striking against her pale skin.

'Talking about her gorgeous man, are you?' she says as she drops her boho bag on the floor and sits down. 'Have you met him yet, Fiona? He's divine!'

'Lucky you,' Fiona says to me. 'What were you about to say?'

'I think I'm in love with Patrick, but I don't know if I can trust him, and it's driving me to distraction.'

'Why, what's happened?' Cassie has poured herself so much wine, she has to bend down to slurp from the rim of the glass so as not to spill it.

I snigger. Fiona looks bemused. I suppose she's not yet used to Cassie's idiosyncrasies.

'I found a receipt for dinner for two in a posh London restaurant, but he had already told me he was in Manchester that night.'

'Yikes,' Cassie says. 'Are you sure? Perhaps it wasn't even his receipt.'

'I know, I know. But it's eating me up.'

'Why don't you just ask him about it?' Fiona suggests.

'Yes, I should do. I don't want to offend him. And he's asked me to lend him money for a rental car because his was badly damaged.'

'You've loaned him money!' Cassie exclaims.

'Yes, for cancer treatment for his sick sister and for the rental car. But he didn't ask for the money for his sister, I offered it,' I say, trying to dismiss the kernel of concern that is bubbling in my stomach at my friends' reactions. 'Really, it's fine.' I'm glad I haven't told Fiona and Cassie quite how much money I've loaned him.

'It's not fine, is it, Fiona?' Cassie says.

'I don't think I'd loan someone money I don't know very well, but it's hard for me to say. What's your gut instinct telling you?' Fiona asks.

'That he's a good guy. He told me he loves me and I'm in love with him too.' I feel my cheeks redden.

'In which case, I shouldn't worry. I can always put something in writing for you, and you can ask Patrick to sign to confirm your agreement.'

'Thanks for the offer, Fiona,' I say, and then change the subject. 'I can't wait to go to Switzerland for Christmas. The kids are having a great time.'

'You're really lucky.' Fiona sighs, slumping in her chair. 'I've got so much work I don't think I'll get much time off. I'm sick and tired of dull property transactions and drawing up wills. Think I might look for another job in the New Year.'

That jogs my memory. 'Talking of wills, we can't start probate for Adam's estate until the inquest has completed,' I say. 'There's still so much legal stuff to do. Actually, I was thinking I should probably change my will. At the moment, everything is left to Adam.' I sigh.

'I'm happy to have a look at it for you,' Fiona offers. 'I'm sure I can fit it in.'

'Thanks, that would be helpful.'

And then my mobile pings with a text. I glance at it and redden.

'Who's it from?' Cassie asks.

'Patrick.'

'What does he say?'

'I can't possibly show you!' I bury my phone deep inside my handbag. Patrick has just spelled out exactly what he would like to do to me right now, and it's making me blush pillar-box red.

14

I expect Patrick to call me after his lewd text, but he doesn't. And I don't call him. I need more time to work out how I'm going to raise the conversation about the receipt. But at 8 a.m. the next morning, his name flashes up on my phone. I stare at it lying on the kitchen table, watching it vibrate, listening to it ring for several seconds. Should I answer? What shall I say? But I'm too late. It stops ringing. I move across the room to make myself a second cup of coffee, but my phone starts up again. I grab it.

'Sorry, I was in the bathroom. I missed your call.'

'How are you this morning?'

'Ok, thanks. And you?' I sound as if I'm speaking to a colleague in the office, not my lover.

'Are you sure? You sound... I don't know, different.'

I plop down onto a chair. 'There is something, Patrick. When you were in the shower yesterday and I was picking up our clothes, a receipt fell out of your pocket. It was for a dinner in London two nights ago. I know I shouldn't have looked but–'

'Hey, it's no problem,' Patrick interrupts me. 'I'd have looked if the shoe had been on the other foot. You're right, I was in

Manchester, but then I had to nip down to London. My client wanted to meet in the Big Smoke. It was really last minute. He's American and one of my best clients, so I have to wine and dine him whenever he's in town. It's really frustrating. He expects me to be at his beck and call.'

'Oh,' I say. 'I thought you said you ate omelettes in your hotel room both nights.'

'I did the first night, but not the second night. You must have misheard me.'

I am silent. I could have sworn he said he stayed in his hotel room both nights. I pray he isn't lying to me. After all the lies Adam told, and possibly the lies that Ajay is still telling everyone, I need Patrick to be honourable.

He breaks the silence. 'Look, Lydia, I get that you find it hard to trust me. Adam treated you like shit. He lied to you and cheated on you with your business partner's wife. But I'm not Adam, darling. You can trust me.'

'Oh,' I say again. Perhaps Patrick is right. I am so bruised from the lies that Adam told me, I'm finding it hard to trust anyone else. But I can't help thinking about the money. Fifty thousand pounds is a hell of a lot of money to lend to anyone, and it's not helpful that I hear Adam's voice in my head, chastising me for being too hasty and too trusting.

'I'll call you later, and I'll come around to yours when I'm back from Maidstone,' he says.

'Um, I'm not sure if–'

But Patrick has already hung up.

I lock up the house and drive to work.

It's mid-morning and I am studying some catalogues from a new supplier when there's a knock on my office door and Ajay walks in.

'Can I ask your opinion about something?'

'Sure, take a seat.' My nerves are on edge and I can't work out why.

'I think I have found a good candidate to take over Adam's position, but would like your input. She's coming for an interview at 2 p.m. and I was wondering if you'd like to sit in with me?'

He passes a CV across my desk. This is clearly Ajay holding out an olive branch. He never involves me in staffing decisions on the operational side of the business, but I suppose filling my dead husband's position is a sensitive issue. And, of course, having an excellent accountant on the team is essential.

'I trust your judgement,' I say, handing the CV back to him after a cursory read. But when I look up, a scowl briefly passes over his face. I thought he would be pleased that I am happy to leave the decision to him, but perhaps I made the wrong call.

'So be it,' he says as he walks towards the door.

'How are things with you and Marianne these days?' I ask.

He freezes and answers with his back to me. 'We are trying to put our marriage back on track. Why?'

'No reason.' But I do have a reason. I want Ajay to know about Patrick. In a weird sort of way, I think I want his approval.

Just a few minutes later, I get a text from Patrick.

Just to let you know that I've repaid the money you loaned me. Can't thank you enough. Px

I check my online banking, and indeed, he has repaid me in full – both for the immunotherapy and the car rental. I groan. I feel terrible for having questioned him, for all that time I have been worrying whether he's ripped me off, for being the eternal pessimist, the doubter. The thing is, when something bad has happened to you, rather than thinking *I've had my dollop of bad luck, I'm in the clear now*, you think, *if it's happened once, it can happen again.*

And it's the same for the kids. For instance, Oliver has developed a phobia of swimming. He used to be quite the little eel in the pool, but now he has asked to be excused from swimming lessons at school. I had to write a note and explain his unusual circumstances. I tried to explain to him that it was one-in-a-billion chance that something could happen to him in a swimming pool, but how can I expect him to believe that after how his dad died?

It's the same for me. Adam lied to me. He cheated on me. Of course I'm going to be wary around other men. Of course I'm going to think that perhaps the fault lies in me. Perhaps I am too trusting or possibly I'm wanting in some way; that is why my husband sought out love elsewhere.

And then Patrick calls me.

'Did you get the money?'

'Yes, thank you. You didn't need to repay me so quickly.'

'Actually I did, Lydia. I get why you're the way you are. I was like you for a long time after I discovered my ex had an affair, but in the end, all that resentment did was eat me up and make me sick. So I get it, darling, I really do. The thing is, I'm not like Adam. I'm single-minded, and both my head and heart are set on you.'

'Thank you, Patrick.'

'Also, I know you are wealthy, far richer than I am, but I hope I can prove myself worthy of you in other ways.'

'I don't care about money. It's not important.'

'Exactly. Sharing values is what matters. Having fun. Being compatible in bed. Talking of which, I would love to ravish you–'

'I'm at work!'

'Even more exciting!' And then he groans.

'It's so frustrating, but I don't think I'm going to be able to see you this weekend, Lydia. Work is crazy in the run-up to Christmas. I hope you don't mind.'

'Ok,' I say. But I am disappointed. I had hoped that Patrick and I could take advantage of Mia and Oliver's absence.

'I've got to go now. Will be in touch. Love you, Lydia.'

As it turns out, I enjoy having the evening to myself, going to bed early and not having to set an alarm clock for the next morning. I spend the day pottering around the house. I know I should be sorting through Adam's office, which I still haven't tackled. I just can't bring myself to do it. Instead, I am tackling a mountain of ironing when the doorbell rings.

I'm confused as to why no one is standing on the doorstep. I glance from left to right and am about to step back into the house when Patrick bounces out of a bush from the side of the house.

'Surprise!'

I jump out of my skin.

'What are you doing here?' I ask, trying to control my racing heart. My nerves are still on edge. It takes me a few moments to realise he's holding out a beautiful bouquet of red roses.

'I'm whisking you away to London for the weekend.'

'But–'

'No buts. Go pack a bag.'

'Where's your car?'

'I've left the car at the bottom of the drive. I wanted to surprise you.'

'You certainly did that!'

An hour later, Patrick and I are in his hire car en route to London. Going against the traffic, we are in the centre of town by 5.30 p.m. Patrick pulls up in front of a beautiful hotel off The Strand, an opulent Edwardian building with curved corners, balustrade balconies and a copula dome. It has a distinctly Parisian feel. A uniformed attendant appears and removes our bags from the boot. Patrick hands him the car key.

The interior of the hotel is breathtaking with twenty-foot-high curved oak window frames, white marble columns and matching marble floor. In the centre of the atrium is an eight-foot-high floral arrangement of amaryllis and ferns, constructed to look like a vast pineapple. I follow Patrick, past dark red velvet banquettes and plush chairs to the curved reception area.

Here, he checks us both in, and we are led by a young porter dressed all in black with gold epaulettes and shining gold buttons to our magnificent room on the fourth floor. The room is furnished in the palest of pastels: muted blush pink armchairs and a baby blue cashmere blanket on the bed to match the blue headboard. The walls are lined with a cream silk wallpaper, and the paintings are equally delicate, abstract landscapes toned to match the rest of the soft furnishings. The marble bathroom has two sinks and a jacuzzi bath with a separate shower.

'I hope you like this,' Patrick says.

'It's amazing!' I throw my arms around him.

'Plan of action is a cocktail here; then we're going to see *The Book of Mormon*, followed by dinner at my favourite restaurant. Tomorrow, I thought you could do the shops in the morning, and early afternoon I've booked you an aromatherapy massage here in the hotel. We'll be home in time for supper. That's when Mia and Oliver will be back from Switzerland, isn't it?'

'Wow! Why do I deserve such a special weekend?'

'Because you are special,' he says, kissing the tip of my nose.

I can't believe that Patrick has been so considerate. He even remembered what time I said the kids would be home.

I AM RELIEVED that I packed my little black dress, the one I wore on the hapless date with Rory the solicitor. I put it on, slide into my stilettos and finish off the outfit with a pair of gold hoop earrings and a simple gold chain. I have a smart, heavyweight black coat and a black-and-gold throw to wear at the theatre and just hope I will be warm enough. Patrick is wearing a suit with a tie. He looks particularly handsome. He takes my hand as we walk to the lift and down to the dining room.

After cocktails we take a black London taxi for the short ride to the theatre. It's years since I've been to a show, and I remember how much I have missed going to the theatre. Even though I have never been a great aficionado of musicals, it is a fabulous performance.

And then to dinner. The restaurant is tucked away behind Covent Garden. Le Goût de L'époque is tiny, with just twenty covers, and if you didn't know it was there, you certainly wouldn't find it. We walk down a short flight of dark stairs and then a heavy navy velvet curtain is pulled back to let us into the room. The ceiling is curved like in a traditional cellar. Every table is laid with white linen and silver cutlery, along with lit candles in filigree holders that throw patterns of flickering light on the walls. A violinist is seated in the far corner playing gypsy tunes, but quietly, so that it's perfectly possible to have an intimate conversation without raising one's voice. The aroma of fine French cuisine makes my stomach rumble.

'Good evening, Mr Grant.' The maître d' nods his head towards Patrick. I'm surprised that he knows his name, but then assume he must have worked it out based on the fact that ours is the only unoccupied table. 'How are you this evening?'

'Very well, thank you.'

He gives us each a glass of champagne and then hands me a menu, and Patrick the wine list with a menu. My menu doesn't have prices on it. I hope that this evening isn't going to cost Patrick too much. I eat a vegetarian starter with beetroot served numerous different ways, followed by loin of venison that melts in my mouth. Normally, conversation flows easily, but there is a strange tension this evening and I can't work out why. Patrick is a little restless, drinking more wine than normal and starting a new sentence before he has finished the previous one.

'Are you all right?' I ask him, leaning across the table and placing my hand on his.

'Yes, yes. Everything is more than fine. I'm so happy.'

And then our plates are removed. I expect the waiter to return with a menu for us to choose desserts, but instead he returns with a bottle of Moet et Chandon champagne.

'Gosh, I'm not sure I can drink much more,' I say quietly to Patrick.

'There's no hurry,' he says.

About five minutes later, the waiter appears with two plates. On each is a large chocolate dome.

'This looks fabulous,' I say.

The waiter places a jug of hot chocolate sauce on the table between us.

'Sir, if you would like to do the honours,' he says, raising his eyebrows at Patrick and then making a strange half bow before moving away. Patrick picks up the jug and pours the steaming hot chocolate over my dome, which melts into a chocolate puddle.

'What's that?' I ask. There is something glinting in the chocolate.

Patrick pushes his chair back and walks two steps so that he is next to me. Then to my utter bemusement he gets down on one knee.

'Lydia, would you do me the honour of becoming my wife?'

My jaw drops open. All the other diners have fallen silent, and everyone is staring at us. Even the violinist has stopped playing. And then, as if he realises that he is missing his moment, he launches into the theme from *Love Story*.

'So?' he asks, reaching for my hands.

'Yes. Yes, of course!' I say.

And he leans over, grabbing my face between his hands and

kissing me passionately. Despite the quiet elegance of the restaurant and its clientele, everyone erupts with applause and shouts of congratulations. The waiter pours us another glass of champagne and Patrick returns to his seat.

'The ring is inside the chocolate.'

'I gathered,' I say, laughing as I try to extract it from the chocolatey goo without making too much of a mess.

'Let me clean it,' he says. He dips the ring in his water glass and then wipes it dry with his napkin. 'Hold out your hand.'

He slips the ring onto my finger, the finger that still has a white mark from the engagement and wedding rings I wore for the last sixteen years. 'You have just made me the happiest man on earth,' Patrick says.

I gaze at the ring. It is huge and utterly beautiful; a large emerald-cut solitaire diamond; I hate to think how much it cost. It makes my ring from Adam pale into insignificance. No wonder Patrick couldn't afford his sister's treatment if he was spending money on a whopper like this.

As we wander back to the hotel, walking this time, arms around each other, I can't help thinking whether I'm being impetuous. I recall my promise to the kids that I wouldn't be giving them a new father. I wonder what friends and family will think, engaged to a new man so quickly after the death of my first husband. Patrick squeezes me as if he can sense my doubts.

'I am so happy,' he whispers into my hair.

'Me too,' I say.

MUCH LATER, when we are lying in each other's arms in the sumptuous bed with the softest mattress and most silken sheets I have ever lain in, Patrick asks, 'Can we get married soon? Perhaps in a month?'

'Why the hurry?'

I can feel his heart beating faster and it makes me love him even more.

'We're not exactly in the first flush of youth. I don't want to miss any more years with you. It just feels so right.'

'Let me think about it,' I say, wondering how I will break the news to Mia and Oliver. 'It's just quite soon since Adam died and–'

'I know, but I want to grasp happiness, and I want you to be Mrs Grant. I'm an old- fashioned man and don't believe in living together before marriage.'

That surprises me, but I don't say anything. I think then of how unhappy I have been during the past few years; the times when Adam was clearly cheating on me, but I let him get away with it for the sake of our family. Those nights I lay in bed with him snoring gently next to me, but feeling lonelier than I might have done if I had been living alone. I had no idea it was possible to feel so forlorn living with someone else.

But Patrick is a different man. He understands my issues with trust, and perhaps he has them too. And the money concerns, well, they have proven to be unfounded so far. I deserve this happiness. So long as I provide security and love to Mia and Oliver, I am sure all will be fine. It will, won't it?

15

The gym has become my refuge of late. It's ironic, really, because I was terrible at sport at school. Always the last to be chosen for teams, I experienced humiliation and bullying because of my ineptitude to catch or hit a ball. And I never learned to swim properly. How ironic that is; perhaps it should have been me who died in our swimming pool.

Occasionally, I use the static bicycles in the gym, but today, as is normal, I am here for a yoga class. The inward focus, breath control and stretches always make me feel better. This afternoon, I got especially lucky, as there were only three of us in the class. Dee, our Aussie teacher, was remarkably good humoured and gave each of us extra attention. So now, as I pull on a sweatshirt, I feel as if I am floating on a zen cloud.

'Lydia!'

I look up. It's Fiona.

'How are you?' She leans in for a couple of air kisses.

'I'm great, actually,' I say.

She stands back and appraises me. 'You're looking fabulous! What's been happening?'

I realise I haven't spoken to her for at least a fortnight.

'Something fantastic has happened,' I say, unable to stop myself from beaming.

She nudges me. 'Go on then, spit it out!'

I glance around me. Silly really, as no one is the slightest bit interested in me. 'Patrick and I have got engaged!'

'Oh my God!' she says, her eyes wide with surprise. 'Oh my God, that's amazing! I'm so happy for you!'

'But please don't tell anyone. I have to pick my moment to tell the kids, and as the police still haven't closed the enquiry into Adam's death, I don't think it's something I should be shouting about from the rooftops.'

She nods. 'I quite understand. But nevertheless, it's so exciting!' She moves as if to put an arm around me but then withdraws it. 'Come on, I need to buy you a drink.'

I follow her to the coffee shop, where caffeine is the strongest substance on offer. 'Tell me all. When did it happen?'

'Two days ago. Saturday night. Patrick whisked me off to London.'

We're at the front of the queue now. 'What would you like?' she asks.

'An apple juice, please.'

She orders the juice for me and a peppermint tea for herself. After paying for the drinks, she picks up the tray and we walk towards an empty table.

'So how did he propose? I want a minute-by-minute account!'

'He whisked me to London. We stayed in a beautiful hotel just off The Strand, and then we went to a show followed by dinner at a fantastic restaurant. Le Goût de L'époque. It's got–'

Fiona knocks over her cup of mint tea. I move away just in time to avoid the burning liquid scalding my legs.

'I'm sorry,' she says, all flustered.

'It's fine,' I say, grabbing some paper napkins and dabbing the spilled tea. 'Let me get you another one.'

'No, no. Don't bother. I'm not that thirsty anyway.'

I frown. 'If you're sure.'

She nods, so I sit back down.

'I interrupted you,' she says.

'Anyway, the restaurant has two Michelin stars, and it's absolutely beautiful. The food was sublime. Then the dessert arrived, and it was a chocolate dome with a little jug of hot chocolate sauce. Patrick poured it over the top and the chocolate dome melted. Inside was a diamond ring. He then got down on one knee and asked me to marry him. It was the most romantic proposal ever!'

'That's lovely,' Fiona says, but there's something a bit off in her reaction. I suppose she's envious. I guess I would be, too, if I had been dating without much success for five years, and then a friend came along and got engaged within seven months of her losing her first husband. I change the subject.

'So what's new with you?'

Fiona reaches for my hand. 'Is that the engagement ring?'

I nod, holding out my left hand so she can admire the whopping diamond.

'It's beautiful,' she says. Her smile is more natural now.

'I know. I can't believe I'm so lucky. But would you mind keeping it to yourself for a while, just until I tell the kids?'

'Of course,' she says. 'What does Cassie think?'

'Her reaction wasn't quite as positive as yours.' I think back to last night, when I rang Cassie to tell her my jubilant news.

'You're what?' she exclaimed.

'Getting married.'

'But, Lydia, Adam only died a few months ago and you've barely known Patrick... for how long? Three months?'

'Four.'

'But that's nothing. Why the need to move so fast?'

'Because I want to, Cassie. We both want to. It feels right.'

'Are you really sure?' she asked.

'Yes. I couldn't be more positive. I love him, Cass. And he loves me. I know it sounds silly, but we're meant to be together.'

'Well, if you're that positive, I'm happy for you. When are you planning on getting married?'

'In four weeks' time.'

'What! Okay, ignore me, Lydia. Just so long as you're really, really sure. But I still think you could hold fire for a few months, just so you can get to know him better.'

'I do know him, Cassie. Anyway, will you be my maid of honour?'

'Of course, hon. You know I'm always there for you.'

'I do, thank you. Let's catch up later in the week.'

THINKING about my conversation with Cassie again, it does feel right. The issues over money are behind us, and Patrick paid for everything during our weekend away, no expenses spared. The beautiful hotel, a massive bouquet of red roses, dinner, and the ring on my finger, which came in a Tiffany's box and must have cost Patrick tens of thousands of pounds. It dwarfs the ring Adam gave me. I don't remember feeling quite so in love with Adam. This feels fresh, exciting, very right. Besides, I may never get another opportunity like this. Both Cassie and Fiona have been single for ages.

'Cassie's just looking out for you,' Fiona says, jolting me back to the here and now. 'You've been through so much this year. I think you're really lucky, and if love has come your way, you need to grasp it.'

'That's what I think, too.'

Of course, Cassie knows me better than Fiona does. And

she knows that I have a tendency to be a bit of a bull in a china shop, certainly more impulsive than she is. But sometimes I wonder if that's what has made me successful in business. I'm prepared to take risks – calculated risks, at least. But my relationship with Patrick doesn't feel like a risk. He makes me feel wonderful, both in bed and out. I feel safe in his arms. But most importantly, I don't want to miss this opportunity of happiness. Does that make me selfish or foolish even? I hope not.

As I'm driving home from the gym, I stop off at the supermarket to pick up some food for supper. The kids will be home on Saturday, and in the meantime, Patrick and I are spending as much time together as possible. I'm midway through making a risotto when the doorbell rings. It's Patrick. He sweeps me into a big hug, and it isn't until he releases me that I see his suitcase.

'What's that?'

'As we're formally engaged, I was hoping I might be able to stay here more often? It's a real hassle for me having to live between my flat and here.'

'I thought you said you were old-fashioned and didn't want to live together?'

'True.' He laughs. 'But that doesn't mean we can't spend lots of nights together! Will you want to carry on living here when we're married? After all, this is the house you shared with Adam.'

'Goodness, I haven't thought about that. I want to do whatever is the least disruptive for the kids. But maybe we should sell this house. Move somewhere new, somewhere that's ours?'

Patrick follows me into the kitchen. 'I think that's a marvelous idea. Something smells scrumptious.' He helps himself to a beer from the fridge whilst I stand at the stove and stir the risotto.

'I'm going to have to choose the right time to tell the kids about us getting married, and if they don't want to move to a new house, then I think we'll have to carry on living here. They might be really upset. Not that they don't like you or anything, it's just they've only recently lost their dad.'

I note a flash of annoyance cross Patrick's face, but after a sip of beer, it's gone and he smiles at me. 'Of course. It's just I want to scream about our engagement from the rooftops. I am the happiest man alive.' He moves across the kitchen and puts an arm around my waist, purring in my ear. 'So, the soon-to-be Mrs Grant, what can I do to help you make supper?'

THE PROBLEM IS, I *can't* tell the children yet. It's Christmas, and Adam's absence will be a gaping chasm for Mia and Oliver, despite us being away from home. Along with the hordes of travelers returning home or going on holiday, I take a flight to Geneva, followed by the train to Sion. It is years since I've been to the Alps, and I have forgotten how stunning the scenery is as the train snakes slowly along the edge of Lake Geneva, the sun glistening on the pale silvery water, so still it could be a mirror, reflecting the glorious white peaks of the mountains and the startling azure blue sky.

Craig is waiting for me at the station, having driven to Switzerland just yesterday.

'How is everyone?' I ask as he kisses me on the cheek.

'On good form. But more importantly, how are you?' He peers at me as if checking me for some rare disease.

'Happier to be here than at home, despite my initial reluctance.'

'Mmm. You look much better,' he says, wheezing as he lifts my two heavy suitcases into the boot of the car.

I wish I could tell him my news; I wish I could wear my sparkling, enormous engagement ring with pride, but instead, it lies hidden in my bedside drawer. If I put it on, it would be an instant giveaway. I wish Patrick were here to celebrate Christmas with all of us.

The chalet is as *hygge* as I anticipated and the children are in fine spirits, bouncing, refreshed and the happiest I have seen either of them since Adam died. Even Mia seems content to converse with me, our previous run-ins seemingly forgotten. And Christmas, well, it isn't so bad. Bea makes a huge effort with a big turkey and Christmas pudding brought from England. I spoil the kids and give them everything on their Christmas lists and more. It isn't until bedtime that Oliver buries his head in his pillow and weeps for his dead father.

Meanwhile, Patrick messages me every morning and telephones me just before going to bed. I feel like a teenager, madly in love, missing him terribly and desperate to announce my happiness to the world.

On Boxing Day, Craig takes the kids off skiing, and Bea and I tog up and go for a walk. Our breaths create wisps of steam as we talk; the snow crunches underneath our boots. I turn my face up to the sun, surprised at how hot the rays feel at this time of year.

'You seem different,' Bea says as she strides along so quickly, I struggle to keep up with her.

'I've met someone.'

'Thought so,' she says, not altering her pace. 'Mia and Oliver are at a very sensitive stage. I hope you're not going to make things worse for them.'

'Excuse me.' I stop still and put my thick, gloved hands on my hips. It takes Bea a few moments to realise I haven't kept pace with her. 'I don't need to be told how to look after my own children.'

'Don't take this the wrong way, Lydia, but sometimes you do. You throw yourself into everything. Work. Love life. I don't know what else you do. Sometimes I think you forget that your children should come first.'

Her words sting and I feel a fury burn at the back of my throat.

'That's not true!' I retort, but I wonder if I'm being totally honest with myself. 'I love my children and do the very best I can for them.'

'It's too soon for you to be in a new relationship.'

'How dare you tell me what I should or shouldn't be doing! You've no idea what I have been through these past couple of years. Don't I deserve any happiness?'

'Of course you do. But there's a time and a place for everything. You need to–'

'Stop listening to my sanctimonious big sister who thinks she knows best!' I retort, turning on my heel and walking back the way we came.

'Lydia, stop!'

But I don't. I march back towards the chalet and then continue along the path in the other direction, tears smarting my eyes. I lose track of how long I walk for. The path is flat and well-trodden, icy patches giving way to sawdust and pine needles. The views are spectacular, long vistas of the Rhone Valley, with towns dotted along the riverside in both directions and magnificent mountains rising far up into the sky. Sometimes I find myself in the forest, where the trees are still laden down with piles of snow, and I breathe in the scent of pine and watch as the snow glistens as if it's made up of millions of little diamonds.

And then I FaceTime Patrick. I hope I'm not disturbing him whilst he's with his sister and her family.

'Darling, how are you?'

I smile at the sound of his voice. 'Look at these views. Aren't they spectacular? I wish you were here.' I hold the phone up so that he can see the mountains.

'Wow! Something else. I'm missing you.'

'I'm missing you too.' I hold the phone so that I can see him, but he's got it on audio only. 'Can you switch over to video so I can see you?'

He lowers his voice. 'Can't, love. I'm with Sandra and the nurse is here. Wouldn't be appropriate.'

'I'm sorry. I'm home the day after tomorrow. Can I see you?'

'Of course. What do your children think about us getting married?'

'I haven't told them yet,' I admit.

'Lydia,' he says, the disappointment heavy in his voice.

'I will tell them. When we're home. I promise.'

'Got to go now,' he says.

'Bye, darling. I love you.'

But he's already hung up.

TWO DAYS LATER, without really patching up relations with Bea, we're back home. This morning, Patrick sent me a text message asking whether I've told the children about us getting married. I haven't replied. The truth is, I haven't plucked up the courage to tell them. We seem to have achieved a sense of equilibrium, and I am so loath to upset it. And Bea's words ring in my ears. But I *do* deserve happiness. Cassie and Fiona know me better than Bea these days, and they're supportive. If I want to marry Patrick, if I want to keep him, I have no choice but to tell Mia and Oliver.

We are having supper and a text pings on my phone. I don't need to look at it to know that it will be Patrick, so I take a large glug of wine, put down my cutlery and tell them.

'Patrick has asked me to marry him, and I've said yes.'

'But what about Dad?' Oliver asks, his lower lip trembling.

'I will always love Dad, but as I explained to you, we were

planning on getting divorced and now... I love Patrick, too. He will never be your dad, but–'

'He's going to move in with us, right?' Mia's upper lip curls.

'Yes. And we were thinking it might be sensible to move house and have a fresh start.'

'But this is Dad's house!' Oliver exclaims.

'And he died here. I don't know about you, but I find that very difficult.'

'It's all about you, isn't it?' Mia throws her cutlery onto her plate, pushes back her chair with a screech, and storms out of the room.

'Mia!' I say, but she ignores me.

'I won't have to call Patrick Dad, will I?' Oliver asks.

'Of course not. He will never be your father, but I hope he can become a grown-up friend, a bit like Cassie is to you. And what do you think about moving house?'

'Okay, I suppose. I don't like the swimming pool. Do you think Dad will mind if we leave?'

'Dad will be with you wherever in the world you are. He lives in your heart.' I stand up and clear my plate away.

'I think I'd better go and talk to your sister. There's more bolognaise in the pot if you'd like some. Help yourself.'

'It's ok, Mum.'

I CLIMB upstairs and knock on Mia's closed bedroom door. As I expected, she doesn't answer. I knock again and open it. To my surprise, there is no resistance. When I switch on the light, it's obvious why. Mia isn't there. I retreat back to the hall and check the family bathroom. It's empty.

'Mia!' I shout through the house. 'I know you're upset, but let's talk.'

I go through each room and then downstairs, checking Adam's office. I even look in the wardrobes and the understairs cupboard. She's not there. In the utility room, I see that her coat is missing. Perhaps she's in the garden? I turn on the floodlights and take a torch.

'Ollie, I'm going outside to look for Mia.'

He has a mouthful and nods at me.

But the back door is locked from the inside. I rush to the front door. It's also locked from the inside. It doesn't make sense. I walked through the whole house; I checked everywhere. I walk all around the garden, shouting her name. It is dark and cold, and there is a fine drizzle that accentuates the smell of rotting leaves. I shine the torch behind shrubs and even up to the branches of the old oak tree, which Mia used to climb when she was going through her prepubescent tomboy stage.

The final place I look is the little pool hut. I haven't been in here since Adam died. My heart is thumping as I open the door, terrified as to what I will find.

Nothing. It is empty.

The pool is covered, but it has no water in it. I got the maintenance company to come and drain it, because we won't be swimming again here.

'Mia!' I shout one last time, the terror evident in my strident tone. An airplane drones high above us on its ascent from Gatwick airport, and then there is silence again, not even the whistle of the wind in the branches or the birds settling down for the night.

I hurry back inside and check the garage and then the front of the house. No Mia.

Bile rises up my throat as I try to control my panic. I attempt some rational self-talk. Mia has stormed off because she's upset. It doesn't mean she's come to any harm. After a couple of deep breaths, I return to the kitchen.

'Mia's disappeared,' I say to Oliver.

'Have you rung her?' He looks at me as if I am a dimwit,

which in my panic, I am. I grab the kitchen phone and call Mia's number. It goes straight to voicemail, which suggests it's switched off.

Oliver sees my expression of dismay. 'Check FindFriends or FindMyPhone,' he says.

'Oh yes, of course.' I fumble with the phone.

He rolls his eyes. 'If you give me your mobile, I'll check for you.'

I hand it to him. I don't need to tell him my passcode. His fingers move quickly, but then he frowns. 'She's got her phone off. Can't help.'

'Oh God,' I mutter.

She can't have gotten far. She's only been gone for ten minutes or so. I run back upstairs and have another look in her room. I fling open her wardrobe, but I checked in there earlier. I ignore the mess inside, and as I'm closing the doors, I feel a cold draught on the back of my neck. I stride to the window and open the curtains. Her window is open. I peer outside, but can't see anything in the darkness.

'Mia!' I shout. There's no answer. Did she climb out of the window? Closing it, I rush to my bedroom, grab my handbag and run down the stairs.

'Come with me, Oliver. We're going in the car to look for her.'

Three minutes later, I'm driving at full pelt along our drive-way, but at the main road, I have no idea whether to turn left or right. I choose right. I drive slowly, and both Oliver and I scour the pavements, but the roads are empty. Besides, as it's dark, she could easily be lurking in shadows. Eventually, I turn the car around and we drive in the opposite direction. She's not there either. I turn the car back to home, saying silent prayers that we will find her sitting on the front doorstep.

But she's not.

Back inside the house, I pace the kitchen. 'I'll need to call some of her friends and see if she's with them,' I mutter, mainly to myself. I try to remember names, but now Mia is at senior school, I don't even know the surnames of most of her friends. It's hopeless. I put my head in my hands and realise what a useless mother I am. I have really taken my eye off things since Adam died and I got involved with Patrick.

Patrick. If I hadn't moved so fast, if I hadn't told the kids we were going to get married, Mia wouldn't have run out of the house. It's my fault. I need to put the brakes on this relationship. We can wait to get married; in fact, we don't even need to get married at all.

'Mum, stop panicking.'

I stare at Oliver. Since when did my twelve-year-old son become the sensible one in our family? 'I'll put a message on Facebook and Snapchat. She'll be with one of her horrible friends.'

'Thanks, Ollie.'

By 9 p.m., we have got nowhere. Mia's phone is still off, and no one has responded to Oliver's Facebook post. I search her room to see if she has taken anything, but it all looks untouched. Only her phone, her wallet and her jacket are missing.

I need to call the police. Let's hope they will do a better job tracking down my missing daughter than they have done in trying to find my husband's murderer.

16

It's 1 a.m., and I have been pacing the house for the past six hours.

'Yes.' I grab the phone on the first ring.

'Lydia, it's me, Cassie. Mia is here.'

'Oh, thank God!' I burst into tears, racked with relief and guilt.

'She's going to stay here tonight, and I'll bring her home in the morning.'

'Is she all right?'

'She's upset. Doesn't think it's right that you're marrying Patrick so quickly. Having said that, she's on board with you moving house.' Cassie lowers her voice. 'She says the house is haunted by Adam's ghost, and she thinks there are evil spirits in the garden. Have you done anything about Mia talking to a grief counsellor?'

'She refuses. Can I speak to her?'

'She doesn't want to talk to you at the moment. She's getting ready for bed. I'm sure after a good night's sleep she'll be fine. Don't worry, Lydia.'

'Please tell her I love her and that everything will be ok.'

.   .   .

THE DOORBELL RINGS at 8.30 a.m. the next morning.

I open the front door to Cassie and Mia and feel such relief at seeing my daughter, I have to swallow hard to stop the tears. Cassie is standing behind Mia and she shakes her head at me and puts a finger to her lips. I let Mia charge past me and up the stairs.

'I suggest I spend the day with you all, and I'll try to explain to her that you're not replacing her father but seeking to live a normal life.'

'Thanks, Cassie.'

'Perhaps stay out of Mia's way for a few hours.'

'Ok,' I say reluctantly as Cassie walks past me and strides to the kitchen. 'Thank you,' I repeat, thinking about how Cassie is my savior time and time again. 'Can I make you a cup of coffee?'

Half an hour later, I hear footsteps coming down the stairs.

'Best if you make yourself scarce,' Cassie says.

I sigh. 'I still haven't cleared out Adam's study. I'll make a start on it.'

'Good idea,' she says, blowing me a kiss.

As I'm walking along the hall towards the study, Patrick calls me.

'Can't wait to see you this evening,' he says.

'Slight problem. Mia freaked out about us getting married. She ran away to Cassie's last night.'

'That's a bit childish for a fifteen-year-old, isn't it?'

'No. The thing is, Patrick, I think she's right. I want to marry you, but perhaps it is too soon. We should let things settle down a bit. What do you think?'

He is silent for a long while, and I wonder if he's still on the line. Eventually, he says, 'Why don't I have a word with Mia? How did Oliver react?'

'He likes you. So long as he doesn't have to call you Dad, he's on board.'

'I think me and Mia need some bonding time. Let me go on the charm offensive and I'll get her onside. I can lay on the charm when I need to. Never failed yet.'

If anything, that makes me feel worse. Is Patrick saying he can get any woman he wants? If so, what is he doing with me? Am I really that special?

'Love you,' he says before hanging up, but it sounds like an afterthought.

I find myself standing in the doorway to Adam's study. This is the one room I haven't tackled properly since his death. Yes, I've dealt with all of the urgent paperwork. I've paid the bills and closed down his Facebook account and the bank accounts that were in his name only. But I have only given the filing cabinet a cursory glance, and I haven't touched his bookshelves. If I want Patrick to move in, I need to tackle this space.

Sighing, I pull open the filing cabinet. It has one long, deep drawer. I take all the hanging files out and dump them on the desk. The first few folders are related to this house: correspondence with the solicitors when we bought it, utility bills, and his car insurance, which he paid for personally rather than putting it through the business. I find some National Savings certificates and ISAs I didn't know he had, and some he set up in the names of the children.

And then I find a folder full of handwritten letters, mainly ones from me in the early days of our relationship. I smile as I read through them. I really loved Adam back then. The rest of the files include certificates from the various accountancy exams he took, paperwork from cars long sold, and receipts. It isn't until I open the final folder that I find a large sealed envelope. I say a silent prayer of forgiveness, rueful that I have to open something that I know instinctively that Adam wouldn't want me to see.

Inside there is a pile of letters, some handwritten, some typed. The letters are dated and go back to Adam's childhood. He would have been in his early teens, the ages that Mia and Oliver are now. They are letters that he wrote to his parents from school, and their responses back to him. I select one at random.

Dearest Adam,
Please, my boy, don't get involved in things you can't begin to under-
stand. Just know that I love your father as I love you. Do well in
your exams. See you at Easter.

Love,
Mummy

WHAT WAS SHE REFERRING TO? The letters are all dated, so I select one written by Adam in the month before.

Dear Daddy,
I know what you've done and it disgusts me. I will protect Mummy
and care for her even if you don't. If you write to me, I will burn your
letter.

Adam

GOOD HEAVENS! What was he referring to? I flick through the earlier letters, but they all seem perfectly normal, mundane even; letters from a young boy, fairly miserable at boarding school, writing to his parents, telling them about his classes and the grades he got in tests. Their missives back to him, mainly written by his mother, detail what they were doing week by week: his father's business meetings and his magisterial duties, his mother's sewing assignments and baking for charity events. There is nothing in any of the letters that explains what Adam's father supposedly did. And now they are all dead, and I suppose I will never know. Was that the start of the deterioration of his relationship with his father?

I am just about to put everything back in the envelope when I notice I've missed something. It's a compliment slip printed with his parents' address, handwritten by his father.

'The will is sorted. Watertight. Nothing for you to worry about. Dad'

Why would Adam have been worried about his father's will? He never said anything to me, either before his father died or afterwards. It makes no sense.

I only realise I have whiled away the whole morning when Oliver puts his head around the door and announces that Cassie has made lunch.

Mia is in the kitchen. 'Mum, I want to say something,' she says before I have the chance to sit down.

'Of course, darling.'

'I don't want you to get married again. I don't like Patrick much, but as Cassie said, it's your life and I mustn't stop you. I was just upset, that's all.'

I fling my arms around her, although she stays quite rigid. 'Of course you are upset. It's perfectly understandable.' I speak softly, my lips grazing her hair.

'Right! Sit down, everyone! Grub's up.' Cassie places a large bowl of steaming risotto in the centre of the table.

I HAD WANTED a winter wedding the first time around, but Adam thought that was a stupid idea, so we got married in

June. Although I won't have the long white wedding dress and all the extravaganza, I can still fulfil that old dream. The decision whether to go ahead was one of the hardest decisions I have ever had to make. The last thing I want to do is alienate my daughter or cause her more grief than she's already suffering, but at the same time I want to grab this chance of happiness. I vacillated so much Patrick started to get annoyed. 'Either you want to marry me or you don't,' he snapped one evening. 'We're not exactly in the first flush of youth, Lydia, and I don't want to waste any more time.'

So I agreed to his timescale. We set the date for 28 January, Patrick's birthday. I knew it would make him happy.

'I'm not a church kind of person,' Patrick said.

'It's fine. I don't mind having a registry office marriage,' I said. I did the full church wedding with Adam and am almost relieved not to have to do it again. 'But let's have a party afterwards. I would like to meet your friends and family.'

'Oh, Lydia,' he moaned, grasping my hands. 'I don't like parties. And I don't want to share you with lots of people. Let's make this intimate and special, just for us. There's nothing worse than having to be on best behaviour for people you hardly know. But most importantly, it probably isn't appropriate. The last time you will have seen all of your friends and family would have been at Adam's funeral.'

He didn't need to say any more. I agreed to keep the celebration small. Tiny, in fact. When I asked him to invite his sister and her family, he shook his head sadly. 'She's too sick, Lydia. Of course you will meet her, but not whilst she's immunosuppressed. It's too dangerous for her.'

'In which case, I won't ask Bea either,' I said, on the one hand relieved that I wouldn't have to face up to her disapproval, but on the other hand, wondering how I will explain it to my sister.

I tried so hard to get Mia onside. I took her out for a

gourmet pizza and tried to explain why it was so important to me to be married to Patrick. I promised her I would never forget Adam, and that Patrick wouldn't replace him. But Mia dismissed my pleas, answering me in monosyllables or just saying, 'Whatever.' In the end, I gave up and neither of us mentioned the wedding again.

I found myself a cream woolen jacket and skirt and some white faux fur of such a high quality it looked real. A dressmaker in town added it to the collar and cuffs, and when I put the outfit on, I feel like Anna Karenina.

So HERE WE ARE, the morning of my second wedding, a cold, grey January Wednesday. Last night, I had a vivid dream. Patrick and I were floating down the aisle of a cathedral, hand in hand, jubilant about our imminent nuptials. We stood there in front of the vicar, and when it came to the line where the vicar said, *If any of you has a reason why these two should not be married, speak now or forever hold your peace,* Adam appeared, fire coming out of his eyes, spitting splinters of glass. 'She is already married to me! This man is an imposter!' he screamed. I awoke, my heart thumping, my body slick with sweat. Afterwards, I tossed and turned and couldn't get back to sleep.

The kids have been allowed to take the day off school, so I let them sleep. I spend a long time putting my make-up on, trying to cover up the dark rings under my eyes. At 9.30 a.m., I wake them.

'I'm sorry, Mum, but I'm not coming.' Mia sits in her bed, clutching her arms around her bent knees.

'But–'

'Don't make me. If you want to marry that man, then what can I do? Nothing. But you can't make me come to the wedding. Please, Mum, I don't want you to be angry.'

I slump onto the end of her bed. 'I'm not angry, Mia. Just

disappointed. I hope that eventually you'll come to love Patrick, not as a father, but as a friend.'

Whilst Mia isn't embracing my union with Patrick, she is at least vaguely civil around him. I have no idea what he said or how he changed her mind, but whatever it was, it worked.

She harrumphs, then swings her legs out of bed. 'Going to the bathroom now,' she says. It's my hint to leave the room.

'I'm not having you stay here by yourself all day,' I say to her retreating back.

'I'm going into school,' she replies. 'Can you order me a taxi?'

By 10.30 a.m., I am ready and so is Oliver, who has agreed to attend. Cassie arrives, holding a large posy of white flowers, which she gives to me. 'Let's get this show on the road,' she says, planting a kiss on my cheek.

A car hoots outside. I wonder if Patrick has organised a car for me as a surprise, so I dash to the door to look. But it's the local taxi firm, a car to take Mia to school.

'Good luck, Mum,' she says as she heaves her school bag onto her back and dashes out of the house.

I try not to let her absence affect my happiness, but what mother doesn't want their daughter at one of the most important occasions of her life? Cassie gives my forearm a quick squeeze. 'Come on, hop into my car and let's go to the registry office.'

Park House is an imposing Georgian building with a red-brick exterior and white columns, built on the edge of a park in the centre of Horsham. The last time I was here was to register Adam's death. It feels like yesterday. Cassie locks the car and starts striding towards the entrance. She has made an effort today, wearing a smart, tailored dress nothing like her normal attire.

'Hey, aren't you coming?' she asks when she notices that I'm still hovering by the car. And then I see Patrick. He is standing by the door, pacing backwards and forwards, a red rose in his buttonhole. When he looks up and notices me, his face lights up. I feel ridiculous now for doubting myself. I smile back and stride towards him.

We get married in the Chairman's Room, a small room with white panels on the walls and doors, large windows that look out onto the park, and pinkish chairs. The officiant's table is in front of an unused fireplace. It looks much like the drawing room of a stately home.

The registrar is a woman in her sixties who does her best not to look surprised that we are only a party of five. Cassie is my witness, and a man whom I haven't met before, called Graham, is Patrick's witness. The service is quick, and before I know it, Patrick and I are man and wife. Afterwards, we walk hand in hand to the restaurant where I had the date with Rory. Cassie walks with her arm flung around Oliver's shoulders. He would never let me do that.

I don't warm to Graham. He doesn't say much, answering questions in monosyllables and seeming disappointingly aloof. I don't understand why Patrick describes him as his best friend, and I wonder if they have had a falling-out in the last day or so.

'How well do you know Sandra?' I ask Graham as we're finishing off our desserts.

'Sandra?'

I frown. 'Patrick's sister.'

'Oh yeah, her. Not very well.'

'You used to, didn't you, mate?' Patrick says.

'Yes, but I haven't seen her in years, have I? Doubt I'd recognise her these days. What's she up to, anyway?'

'I told you. She's got cancer.' Patrick scowls at Graham. The dynamic between the two of them is weird, and I can't put my finger on it.

Shortly after coffee, Graham stands up. 'Sorry I've got to

break up the party. Congratulations again to you both.' He holds up his empty champagne glass.

'I'll see you out,' Patrick says. He follows Graham as he walks to the door. I have my back to them, but Cassie frowns as she watches them talk together.

'What is it?' I ask.

'Nothing,' she says, shaking her head. 'Nothing.'

And then it's time for us to leave; time for Patrick and me to go to the fancy hotel that he has booked. Cassie throws her arms around me and squeezes me hard. 'Have a wonderful wedding night,' she says. 'And don't worry about Mia and Oliver. We'll have fun tonight, won't we?' She nudges Oliver, who throws a weak smile.

'Bye, my love,' I say to my boy. He doesn't reply.

We walk to the car park where Patrick has left his hire car, packed with a small suitcase that I gave him yesterday with my overnight things. I suppose, if I'm honest, I'm disappointed. There is no white ribbon on the front of the car; nothing to suggest that we are newly-weds. And then I chastise myself. I had all of that last time; I don't need it now. I have all I need: the love of a wonderful man.

17

Two days after our wedding, Patrick moves in. The kids are at school, and I wait expectantly, hovering at the front door. We have never discussed how much stuff he intends to bring, and I wonder if we'll have sufficient space. Will I need to get rid of some of our furniture to make space for Patrick's? Perhaps I should remove the picture hanging over the fireplace and suggest he hang his ocean painting there instead. It's a more attractive piece of artwork than the abstract landscape that Adam chose and insisted on displaying, chosen because it was painted by a famous artist rather than being a picture he loved. I decide to leave it for now. We can always change things around later.

Just after 10 a.m. I hear the crunch of tyres and I pull open the door. Patrick hops out of his car and opens the boot. He reaches in and tugs out one large suitcase and a small bouquet of red roses. After shutting the door, he carries the case to the front steps, puts it down next to him, places the bouquet on top of it and pulls me towards him.

'Hello, Mrs Grant. How are you?'

'Very well, Mr Grant. And you?'

He gives me a quick kiss and pulls away, leaving me wanting more.

'Lead on,' he says.

'What time is the lorry coming?'

He stops still. 'What lorry?'

'The removals lorry with all your stuff. Or is it a van?'

'There is no lorry, Lydia. This is it. The sum contents of my belongings. As I told you, my ex took all of our furniture, and my sister has an old Welsh dresser that belonged to our parents. There was nothing else worth keeping.'

'Oh.' I frown. 'But what about all the furniture in your flat? And the lovely seascape picture in your lounge?'

'I'm renting out the flat furnished.'

I realise we haven't discussed any of this. I have been so swept away in the whirlwind of our romance, so engrossed in managing the fallout from Adam's death, my wedding to Patrick and the problems we are facing at work, I haven't given a moment's thought to the practicalities of us merging our lives together. I had assumed he would be selling his flat and we'd add that money to what I get for the sale of this house, and together we would buy our new family home. He must notice my confusion. He runs the palm of his hand over my cheek.

'I thought we could use the rental income from the flat for our day-to-day living expenses. I know you have lots of money, Lydia, but I want to contribute my fair share. I hope you understand?'

'Yes, of course.'

But I can't get over Patrick having so few personal belongings. I find it quite odd for a man approaching fifty. He follows me upstairs into the master bedroom. I cleared out all of Adam's clothes and shoes. Most of it went to a couple of charity shops in Horsham, but I kept Adam's black-tie suit and stored it in the loft. Perhaps Oliver will wear it one day.

'This space is for you,' I say, flinging open the cupboard doors in our dressing room.

'All of this?' His eyes are wide. 'I don't have very many clothes, Lydia. I've never been one for accumulating stuff. Fashion doesn't interest me.'

I wonder if this space is making him feel uncomfortable. It's the last thing I want.

'Anyway, I don't want to get too embedded here, as we'll be moving soon.' Patrick unzips his suitcase. 'Have you spoken to any estate agents?'

'Not yet,' I say.

'Well, there's no time like the present. Why don't you make a few calls whilst I unpack?'

'Sure,' I say, backing out of the bedroom, wondering why that sounds more like an instruction than a suggestion.

I RING the estate agent we bought the property from originally. An assistant takes down my details and tells me that her boss, Gail Smithers, needs to come and value the house. It seems they are hungry for a sale, so we agree that she will visit in two days' time. Unsurprising in these times of economic downturn.

It doesn't take Patrick long to unpack, and soon he bounds down the stairs and into the kitchen.

'Can you make me an espresso, Lydia?'

'Sure.'

He flicks through a few papers that I have on the end of the island unit, invoices and suchlike. I have to restrain myself from asking him to please leave my papers alone. As I hand him the small cup and saucer, he gives me a kiss on the cheek and walks out of the room with them. I open my mouth to ask him where he's going, but then close it again. I must remember that Patrick is no longer a guest in this house. This is his home, too.

I settle at the kitchen table and open my laptop, answering

a few work emails, and soon enough it's lunchtime. I put some pasta on to boil and go in search of Patrick. He's not upstairs. He's not in the living room. And then I hear his voice.

Patrick is in Adam's study, and it sounds as if he's on the phone. Softly, I open the door.

'I've got to go. Bye.' Hurriedly he switches off his phone and glances up at me. He is sitting on Adam's chair with his laptop open on Adam's desk. It makes me shiver.

'You don't mind me installing myself in here, do you?' He peers at me, a look of concern on his face.

'No. No, of course not.' But I do. A little bit. I'll get used to it, I suppose. I remind myself that I didn't love Adam for a long while before he died. This is the man I love now.

'I can sort through the remainder of Adam's things if you'd like,' Patrick says, eyeing the bookshelves and half-packed boxes. I wish I had done more sorting beyond the filing cabinet. 'It might be easier for me to go through everything, as I don't have an emotional attachment.'

'That's kind of you, but I'll do it. I'm sorry I didn't clear it all away before you arrived. Anyway, I'm making pasta for lunch, if you'd like some?'

'Thanks.' He turns back to his laptop.

I have arranged for a mother of one of Mia's school friends to bring them home this afternoon so that I can spend the day with Patrick. Not that we do. He works all afternoon.

Shortly after five p.m., Mia walks into the kitchen, her skirt rolled at the waist so the hemline is almost indecently short. She dumps her rucksack on the floor and opens the fridge.

'Where is he, then?' she asks.

'I assume you mean Patrick?'

'Yeah. Lover boy.' She sticks her tongue out and makes a mock retching movement. Oliver sniggers.

'He's in the study. We'll all have supper together in about an hour.'

'In Dad's study?' Oliver asks. He looks pained.

'Yes. It's Patrick's now.'

'I bloody told you!' Mia slams the fridge door closed. She grabs her rucksack and a bottle of freshly squeezed orange juice and stomps out of the room.

'Are you ok, sweetheart?' I ask Oliver.

'Yeah. Why wouldn't I be?'

An hour later, I go upstairs to tell the kids that supper is ready. Mia is hunched over her laptop, headphones on.

'Supper,' I say. She nods but doesn't look at me.

Oliver isn't in his room doing his homework as he normally does straight after returning home from school. As I walk downstairs to look for him, I'm surprised to hear laughter coming from the living room. Then I hear Patrick's deep, mellow voice followed by further peals of laughter from Oliver.

'What's going on?' I ask, pushing the door open.

'We're playing a computer game,' Oliver says. 'Patrick's brilliant at it. Hey, watch out!'

'You won that round,' Patrick says, leaning back in the armchair.

'Have you done your homework?' I ask.

'No. Look, look, Patrick!'

They both peer at the television screen. I have no idea what game they're playing.

'You're good, man!' Patrick says. He high-fives Oliver.

'You need to do your homework straight after supper,' I say.

'Yeah. Yeah,' Oliver says dismissively.

'It's more important to have fun when you're fourteen years old, isn't it, Ollie my boy!' He thrusts his knuckle towards my son.

'I'm only twelve!' Oliver says.

'You're very mature for a twelve-year-old.' Patrick looks impressed. 'And bloody good at gaming.'

'Um, no swearing, please, Patrick.'

'Well, your mum is a right spoilsport, isn't she, Ollie? I think we'll need to work out how to loosen her up.'

Oliver's smile is the widest I have seen it in months. Whilst I'm happy that Patrick and Oliver are bonding, this love-in is too much. I'm going to have to have a word with Patrick about discipline. It's quite obvious that he hasn't got children of his own and doesn't understand the need for routine.

'Supper will be getting cold.'

Patrick stands up and stretches. Oliver groans but switches off the game. They follow me to the kitchen.

Mia is already seated at the table, but she has her headphones on.

'Can you take your headphones off, please.'

She pretends not to hear me and carries on picking her nails.

'Mia!' I say a bit more loudly. I still get no response.

A flash of anger darkens Patrick's face.

'Is she always this rude to you?' he asks quietly.

'No. She's struggling at the moment.'

Mia pushes her headphones off. 'I'm not struggling, I just don't want...'

She scrapes her chair away from the table and stands up, tears welled up in her eyes. 'I'm not hungry,' she mutters as she dashes out of the room.

'I thought I had sorted things with her,' Patrick says. He clenches his teeth together.

'I'm sorry,' I say. 'It's hard for Mia to adjust to everything. Plus she's got all the normal teenage hormone stuff going on.'

'Well, she mustn't spoil our evening. I found a bottle of champagne in your cellar and have popped it in the fridge. I think we should celebrate.' Patrick walks over towards the fridge and removes the bottle. 'Where are the champagne glasses?'

My smile is forced. It is so strange that Patrick is helping himself to my things. As I stride to the cupboard where we keep our glasses, I tell myself to snap out of this. What is mine is his. I place two empty champagne glasses in front of Patrick. He uncorks the bottle with a pop and pours me a glass.

'And how about you, young man? Fancy a sip to celebrate your mum and me living together?'

'Um, I'm not allowed any. I'm too young.'

Patrick rolls his eyes. 'One day, when your mum is out, then. But don't tell her!' he says in a mock whisper.

After we have finished dinner, Oliver returns upstairs to finish his homework.

'Do you need any help clearing up?' Patrick asks.

'No, it's fine. Go and relax,' I say. After I have loaded the dishwasher, I put a portion of the chicken stew, rice and vegetables on a plate and place it on a tray. I carry it upstairs. I'm about to open Mia's bedroom door when I hear voices inside. It sounds as if Patrick is talking to Mia but in a low voice, so I can't make out what he is saying. I hesitate a moment and then knock on the door.

'I've got some food for you, Mia,' I say.

She is seated cross-legged on her bed. Her eyes are red from crying. We refurbished Mia's bedroom a little over a year ago, transforming it from a pink Barbie-inspired room into something surprisingly sophisticated with a teal-velvet-covered headboard, a copper pendant light and copper accessories. Patrick is perched on the window seat, his arms crossed, the teal blinds pulled down behind him. I can't quite put my finger on the atmosphere. It reminds me of the ozone-scented air after a heavy storm; a relief that the worst is behind us.

'I've just had a little word with Mia, and she's got something to say to you, haven't you, Mia?'

'I'm sorry, Mum. I won't behave like that again.'

'It's ok, love.' I place the tray on the end of her bed.

Patrick throws Mia a look that I don't understand and then leaves the room.

'What was that all about?' I ask.

'Nothing,' Mia says, shaking her head. 'I'm okay now, and I'm sorry for being rude.'

'It's all right, my darling. I know how difficult things have been.' I try to give her a kiss, but she wriggles away and grabs the plate of food.

'Thanks for this,' she says, spooning large forkfuls into her mouth.

I don't know what Patrick has said to Mia, but I don't recognise this polite version of my daughter.

THE NEXT FEW days are uneventful. Gail Smithers has a good look around the house and values it for twenty percent more than we bought it for. If she knows about Adam's death, she doesn't mention it. Instead, she tells me that she has a number of properties on her books that might be suitable for us, all at a fair whack more than what she proposes we sell our house for. She says she can think of at least three clients whom she wants to show our house to. I am buoyed up by her positivity.

Today was packed full of meetings, and I realise I'm going to be home late. I message Patrick, who offers to collect the kids from school and to make supper. I smile. Adam used to help out, but only if I asked him to. I finish off my work and it's gone six thirty by the time I put my key in the front door.

'Hello!' I shout, dumping my coat and my bags in the hall and walking down the corridor to the living room.

'Oh!' I exclaim, my hand in front of my mouth as I look around the room. Logically, I know that this is my living room, filled with my furniture, but it looks nothing like how I left it this morning. The large cream sofa has been moved to the other side of the room and has its back to the wall. The armchairs are placed facing it, nearer to the fireplace. The antique satinwood bookcase is now on the wall adjacent to the patio doors, and the console table is a few feet in front of the doors. On it is a large arrangement of dried flowers that I keep in the hall, along with some ornate silver candlesticks. Even the long, silken-haired rug has been moved.

'Do you like it?' Patrick asks. He is seated on the sofa a little too closely to Cassie, who has her legs curled up underneath her.

'Um, yes. It's different. Hi, Cassie. I didn't know you were coming over this evening.'

'I wasn't. I rang up earlier for a chat; Patrick answered and invited me for supper.' She lays her hand on Patrick's forearm. I notice a nearly drunk bottle of wine on the coffee table.

'Not only is he handsome and witty, but he's a great cook and a fine interior decorator. You've got a good un here, Lyd.' She sucks her index finger and blinks slowly.

I smile awkwardly. Cassie is drunk, and she's flirting with my new husband in my lounge that I no longer recognise. For a moment, I feel like a stranger in my own home. And I don't like it.

'I'm just going to get myself a drink,' I say, turning around.

'No, you stay here. Let me get it. I need to check on the food anyway.' Before I can object, Patrick has launched himself across the room. He lifts my chin up and kisses me on the lips, sliding his tongue into my mouth.

'Eww – get a room!' Cassie laughs.

He gently slaps me on the bottom as he walks out. I slump onto one of the armchairs.

'You are so lucky,' Cassie moans. 'I wish I had a gorgeous man like Patrick.'

18

I am wide awake at 4 a.m. After lying still for about an hour, worried about waking Patrick and my forthcoming appearance on TV, I slip out of bed and tiptoe to the bathroom. As I peer at myself in the mirror, I hope that the make-up artist will be able to hide my dark circles and extra wrinkles. It seems that the stress of the past few months has taken its toll on my face. With my dressing gown on, I go downstairs to the kitchen, make myself a cup of tea and study the instructions for the new electronic knitting machine.

This morning, I will be presenting on BUYIT TV, trying to persuade viewers to spend a little under two hundred pounds on a new-to-the-market knitting machine that promises to make knitted garments in a fraction of the time it takes to hand-knit them. Of course, knitting machines have been around for years, but they have either been very expensive and complicated or too simplistic. YarnItNow is an American company, and their new machine, called Knit It Qwik, promises to appeal to the mass market. Within a couple of months of launching the Knit It Qwik, a rival machine was launched by a Chinese competitor. It's so often the case in our crafting industry.

I tried out the machine yesterday in the office and have managed to produce a couple of reasonable-looking scarves, so I'm confident I will be able to operate it on live TV without any hiccups.

After listening to the news on Radio 4 and checking that the trains are running normally, I return upstairs and get dressed.

'Wake up, sleepyhead,' I say to Patrick as I nudge him gently.

He opens his eyes and reaches for me. 'Get into bed,' he slurs.

I pull away and laugh. 'Can't. I've got to go to London. I'm dressed.'

'And I'm horny.' He lunges at me, but I dart out of the way.

'Tonight,' I say.

'Fuck it, Lydia,' he growls. I am surprised that he looks so pissed off. He rolls over with his back to me.

'I'll wake the kids up, but please remember you're taking them to school this morning.'

He grunts.

'Bye,' I say. 'Have a good day.'

He doesn't reply.

I leave later than I wanted to, because I need to make sure that Mia and Oliver are both dressed and eating their breakfast. There is still no sign of Patrick.

'Can you make sure Patrick is up and ready to take you to school?' I tell Oliver. 'Have a good day both of you.' I blow them kisses and leave.

I GET to the station just in time to catch the 7.50 a.m. from Horsham to London Victoria. The train is busy and I have to walk down two carriages before I find a seat.

Just as we're pulling into Crawley, my phone starts vibrating. It's Ajay.

'Are you prepared?'

Gone are the days where we preface conversations with pleasantries. Now it's all about business.

'Yes, of course.'

'It's just you haven't presented in a long while, and it's easy to get out of practice with these things.'

What he means is I haven't shown my face to the media since Adam died.

'I'm fine,' I say. But actually I'm not. I am tired and nerves rumble in my stomach. I wish I had eaten more than a banana for breakfast. But I don't need Ajay to tell me how important it is that I present well. Cracking Crafts needs all the sales we can get, and the margins with BUYIT TV are excellent.

'Call me the second you're off air. I need to know the numbers.'

'And goodbye to you, too,' I mutter under my breath as I listen to the dial tone. The woman opposite me throws me a sympathetic glance.

BUYIT TV's offices are just off the Earls Court Road in a modern office block constructed from glass and steel. It sticks out like a sore thumb next to its traditional red-brick neighbours with their ornate white cornicing. My heart is thumping as I walk through the rotating doors and pace towards the reception desk.

'I have a meeting with Andrew McFeatry.'

The receptionist has glossy long blonde hair, super-sized black false eyelashes and heavily stenciled eyebrows. Her teeth flash bright white as she smiles at me, and the bright blue of her shirt echoes the turquoise of her eyes. I assume she's wearing coloured contact lenses. Most of the staff here are like her. Pretty young girls, with drawling, privately educated voices that rise in pitch at the end of sentences, eager for a break on television, which ninety-nine percent of them won't get. She rings Andrew.

'Mr McFeatry says please go straight up.'

I nod. I know my way around here. Even though I haven't presented in months, I have demonstrated products on BUYIT TV probably half a dozen times a year for the past seven years. I walk to the bank of glass lifts and press the button. When I emerge on the fifth floor, Andrew bounces over to greet me.

'Dear Lydia,' he says, grasping my shoulders and giving me an air kiss above each cheek, 'I am so sorry for your loss, but I understand you've already moved on. Who is he, then? Pictures, please!'

Quite how Andrew is so up to date with my personal life, I have no idea.

'I'll show you later. If we're on air at 11 a.m., I need to get a move on. Make-up will have a lot of work to do,' I say, pulling a face.

'You're beautiful as always,' Andrew fawns as we walk side by side towards the dressing rooms.

I haven't met the make-up girl before, but she seems unfazed by my face and quickly gets to work. I try to swot up on the instructions for the knitting machine, even though I already know them inside out. She is putting the final touches to my face when my mobile phone rings. She frowns. We're meant to switch our phones off on this floor. There's nothing I can do, as she's applying a last coat of mascara.

'Sorry,' I say.

She sighs. 'Do you need to get that?'

I fumble in my bag and find my phone, switching it onto silent. But then it starts again, vibrating in my hand. My heart leaps. It's the kids' school. I have to answer it.

It's the school secretary. 'Mrs Palmer, sorry, Mrs Grant, I'm afraid that something has happened to Mia and we need you to come to school straight away.'

'What do you mean something has happened? Is she ok?'

'Yes, she's fine.'

'Has there been an accident?'

The make-up artist sighs and looks up at the clock. I have five minutes until I'm meant to be on air.

'No, nothing like that. But we need you to come as soon as possible. There has been an incident.'

'I can't!' I say, a ring of panic in my voice. 'I'm in London, about to go on television.'

'Please arrange for one of Mia's other guardians to come, then. This really can't wait until the end of the day.'

Andrew pops his head around the door to my dressing room.

'All ok, darling?'

I grimace at him. 'I'll do what I can,' I say before ending the call to the school secretary. 'Got an emergency with my daughter,' I tell Andrew. He rolls his eyes. Proud to be childless and gay, he is thoroughly disinterested in children.

'Four minutes,' he says, pointing to his watch and letting the door close.

My fingers are shaking as I dial Patrick's phone. He answers after the sixth ring.

'Patrick, please can you go to the kids' school for me? There's been a problem and I'm stuck up here in London.'

'Sorry, Lydia. No can do. I've just arrived in Southampton and am about to go into a meeting.'

'Oh.'

'Must go. Speak later.' He hangs up on me.

I call Cassie, and whilst I'm holding the phone up to my ear, the make-up artist comes towards me, brandishing the mascara wand. Cassie's phone goes to voicemail. Hardly surprising that she has her phone off during the day whilst she's teaching.

One of the runners opens the door. 'You're on in sixty seconds, Mrs Palmer.'

I don't correct her. Instead, I jump up, tug my skirt down and follow her out of the room. And in this moment, I'm missing Adam. I know it's crazy and hypocritical, but at least if Adam were still alive, he would have dealt with the school. But now I'm alone. I can't rely on Patrick to help out with the kids, and why should he? They're just an appendage to me. It's not fair to expect any more from my new husband.

And Mia. What has happened to her? Is the school secretary holding something back from me? If she was hurt or ill, the woman would have told me, wouldn't she? I want to scream. How am I going to concentrate when I'm worried about my girl?

I take a very deep breath, pull my shoulders back and walk onto the set. The lights are glaring and warm, and Andrew is already there looking at the knitting machine. The runner pushes an earphone into my ear.

'Long face, Lydia,' Andrew says, pulling the corners of his mouth up. But I can't look at Andrew; my eyes are drawn to the machine on the presenting table.

'What the hell?' I exclaim. This isn't a Knit It Qwik. This machine is bright pink and has the wording NitNakNok emblazoned on it.

'This is the wrong product!' I turn to Andrew and wave at the producer. 'This is a screw-up!'

'You're on air in five. Four. Three. Two. One. On air.'

'Good morning, everyone! Welcome, Lydia! What crafting wonder have you got for us today?'

My heart is thumping so hard I can hear it pounding in my ears. I wonder if I can even speak. How the hell am I going to get this machine to work? I've never seen it before, and it looks nothing like the Knit It Qwik, which I've swotted up on.

'Good morning, Andrew. Good morning, everyone,' I say, amazed that my voice sounds relatively normal. 'I'm thrilled to be here.'

'What is this unusual-looking machine, Lydia?' Andrew asks, running his hands over the top of it.

'We have here a knitting machine. It lets you knit things up super quickly, but unlike earlier versions on the market, this isn't cheap and plasticky, and it won't fall to pieces nor is it super expensive or very complicated.' It is extremely plasticky looking to me and a lurid pink.

'Exactly. And at £185 it is discounted by twenty percent off its normal retail value. But you won't find this just anywhere, will you, Lydia?'

'Um, no. We have exclusivity here on BUYIT TV.' A little voice bellows inside my head. *Do we?* I don't know anything about this damn machine.

'So, Lydia, what are you going to make us today?'

'I thought I'd knit up a quick cushion to show you how easy it is.'

I lift up a ball of lurid yellow yarn that is lying next to the machine and attempt to thread it. All the while Andrew is gushing how these machines are selling out fast and what amazing home-made presents you'll be able to make if you purchase one.

But I can't thread it. The mechanism is totally different to the Knit It Qwik. I turn the crank and there's a loud crunching sound.

'What the fuck!' the producer yells in my ear. I can feel blood rushing to my face and pray that the heavy coat of foundation will block it out.

I cannot afford to screw this up, but if I don't know how to use the machine, that's exactly what I'm going to do. I think of Ajay. I think of our staff and everyone who is relying on me to do a good sales job. And then I think of Mia, and I want to run off the set right now.

'Lydia?' Andrew says.

'So last night, I made some fabulous cushion covers. And it

would be super easy to make a jumper, knitting flat panels up in a couple of hours. This really is the easiest and quickest way to make fantastic garments that look as if they've been hand-knit, but can be made in a fraction of the time.'

'Can you show us how it works, Lydia?' Andrew asks.

'Well, I'm not as familiar with this machine as I should be, so...'

'Cut!' the producer screams in my ear. 'Andrew, onto the next item.'

'Next up, we have a fabulous embroidery kit. You can sew up your own cushions in these incredible and unique designs. And look how divine this is.'

'Lydia, get off the set,' the producer says. 'Away from camera three.'

I bite my bottom lip as I slip away off the set. The runner grabs my earpiece. Everyone else is ignoring me. That was an unmitigated disaster. I doubt if we made a single sale, and if we don't sell our products, then BUYIT TV will delist us and we'll lose a lucrative sales channel. Why was the wrong machine on set?

Back in the dressing room, I call Lucinda, my sales contact, who is a couple of floors down in this building.

'What the hell just happened? I came onto set and there was another brand of knitting machine. All the paperwork said that I would be presenting a Knit It Qwik! And I know, because I completed the forms myself.'

'Calm down, Lydia. Let me look through the file.' With her strong estuary accent, she's not like most of the other girls in the office, and she doesn't sound like a Lucinda. I pace the room, fuming.

A moment later she comes back on the line. 'I got a phone call from Ajay Arya last week confirming that you would be presenting the NitNakNok instead. The product was sent through three days ago. There must have been a communication breakdown at your end.'

Shit. What the hell has Ajay done? It doesn't make sense that he would undermine me. We both need Cracking Crafts to be successful. When I screw up here, it's a disaster for the business, a business we're equal partners in. And then I begin to doubt myself. Did Ajay tell me? Was there an email I've overlooked perhaps? I've had so much going on recently, it's quite possible that I have screwed up. Did I research the wrong machine? All I know for sure is that I have totally mucked up. We will have made no sales, and quite possibly BUYIT TV will delist us. And if that happens, we will lose a major revenue stream, and I will have put our business in jeopardy.

Quickly, I gather up my coat and bag and hurry out of the building. It isn't until I'm outside on the pavement, jostling with other Londoners, their heads down, in a hurry to go about their business, that I remember the phone call from the school. It was less than an hour ago, but it seems like a lifetime. And now I feel even more wretched. How could I forget that my daughter needs me? Business problems are irrelevant in comparison to her well-being.

I try calling her mobile phone, but frustratingly, and unsurprisingly, it is turned off. I leave a message.

'Darling, I don't know what's going on, but I'm leaving London now. I should be at school within the next couple of hours. Call me.'

She doesn't.

It is strange driving to the kids' school and being able to park directly outside, not having to jostle for a parking space. I dump the car and hurry up to the gates. After I press the electronic buzzer, I explain that the school secretary has asked me to come in urgently. The gate opens. The school is quiet, and I make my way through to the main building where I have to press another buzzer.

'Mrs Kenner is expecting you,' the secretary says. My heart sinks. I am being called to speak to the head of the school. The only time I have had a conversation with her was on the school's open day, and even though she was doing her sales spiel, I found her impressive; the sort of woman you would definitely want to be on your side. I follow the signs to the head's room, and just as I'm turning the corner, I see Mia sitting on a chair, her head bent low.

'Darling!' I exclaim, hurrying towards her. She looks up at me, her eyes red and her cheeks tearstained. 'What's happened? Has someone done something to you?'

She cowers away from me, but before I can say anything else, the door opens.

'Mrs Grant, thank you for coming into school. Please come in.' Mrs Kenner holds the door open and I step into her study. She is a tall woman with short-cropped grey hair, a slash of cerise lipstick and massive pom-pom black-and-turquoise earrings. Wearing a cerise boiled wool jacket and black trousers, she looks more like the head of an advertising agency than the headmistress of a leading co-ed day school.

'Please have a seat.' She sits down behind her wooden pedestal desk piled high with papers. 'I won't beat about the bush. I'm suspending Mia for a week as of today.'

'Why?'

'She was caught smoking weed in the girls' toilets.'

'Mia, smoking drugs!' I can't believe it. 'She must have been set up. There's no way that Mia would do something like that. And where would she find weed anyway?'

'That's something we are investigating, and the reason why she's being suspended rather than expelled. We don't believe that Mia fully appreciated the consequences of her actions. We are also aware that she was, up until this term, an exemplary student, and her form teacher is in no doubt that the tragic death of her father has caused her a great deal of anguish. I think it would be helpful if Mia had a course of counselling. Is that something you could organise?'

'Um, yes. Of course. I already suggested it. Has Mia got in with a bad crowd of kids?'

Mrs Kenner bristles. 'We don't have bad kids at this school, Mrs Grant. If Mia does anything similar again in the future, please be in no doubt that she will be expelled immediately.'

'Yes, of course.' And now I feel like I've been hauled up in front of the head, my knuckles about to be rapped.

Mia and I walk to the car in silence. I cannot believe that my little girl has been caught smoking dope. How many times did Adam and I expound the dangers of drugs and alcohol? She climbs into the passenger seat, but I don't turn on the engine.

'What happened, Mia?' I ask, my voice quiet.

She bursts into tears. I pull her towards me and give her a hug.

'I know it's been a terrible few months for you, darling. I know you miss your dad. But you need to talk to me. It's no good bottling it all up.'

'Sometimes I hate you, Mum,' she says as she pulls away. 'You care more about Patrick than you do about us. It's not fair.'

I know that I mustn't burst into tears too, and I fight the dismay that is tightening my throat and threatening to break me down. I turn on the car engine and gently pull away from the curb.

Am I really such a terrible mother?

19

Mia won't talk to me, and I know that in her current state of distress, it would be futile to push her. She rushes to her bedroom and I sit at the kitchen table, trying to take stock of my horrendous day. I turn on the laptop and search through all my emails from Lucinda at BUYIT TV and all my emails from Ajay. There is nothing to suggest that the brands of knitting machines had been swapped. I pull up copies of the contract, and all the paperwork states that I will be presenting the Knit It Qwik. It doesn't make any sense.

Reluctantly, I call Ajay.

'What happened?' he asks the moment he hears my voice. 'I was watching BUYIT but your face was shown for a couple of seconds and then the cameras switched to another presenter.'

'They pulled it. I had prepped for the Knit It Qwik, but another brand of machine was there and I didn't know how to use it.'

'For fuck's sake, Lydia. Are you telling me we had no sales?'

'Yes, and it's because you rang up and switched the brand.'

'I don't know what the hell you're talking about!'

'The conversation you had with Lucinda three days ago? I don't understand what you're doing, Ajay!'

'I haven't spoken to Lucinda for weeks! I know you've been under a lot of stress Lydia, but you're losing your grip. You need to sort this!'

'But–'

He interrupts me. 'This one is down to you.' He hangs up on me and I let out a screech.

Although it's way too early, I pour myself a glass of wine. I deserve it after such a dreadful day.

OLIVER IS DROPPED off by a friend's mother, and Patrick arrives home not long afterwards. He sweeps into the kitchen and pulls me towards him.

'How was it?' he asks, holding me by the shoulders as he stands back.

'A terrible day. Everything has gone wrong. Mia has been suspended, and Ajay organised for the wrong machine to be on set, so I screwed it up.'

Patrick frowns. 'Why would Ajay do that?'

'Search me.' I shrug. 'He's denying it, but Lucinda at BUYIT TV has no reason to lie to me.'

'Mmm.' Patrick scratches his chin. He walks over to our vast American fridge and takes out a beer, flipping off the lid and drinking it straight from the bottle.

'Come and sit down,' he says, taking my hand and pulling me towards the table and chairs. When I'm seated, he walks to the kitchen door and closes it.

'There's something I want to share with you that I haven't mentioned before. I did a bit of digging into Ajay for you.'

'What! Why?'

'The police have got some new evidence that incriminates Ajay.'

'How do you know?' That doesn't make sense.

'I think the police might be questioning him this evening.'

'What?'

'Look, I don't want to worry you, Lydia, which is why I haven't said anything before. I've got a mate in the police, and I took him for a drink last week to pump him for information on Adam's case. He rang me yesterday and said that someone has come forward with some new evidence, and they might be pulling Ajay back in for further questioning.'

'And why hasn't DI Cornish let me know?'

'It's strictly off the record, Lydia. This mate owes me a couple of favours, and I asked him to keep me in the loop. And the last thing I wanted to do was worry you unnecessarily in case it comes to nothing. But, you see, there's something else as well.' He pauses as if he's still undecided whether to tell me.

'What?'

He sighs. 'Ajay was done for grievous bodily harm when he was in his early twenties. Did you know that?'

'No! Ajay? Surely not.'

'I'm afraid it's true, Lydia.'

'No!' I shake my head. Until Adam's death, I would have described Ajay as one of the gentlest people I know, but now it seems as if I have got him totally and utterly wrong. And it makes even more sense that the police considered him a suspect. With a history of violence, it's beginning to stack up that he may have murdered Adam when he found out that Marianne was having an affair with him.

'According to my mate, Ajay glassed someone in a pub.'

'Are you sure?'

'One hundred percent.'

'But why did you get him checked out?'

Patrick strokes my cheek. 'Because I love you. You're my wife and I need to look out for you.'

Patrick sighs and takes a swig of his beer. 'I don't trust the man. The police would not have interrogated him in the way you said they did regarding Adam's death if they didn't have something on him, and now someone has come forward to say they saw his car near your house on the day Adam was killed.'

'But why's it taken them so long to come forward?'

Patrick shrugs. 'I guess we'll find out in due course. Ajay spent six months in jail. He was released early for good behaviour and because he showed remorse. If he can do that, and he has kept it hidden from you all of these years, you can see why I don't trust the man. I want to make sure you're safe.'

'But Ajay isn't going to harm me!' I exclaim.

'Why not?' Patrick raises his eyebrows. 'If he killed Adam... Perhaps this is his extreme way of getting one hundred percent control of Cracking Crafts?'

I laugh. 'Come on, Patrick, that's absurd. You don't know Ajay like I do.'

'I don't want to labour the point, Lydia, but you didn't know Adam was having an affair with Ajay's wife, you didn't know that Ajay has a criminal record for violence, and you didn't know that your daughter was smoking weed.'

'Woah!' I say, holding my hands up. 'How do you know that Mia was suspended for smoking weed? I only told you she was suspended.'

'She messaged me this morning. She was terrified about your reaction.'

I don't know what to say now. I should be pleased that Mia has confided in Patrick, but it makes me feel like even more of a failing mother.

'Hey, you.' Patrick takes my hands. 'Cheer up. None of this is the end of the world. The most important thing is that you and the kids are safe. If Ajay is undermining you or the business, then you need to get rid of him.'

'I can't get rid of Ajay! We're equal partners.'

'Think about it, Lydia. The man had a motive to kill Adam;

he has previous; he has lied to you about the machine you were presenting and undermined the business. If he devalues the business, he can try to oust you and buy the business for much less than its true market value. And now the police are likely to call him in again. It could be happening right now. I am honestly scared that he is going to do something to you. Let's think this through. If you die, what happens?'

It's a rhetorical question, because Patrick carries on talking.

'I assume your shares go to your estate, which means that whoever is your children's guardian will, in theory, have to protect their interests. In practice, it means that Ajay will be sole director in Cracking Crafts, and that means he'll have full control.'

'Yes, but...'

'Look, why don't we go and talk to Ajay tomorrow?' he suggests. 'Let's get things out in the open.'

'We?'

'I'm your husband. I want to support you. I think you need to have a conversation with Ajay. Perhaps ask him to step away for a few weeks, just until things settle down a bit more.'

'I can't run the business without him. It's too big.'

'Darling, your safety is more important than the business. Just think about it.'

AND I DO. I can't sleep. If Ajay found out that Marianne and Adam were having an affair, he could have killed Adam to get him out of the way. He and Adam had been clashing for months about the business, so it would have suited Ajay to 'get rid of' Adam. He would have known that I would never boot my own husband, even if we were getting divorced.

And now... perhaps he does want sole control of Cracking Crafts? Perhaps he's undermining me and setting me up for failure? Or worse, perhaps he's considering killing me as well.

When Patrick rolls over in bed and throws a heavy leg over mine, I snuggle up closer to him. Thank goodness for Patrick. He makes me feel safe.

MIA COMES DOWN for breakfast still in her pyjamas and dressing gown.

'You'll need to get dressed,' I say. 'You'll have to come into work with me for the next few days.'

'Why can't I stay here? I'm nearly sixteen.'

'And you've been suspended for smoking dope. That doesn't exactly make you trustworthy in my eyes,' I say.

She scowls. 'I've got schoolwork to do. I'm not going to be lounging around in front of the telly or going out to meet my dealer.'

'Dealer?' I hold my mug of coffee in mid-air.

'Chill, Mother! I'm only joking. I don't have a bloody dealer. Some boy at school gave it to me because I was feeling shit. He was just trying to be nice. Said it'd make me feel better.'

'Oh, Mia, I know you've been feeling rubbish, and that's why we need you to talk to a counsellor. I've been saying that for a while, and Mrs Kenner suggested it, too. It's been a horrible few months. But I'm not leaving you here alone. You can bring your work and sit in the boardroom. Ok? And if you get bored, I'm sure Nicky can find some things for you to help out with.'

Mia has always had a soft spot for my secretary, Nicky. She thinks she's cool, probably because we let slip years ago that she's an ex-convict.

Patrick strides into the kitchen. He's wearing a suit and tie. 'I have a meeting in Brighton later, but I've got time to come with you to your office first. We'll need to go in separate cars.'

'Ok,' I say reluctantly. I'm still not sure that it's a good idea to confront Ajay. Mia plonks her crockery in the sink. I don't have the energy to tell her to put it straight into the dishwasher.

'You don't sound convinced,' Patrick says quietly. 'Remember what I told you yesterday. I don't want you to take any chances. And especially if Mia is going to be here or with you at work this week. I want my girls to stay safe.'

I smile when Patrick calls Mia and me his girls.

An hour later, I have dropped Oliver off at school, Mia has spread her books across the boardroom table, and I'm in my office, having another look at BUYIT TV's paperwork. I want to be absolutely sure we're not accusing Ajay of something in error. But it seems that everything tallies with what I thought. The internal phone rings.

'Patrick is here,' Nicky says.

'Please send him in.'

Patrick strides briskly into my office and leans over my desk to give me a kiss. 'Ready?' he asks. I nod although I'm not.

I knock on Ajay's door, even though I can see him sitting at his desk, his fingers flying across his keyboard.

'Come in,' he says, without looking up.

We both walk in and Patrick closes the door behind him. Ajay stares at us with a bemused expression. 'Everything all right?'

'Um, no, not really. The thing is, um, there's no easy way to say this, um.' I simply can't get my words out. Patrick takes over.

'Ajay, it's in the best interest of the business, and of Lydia, if you take some time off. Perhaps a few weeks' paid leave, just until the police finally decide who was responsible for Adam's death and so that there aren't any more screw-ups, such as the fiasco with BUYIT TV yesterday.' Patrick stands with his arms crossed in front of him.

Ajay explodes. 'What gives you the right to come in here

and tell me what to do! This is my bloody company, and you have nothing to do with it!'

'He's here on my behalf, Ajay. To support me,' I say lamely.

'And you want me to get out, is that it?' He slams the palm of his hand onto the desk. I take a step backwards. Patrick grasps my hand. I know now what Patrick means. Ajay has a temper I've never witnessed before. 'You have no right, either of you. In case you've forgotten, Lydia, we are equal shareholders and co-directors. I have put my everything into Cracking Crafts, and it's my life as much as it's yours. Or at least I thought it was. How dare you try to fire me!'

'I'm not trying to fire you. I just think it might be easier for everyone if perhaps you work from home for a while. I'm not comfortable–'

'Lydia told me about what happened at the television station yesterday,' Patrick says.

'This is none of your bloody business! Get out. Now!' He points his finger at Patrick. His hands are shaking with fury.

'No,' Patrick says softly. 'I'm here to protect my wife. I'm sorry, mate, but it's you who has to go.'

20

I have never witnessed anyone fly into a rage as Ajay does. His eyes are bulging, his nostrils flared and his teeth are bared, pink gums glistening with saliva. He swipes a pile of files off his desk and onto the floor. They land with a clatter.

'Get out of my office!' he shouts.

I back towards the door, tugging Patrick's hand.

'No, you stay here, Lydia!' Ajay growls. 'Patrick, you're nothing to this business. Get out!'

'She's not staying here without me,' Patrick says, holding his ground.

There's a knock on the door. We all freeze. I am the first to turn and open the door, relieved to have an excuse to walk away.

'Is everything all right, Lydia?' Nicky asks, frowning whilst glancing from Ajay to Patrick and back again.

'Everything's just fucking fine!' Ajay snarls. He grabs his jacket and his briefcase and pushes past Patrick. Both Nicky and I stand back to let him go.

'What?' Nicky says.

'Don't ask,' I murmur.

She edges away.

'Shit,' I say as Patrick and I are left alone in Ajay's office. I am trembling.

'It's for the best, Lydia. After that little display, I think I'm right. I don't want him around you or Mia. At least not until we can be sure that he doesn't have evil intentions towards you or the business. Just let things settle.'

'It's easy for you to say that, but without Ajay I have to be fully responsible for this multimillion-pound business. I don't know about logistics or accounting. Adam and Ajay did all of that. It's too much for me.'

'You're a strong woman, Lydia. You'll cope.'

I don't agree. All I want to do right now is bury myself in a dark hole, away from everyone, where I can be free of responsibility. I don't want this hassle. But then I think about this wonderful business and all the years we have spent growing this, and I try to imagine my life without it. I can't. I love Cracking Crafts. It's my identity and my passion. I just need to get a better grip on things. And first of all, I must concentrate on my children.

'I've got to get off now,' Patrick says, interrupting my thoughts. He gives me a quick kiss on the cheek. 'Leave your phone on and call me if there's the slightest hint of trouble. And call the police if you're worried. Promise?' He looks deep into my eyes.

'I promise,' I say.

'At least it's Friday. I'll see you later.'

Ajay doesn't return, and I'm relieved. I really couldn't face a showdown. My head pounds and it feels as if my heart is beating too fast whilst my throat is choking. I'm overwhelmed, and there's nothing I can do about it. Cracking Crafts is my responsibility. I remind myself that I love this business, that we have a good team and a new accountant, and we are a well-oiled machine.

Later that evening, after supper, I tell the kids and Patrick that I've got a headache and am going to bed early. I leave them to clear up. After running myself a bath, I'm about to nip back downstairs to get a glass of water when I see Patrick talking in hushed voices to Mia in her bedroom. She looks delighted about something he says. It brings a smile to my face. At least the kids are getting on well with Patrick now. Oliver plays computer games with him most evenings, and I still struggle to get him to do his homework.

No one has cleared up from supper. The dishes are on the side, dirty plates in the sink. I sigh. Why can't my children clear up after themselves? Why doesn't Patrick lift a finger to help? The first couple of weeks he lived here, he bent over backwards to help, cooking and clearing up, but now he does nothing. I can't help but think of Adam. As much as we argued, he did his fair share around the house, cooking a meal at the weekends and helping me clear up after dinner when I asked for assistance. But Patrick expects me to do everything. I'm going to have to talk to him about it, but not tonight. I'm too tired.

After washing up, I walk back upstairs and go into Mia's bedroom to say goodnight. It looks as if most of the contents of her wardrobe have been piled up on her bed. She's wearing a very short black leather-look skirt that I've never seen before and a sparkly silver top that shows her burgeoning cleavage. It makes her look ten years older than she is, and with her big eyes, it's not the image I want my daughter to portray.

'What are you wearing?'

'Danni loaned me these.'

'And why?'

'Because I've got nothing suitable, obviously.'

'Suitable for what?'

She turns her back to me.

'Mia, please answer.'

'The party tomorrow night.'

'What party?'

'Danni's sixteenth.'

'You've been suspended from school. You're not going.'

'Yes I am! Patrick's already said it's fine.'

'Patrick is not your father.' As soon as the words leave my lips, I regret them. She throws me a withering look. 'Look, I am responsible for you and for making these types of decisions, and I don't think it's appropriate.'

I jump as Patrick puts an arm around my waist. 'What's going on?'

'Mia is telling me about this party. I don't think she should go.'

'She'll be fine, won't you, Mia? I've already told her that I'll collect her at 1 a.m. It's not like the party is in a club or anything. Mia said it's at a friend's house in Crawley.'

'Whoa!' I exclaim. 'One a.m.! Crawley! But we don't know who these people are or whether the children will be supervised.'

'I'm not a child,' Mia pouts, her hand on her hip.

'You certainly don't look like one in that outfit,' Patrick says. 'Perhaps wear a few more clothes, Mia?'

She tosses her hair.

'Look, Lydia, I've already told Mia that she can go, but let's agree. You're not wearing that outfit. Ok, Mia?'

'Ok,' she says, a grin creeping across her face.

I have just been totally outmaneuvered, and I'm furious. I stomp to the bedroom.

SLEEP EVADES ME, and I'm still tossing and turning when Patrick comes to bed. Some time later, I hear a phone vibrate. Patrick slips out of bed and I listen to him pad down the hall. Eventually, I fall asleep, and when I next awake, there is a grey light coming through the curtains and he's snoring gently by my side.

I SPEND the day fretting about the party that Mia is going to. She's only fifteen, and I don't think it's appropriate that she is staying out until 1 a.m. It hardly gives the right message to allow her to go when she's on suspension from school. In the end, I decide to suggest a compromise. She's in her room, seemingly working on some homework. She doesn't hear me, as she has her headphones on. I know that generally she's conscientious and does well at school. I'm sure the weed smoking was a one-off and that it's a direct consequence of the turmoil she's suffered at home. She jumps when she sees me.

'Mia, I'll let you go to the party, but you're going to leave at 11 p.m. I don't want Patrick having to collect you so late.'

'No! Patrick already said it's ok.'

'And I say it's not, and what I say goes.'

'You're such a cow! Patrick is way nicer than you. I'm glad he's my stepdad!' She shoves the headphones back over her ears and turns her back to me.

Patrick is in Adam's study. I know I need to stop calling it that, but I'm not sure I ever will. I'm looking forward to moving house, to give us that chance to start again as a new family. He is peering at his laptop, and when I knock at the door and he sees me, he slams down the lid.

'I think it's better if you collect Mia at 11 p.m. from the party tonight. It's too late for her to stay out.'

'Hey, Lydia, you need to chill! In a few months, she'll be old enough to start a family. Good heavens, by the time I was her age, I'd been around the block many times, and I'm sure you had, too!'

I bite my lip. I certainly had not been around the block in my teens. 'But I don't want you going out so late to collect her.'

'All right. Let's compromise. She'll leave the party at 11.30, so we'll be back home by midnight. You need to stop worrying.'

It's all right for you to say that, I think. *She's not your daughter.*

At 7 p.m., Mia comes downstairs with her coat wrapped around her slender frame.

'Where's Patrick?' she asks.

'In the study. I'll drive you to the party.'

'No! Patrick already said he'd take me.'

I don't hear him walk up behind me, so I jump when he speaks. 'She's right. I'll take her. I've got an old friend who lives in Crawley, and I've agreed to go out for a drink with him so I don't need to come back here in between.'

'But you won't drink, will you?'

'Lydia!' he chastises. 'You must know me better than that by now. Mia will be safe and so will I. Come on, young lady. Let's get a move on; otherwise you'll be late for that party.'

'No alcohol and no smoking,' I say to Mia's retreating back.

I am on edge all evening and feel such a sense of relief when I hear car doors slam shortly after midnight. I hurry upstairs and into bed.

'How was it?' I ask Patrick as he tiptoes into the bedroom. I switch my bedside light on.

'Fine, and Mia is home in one piece.' He starts peeling off his clothes and then walks into our en-suite bathroom. I listen to him turn the shower on and then brush his teeth. When he gets into bed, I turn towards him and run my fingernails down his torso.

'Not tonight.' He sighs. 'I'm tired.'

I edge away from him. We both lie there, still, in the darkness. I try to remember when the last time was we made love. It must be weeks. And we're still newly-weds. I know we're not in the first flush of youth, but that can't be right, surely? I resolve to make more of an effort.

MONDAY MORNING, and I have never been so reluctant to go into work. I am sure that Ajay will be there, ready to pounce on me, to demand an apology. Patrick is in London today, and I have no backup. Ajay's office door is shut and he's not seated at his desk, so I return to the open-plan office and walk up to Nicky, who is typing rapidly.

'Is Ajay not in?'

'No.'

'Have you heard from him?'

'No, but I can give him a call if you like?'

'That's fine, Nicky. I'll ring him myself.'

On the one hand I'm relieved that he isn't here; on the other, it makes me more worried. I can't see Ajay just walking away. Also, without him I'm going to have to make all the decisions by myself. I'm capable of doing it, but I don't want to. We have been so comfortable over the past few years, each with our own set of responsibilities. As I sit down at my desk, in my brightly coloured office, I have a lightbulb moment. Patrick is a management consultant. He goes from business to business helping them out, predominantly sorting their IT issues, but I'm sure he would be able to help us here. After all, most of Ajay's role is logistics and systems stuff. I decide to ask him tonight.

A couple of hours later, Shireen, our new accountant, knocks on my door.

'I've got a bunch of payments I need you to sign off on, and I just wanted to discuss a few issues with you,' she says, hovering by my desk.

'Have a seat,' I say. She looks too young to be a fully qualified accountant, with pimples on her forehead and bright innocent eyes behind large glasses. I sign where she tells me to. Then she stands up, fingers the hem of her jumper and clears her throat. I look at her expectantly and she flushes.

'There are a few problems,' she says, shuffling a bit more. 'I hope you don't mind me saying, and I've already told Ajay this, but you've got five stores that are doing really badly, incurring big losses, and costs continue to rise. Look, I prepared you a graph.' She leans forwards and shows me the graph, and it's obvious to see that we're hemorrhaging money.

'What did Ajay say?' I ask.

Shireen looks at me, her face owl-like behind black-rimmed glasses.

'He didn't. But I just thought you should know.'

'Yes, thank you.'

'I'll go now, then,' she says needlessly. She collects her papers and backs out of the room.

I knew things were bad, but not that bad. And now that we've probably lost BUYIT TV's account too, I suppose it's up to me to take action. I miss Adam, and I miss Ajay. I wonder if I should call him and apologise. But then I remember his fury and the possibility that Ajay may have killed Adam, and I realise I have to do this alone. I lean back in my chair and close my eyes.

LATER THAT EVENING, Patrick is watching football on the television.

'Can I talk to you?' I ask as I snuggle up beside him.

He turns the sound off. 'What's up?'

'I was thinking. You're a management consultant. Could you come and help me in the business?'

'It's flattering of you to ask me, but I'm really stretched at the moment, Lydia. Besides, I'm not sure my skill set is what you need.'

'I need someone to bounce ideas off. Someone to tell me to stop worrying and to help me close down the stores that are failing.'

He tips my chin up. 'You're strong, Lydia. And bright. And beautiful. You can do this.'

'I don't know, Patrick. I love the business. It's like my third child, but sometimes I wonder if it's grown too big.'

'You're a worryguts,' he says, planting a quick kiss on the end of my nose. Then he switches the sound back on the television, turning the volume up several notches.

21

I haven't heard from Fiona in a while, so I'm happy to get a text from her asking if I'm free to meet up for a drink sometime this week. Rather than texting her back, I pick up the phone.

'Am I disturbing your work?' I ask.

'I'm amending a will, so I'm happy to be disturbed. How are you?'

'Too much going on at the moment.' I sigh. 'And I still need to get you to change my will.'

'Have you got time to meet up?'

'That's why I'm calling. Why don't you come over for supper? You haven't met Patrick, and it would be nice for you to get to know the kids. Are you free tonight?'

She hesitates. After a long pause she says, 'That would be lovely. Thank you.'

'Seven p.m. suit? It's a school night, so we try not to eat too late.'

'Sure. Thanks, Lydia.'

. . .

FIONA RINGS the doorbell on the dot of 7 p.m. Patrick hasn't come home yet, which is unusual for him. He normally messages me if he's running late. Fiona leans down to give me a kiss and I stand back to let her in. She lets out a slow whistle.

'Wow, your house is stunning!'

I realise that this is the first time she has actually been to my home. We've met up numerous times over the past year, but for some reason or another, it's always been when we're at the gym or when we have gone out for a meal or a drink with Cassie.

'Thanks. We've actually put it on the market. The agent is organising an open house, so hopefully it will be sold before long.'

'Oh, that's a shame. It's lovely. But I suppose with everything that's happened and your new relationship, you'll be wanting a fresh start.'

'Exactly.'

We walk into the kitchen, and as everyone does the first time they come into this room, she looks around with amazement, taking in the dramatic oak beams and the beautiful handmade kitchen units.

'What can I get you to drink?' I ask.

'Just a small glass of white wine. Thank you, Lydia.'

'I hope you don't mind,' I say as I open the fridge, 'but I've only got ready-made meals. I haven't had the time to prepare anything. I've had a bit of a run-in with my business partner, and everything is getting on top of me a bit.'

'Goodness, that's not surprising. You've had a hell of a few months, and I guess your business must be all-consuming.'

'Yes. It's quite a responsibility.'

'The food smells good.'

'It'll be ready in a moment. I'll just give the kids a shout. I'm not sure what's happened to Patrick. He's normally home by now. Have a seat.'

I call upstairs for the kids. Oliver hurtles down the stairs, and Mia arrives a couple of minutes later. She's been much calmer this week.

'Hello, I'm Fiona.' She extends her hand to both the kids. She seems awkward around them, not quite knowing what to say. I dole out the food and then make my apologies, saying I need to call Patrick to find out where he is.

I am worried, but I try not to let it show. Images of ambulances and car accidents flash through my mind, but Patrick answers on the fifth ring.

'Where are you?' I ask a little snappily.

'At my client's.'

'But I sent you a message telling you that Fiona was coming around and we were having supper at 7 p.m.'

'Have you forgotten?' he asks.

'Forgotten what?'

'I told you last night that I would be working late tonight and staying over in Southampton.'

'No, you didn't.'

'Lydia, love, I absolutely did tell you. You've got too much on at the moment, so it's not surprising you've forgotten. Don't you remember, you even saw me carry my overnight case out to the car? Anyway, what's the problem?'

'None. I just wanted you to meet Fiona.'

'Another time. Heard anything from Ajay?'

'No.'

'That's good. Got to go now, Lydia. Sleep tight.'

I put the phone down. I am sure that he didn't tell me he was staying the night in Southampton. I wouldn't have asked Fiona over this evening if I had known Patrick wasn't going to be here. And I am certain that I didn't see him carrying his little suitcase. That would definitely have stuck in my mind. Frowning, I walk back to the table.

'Everything all right?' Fiona asks.

'Yes. There must have been a mix-up. I'm sorry, but Patrick won't be joining us.'

'Not a problem. We'll have more time to gossip. And anyway, if we're going to talk about your will–'

I cut her off. I do not want her mentioning wills in front of the kids. Oliver is still terrified that I'm going to die on him too, and that he'll be left an orphan.

Fiona tries to make conversation, but it's very obvious she doesn't have experience of teenagers. Giving up on conversing with them, she turns to me. 'Have you got any holiday plans?'

'No,' I say, finishing my second glass of white wine. Fiona has barely touched her first. 'With the house move and everything, it's not the right time.'

'I want to go skiing,' Mia says.

'And I want to go scuba diving,' Oliver retorts.

'I might be going scuba diving,' Fiona says. 'Cassie and I are planning a holiday away together. We're thinking about Egypt, so we can get a bit of warmth, and I've always fancied diving.'

'Oh,' I say. I'm taken aback. Cassie hasn't mentioned anything to me about going away on holiday with Fiona, and I'm surprised that she even has the money.

'Cassie and I have so much in common,' Fiona says as she carefully places her cutlery on her empty plate. 'She's such a lovely, warm person.'

My smile feels forced and unnatural. I'm jealous. Yes, I know it's ridiculous and I have no right to be, but Cassie and I have been best friends for years. Fiona is the newcomer. I hadn't realised that they were hanging out together so much. But it does make sense. They're of a similar age and both single. Why shouldn't they go on holiday together? Besides, I'm married again and have kids living at home.

'Yes. Cassie is the best,' I say. 'I hope you have fun.'

'If you weren't so busy, we would have suggested you come

with us. But I expect your new husband might not be best pleased.'

'You're right. We still need to take a honeymoon, and we've promised the kids a holiday as soon as things calm down.'

Fiona doesn't stay late, explaining that she has a busy day tomorrow and promising that she'll get to my will as soon as she can. It suits me that she leaves early. I'm exhausted. I have a hot bath with water turned blue thanks to my heavenly scented lavender bath oil; I'm in bed by 10.30 p.m. I send Patrick a text message wishing him goodnight. He sends me one back. *Sleep well. I love you xxx*

I am in a deep sleep when something tugs me awake. My heart is thumping as I come to and switch on my bedside lamp. The phone is ringing. The landline, not my mobile, which I switch off before I go to sleep. My first thoughts are of Patrick. *Please God, don't let anything have happened to Patrick.* I grab the phone.

'Hello?'

There is silence.

'Hello,' I repeat. Still no one answers. I wait for a few seconds, listening in case someone comes onto the line, and then I'm straining to hear if I can make out breathing. But no. There is silence. I hang up. I dial 1471 to double-check who has made the call, still worried it might be Patrick. The number comes up as withheld. I switch on my mobile and send Patrick a text message just in case he's still awake.

Just woken by a silent call. Wanted to check you're ok. x

He sends me an immediate text back. *Yes, fine. Still working. Go back to sleep.*

I miss the kisses he normally places after his initial. I place the mobile on my bedside table, leaving it on this time, and try to fall back to sleep.

And then it happens all over again. I jerk awake and grab the phone. 'Who's there?'

Again, there is silence. It's 3 a.m., and this isn't funny. I'm annoyed, so I put on my navy fleece dressing gown and go downstairs to make myself a cup of chamomile tea. As I'm waiting for the water to cool down, I think of Ajay. Would he do something as petty as call me in the middle of the night to scare me? I'm nervous now, so when I go upstairs, I put the house alarm on. I write little notes and shove them under the kids' doors, telling them not to come downstairs without switching the alarm off.

The chamomile tea does nothing, and sleep evades me for the rest of the night. When I turn over onto my side, all I hear is my heartbeat pumping faster and faster. My mind is a cauldron of concerns and worries. The children, the business, Ajay and even Patrick. I think of what Patrick's police friend said, that they would be reinterviewing Ajay. Why hasn't DI Cornish or DC White contacted me to tell me what's going on? I'll have to take matters into my own hands.

On the dot of 9 a.m., I call DC White.

'I've heard on the grapevine that you have some new evidence. Can you tell me more?'

There is silence. 'Are you still there?' I ask eventually.

'I assume you have spoken to Mr Arya?'

'No.' And then I realise I should have said yes, as now he might want to know how I came by the information. I quickly change my mind. 'Um, yes. Look it's very awkward for me having to work with him. I need to know if I'm safe.'

'It is true that new evidence has come to light.'

'Please, you've got to tell me!'

'Keep this to yourself, Mrs Palmer.' I don't correct him for using my previous name. 'A neighbour has come forwards to say that they saw a red saloon car leaving your driveway on the night of your husband's death.'

'Ajay's car?' My heart is pounding now.

'We are investigating that possibility.'

'But why has it taken months for them to come forwards?'

'The car was seen by your neighbour's Australian relative. He left the country before Mr Palmer's death made the headlines. We understand that the neighbor was chatting about the murder with his relative during a long-distance telephone conversation. It was only then that the relative remembered what he had seen."

'Really?' I find this so hard to believe, but then again, why would a stranger lie about something like this? 'And you think it's Ajay's car?' I ask in a small voice.

'We are investigating. Please be assured that should we make an arrest, you will be the first to know.'

'But have you interviewed him? Is he on bail?'

'I'm sorry, but I can't tell you any more at this stage. I have to go now.'

I grit my teeth in frustration as DC White ends the call.

22

Over the next few days, I wait for another call from DC White or DI Cornish, but it doesn't come. The more I think about Ajay's involvement in Adam's death, the more it makes sense... yet the stranger it seems. Ajay is an intelligent man. Surely he wouldn't have driven his distinctive car to our house; any of us could have seen it. Yet Ajay doesn't reappear at work.

With everything that has been going on, insomnia combined with the fact that I'm having to work all hours in order to cover for Ajay's continued absence, I totally forget what day it is. Patrick wakes me by getting out of bed first. I glance at my alarm clock with concern, worried that I've over-slept. But I haven't. It's just before six a.m. Why has he got up so early? I'm annoyed to be woken and am dozing when he comes back into the room.

'Wake up, sleepyhead.'

I force my eyelids open. He is standing at the bottom of the bed, holding a massive bunch of red roses and a balloon.

'What?' I'm still groggy with sleep.

'Happy birthday! Have you forgotten?' He laughs.

I flop back onto the pillow. 'Yes! And I'm quite happy not to be reminded that I'm another year older.'

'Spoilsport,' he says, laying the bouquet on top of the chest of drawers. He bounces onto the bed, almost squashing me. 'Here!' He holds out a very small box wrapped in gold paper and tied with a gold bow.

'Thank you,' I say, shifting myself up in bed. I unwrap the paper and carefully open the box. Inside is a stunning pair of emerald-cut earrings, in a simple rectangular design to match my engagement ring. They are tasteful and beautiful. I take them out of the box.

'Put them on,' he says as I lean back into the crook of his arm. I do as I'm told.

'You are the most beautiful woman, Mrs Grant,' he says, running his fingers down my neck. And then my alarm clock goes off and I freeze.

'I've got to get up,' I say, gently easing myself away from him.

He groans. 'Guess I'll have to wait until tonight, then. You'll need to wear a dress. We're going out.'

When the children come downstairs, it's evident they haven't remembered it's my birthday. I can't help but think of Adam. He used to make sure they both made me a birthday card. I remind myself that I don't miss him, that I'm much happier with Patrick.

'Why have you got a balloon?' Oliver asks.

'It's your mother's birthday. Didn't you remember?' Patrick frowns.

Oliver jumps off the chair and rushes over to embrace me. 'I'm sorry, Mum. Happy birthday.'

'It's fine,' I say, even though I can't shake the feeling of sadness.

. . .

AT WORK, my day gets worse. I receive a letter from BUYIT TV informing us that we are being dropped from the vendor list, and we will no longer be able to present our products on their channel. I'm not surprised, but I'm still upset. It's all my fault. If I hadn't screwed up a week ago, we would still have the important revenue stream. Or perhaps it was Ajay, trying to undermine me? Either way, it's a disaster. Now I will need to contact all the other TV shopping channels and see if anyone else will give us a go. I'm not hopeful, because they will know that we have had a longstanding relationship with their competitor. After staring at the letter for many long minutes, I make a decision. I need to talk to Ajay. We must sort things out. I can't stand this stalemate, not knowing where he is or what he's doing.

I call his mobile. The phone rings, and then it eventually goes to voicemail.

'Ajay, we need to talk. Please, can you call me?'

I wait all day, but he doesn't.

THE LAST THING I feel like doing is going to a fancy restaurant to celebrate my birthday, but it seems that I have no choice. Mia comes into the bedroom as I'm getting changed, undecided what to wear.

'You're looking smart,' I say, noting her short black velvet dress.

'Patrick wants me to choose what you're going to wear tonight.'

'You!' I say with surprise.

She scowls.

'Are we all going out?'

'Yes,' she says as she marches into my dressing room.

'Wear this.' She holds up a sleeveless red satin dress that I haven't worn in two years.

'It's very dressy,' I say. 'I'm not even sure it fits.'

'You look good in it. It'll be fine.' She speaks with the certainty of youth.

I do as I'm told.

As I am walking down the stairs, the doorbell rings.

'It's the taxi,' Patrick says. He is wearing a smart navy suit with slim-fitting trousers and a red tie. After locking up the house, I follow him and the children to the taxi.

'Where are we going?' I ask.

'You'll have to wait and see,' Patrick says. Oliver giggles. Twenty minutes later we pull up in front of one of the most upmarket hotels in Sussex, with an acclaimed three rosette restaurant. I hope the children will be able to eat the food. Despite my exhaustion, I chastise myself. I will enjoy the evening. I'm here with my family, the three people in the world whom I love the most.

We walk into the imposing oak-paneled entrance hall, where a receptionist bustles over to us and offers to take our coats.

'It's this way, Mr Grant,' she says, flicking her ash blonde mane. We stroll along a corridor lined with foreboding oil paintings, and then she opens a door, standing back to let us go in. As I walk through, there is a collective roar.

'Happy birthday, Lydia!'

My hand rushes to my mouth and I have to blink away tears. There must be thirty people in the private room, all holding glasses of champagne. Thirty people who are important in my life, including Cassie, Fiona and a couple of key staff from work such as Nicky. Ajay and Marianne are conspicuous by their absence.

I turn to Patrick, feeling overwhelmed. 'Did you organise this?'

'Yes, with a little bit of help from Mia and Cassie.'

Cassie walks over and hugs me. Her hair has changed

colour again. It's now platinum blonde, and it matches her silver shimmery dress.

'Thank you,' I whisper.

The room is beautiful, with more oak walls, intricate cornicing, and large candelabras positioned in the corners. Three tables are covered with starched white linen and laid with silver cutlery. Waiters move silently between the guests, proffering silver platters of canapes and trays of champagne. As people come over to say congratulations, it strikes me that the last time I saw most of these people was at Adam's funeral. And there are quite a few people whom I haven't yet introduced to Patrick.

After hugging my sister, Bea, Fiona eases her way towards me. 'Happy birthday,' she says, air kissing, as she hands me a small gift-wrapped box. Mia takes the gift and places it on a square table next to the door where there is already a pile of colourfully wrapped presents. I don't remember having a birthday party like this, ever.

'I want to introduce you to Patrick,' I say, grabbing Fiona's hand and leading her to the other side of the room, where my divine husband is talking to my brother-in-law, Craig.

'Can I interrupt?'

'Patrick, this is Fiona.'

'Hello, lovely to meet you,' he says. Fiona's eyes don't leave Patrick's face. It gives me a little surge of pride. Yes, my husband is handsome and he's kind, and he organised this evening especially for me. I take a sip of champagne and feel warmth course through my veins. And then I notice Mia. She is staring at Fiona, a frown on her face.

I start walking towards her to check if everything is all right, but I get stopped by my elderly godmother, whom I haven't seen since Adam's funeral. When I next see Mia, she is laughing at something that Finlay is saying.

A while later, we sit down for dinner at three tables of ten,

Patrick seated on my left and Craig on my right. After a sumptuous meal of salmon mousse wrapped in smoked salmon followed by roast duck, Patrick stands up and chimes a spoon on his wine glass. Everyone falls silent and turns to look at my husband.

'Thank you all for coming. As you know, we're here to celebrate my beautiful wife's birthday. Most of you will have been surprised that we married so quickly, particularly after Lydia, Mia and Oliver suffered such tragedy with the death of Adam. His were big shoes to fill. But the thing is, I knew from that very first time I met Lydia that she was the love of my life. I knew that I was the luckiest man to find her, and I knew that I could never let her go. I never imagined I could find such love in middle age, and I wanted to share every possible moment of the rest of my life with this wonderful woman. So please forgive us for not having a big wedding, for acting with, what some might view as, inappropriate haste. That's what love does to you. Please raise your glass to my wife, Lydia Grant. Happy birthday!'

Everyone bounds to their feet and lifts their champagne glasses, wishing me a happy birthday. Tears of joy prick my eyes. And as Patrick sits down, I grab him and plant a kiss on his lips.

'Thank you,' I murmur. 'You have no idea how happy I am.'

The rest of the evening passes in a blur as I chat with friends and family, and then around midnight, guests start to leave, until it's just Cassie and the four of us left in the room. Oliver has laid his head on the table and looks as if he's fast asleep. Mia is typing furiously on her phone.

'Happy birthday, gorgeous.' Cassie gives me a kiss on the cheek.

'Has Fiona gone?' I ask Cassie, realising that she didn't say goodbye.

'Yes, she left before the coffee arrived.'

'Oh,' I say.

'She said she wasn't feeling well.'

'Anyway, I just want to thank you for a wonderful evening.' Cassie smiles.

'It's me who needs to thank you,' I say. 'And you need to thank this man.' I loop my arm through Patrick's, and I think I see Cassie's smile quiver. I feel for her. I hope that both she and Fiona find partners as gorgeous as mine.

'Right, we need to go. Mia, can you wake your brother?' Patrick says. With his arm around my shoulders, we walk out of the hotel, to where another taxi is awaiting us.

HALF AN HOUR LATER, we are home and I am slipping out of my dress. 'That was a truly wonderful evening and such a surprise. I can't thank you enough.'

'It was fun to meet your friends and family,' Patrick says, undoing his shirt buttons.

'You should have invited your sister. I can't believe you still haven't introduced us.'

Patrick has his back towards me. 'I didn't want to ruin your day by telling you, but she's back in hospital.'

'Oh no. I'm so sorry. Is the treatment not working?'

'I think it is, but she has terrible side effects. I visited her earlier in the week.'

'You did?' I frown. 'You didn't tell me.'

'You had quite enough to worry about with the business and Ajay. No need to burden you with more concerns.' He drops his shirt onto the floor and strides towards the bathroom.

'I'd like to meet Sandra,' I say. 'Next time you're visiting her, can I come?'

'Sure.'

A few minutes later we're both in bed. I turn towards Patrick and kiss him. He sighs and pulls back.

'I'm really tired, Lydia. Do you mind?'

'Of course not,' I say. But I do. Tonight of all nights we should be making love. Tomorrow is Saturday and we don't even have to get up early. Perhaps in the morning, I think to myself.

At 8.30 a.m., Patrick bounds out of bed and offers to take Oliver to football practice. I eagerly accept. Mia still hasn't surfaced, so I have a couple of hours to sort through bills and do all the mundane household stuff that I used to share with Adam, but now have to do alone. I switch on my laptop and click onto online banking. I have three accounts. My current account, a savings account and the new joint account that Patrick and I set up together. I click onto that and notice with dismay that it's overdrawn. How is that possible? And then I see the two very substantial payments. Three and a half thousand pounds was spent at a jeweler's in Horsham earlier in the week. My new earrings, I suppose. And just under five thousand pounds was spent at the luxury hotel where my party was held yesterday.

'Shit,' I mutter out loud. It's not as if I can't afford it. I can. There is a large six-figure sum sitting in my savings account, but that's not the point. Naturally, I assumed that Patrick would have paid for my earrings and the party himself and not taken the money out of our joint account, which is predominantly topped up by my money. Well, perhaps it's fair enough to use our joint money for the party, but to use it for my earrings...

It feels mean, especially as he knows that I will see how much he spent. Patrick doesn't have anything like as much money as I do, but then again, I don't know how much he earns, or exactly what he has. I assumed he was well off, because how else could he afford to pay for his sister's immunotherapy?

I sit there for a long time trying to quell the unease. Eventually, I decide I must let it go. Money must not become an issue between us. Patrick is a kind, loving man and, as I reiterate to myself, what is mine is his.

23

On Monday morning, I stride into work feeling positive. I have had lots of messages from friends and family thanking us for the dinner, commenting that Patrick is a delightful man, and how happy they are that I've found happiness again. I've forgiven him for using my money on the earrings and the party. It's not as if Patrick has ever taken advantage of my wealth, so I've put that initial disappointment behind me. Now I need to concentrate on Cracking Crafts.

I am wearing a bright red jumper, and despite the pouring rain, it cheers me up. Just because we've lost the BUYIT TV account doesn't mean we're facing financial ruin. I say good morning to Nicky and the rest of the team and stride down the corridor to my office. I open the door and jump.

Ajay is sitting in my chair.

I take a step backwards. 'What are you doing?' I ask.

'Waiting to talk to you.'

'Where have you been all of last week? Why didn't you get in touch?'

'I needed time to think, Lydia, and now I have. I want to buy you out of Cracking Crafts. I can turn the company around. You've taken your eye off the ball, and it's outgrown you.'

'No! Absolutely not. This business is my life. I set it up and I'm not selling.'

'That's a very rash, ill-thought-out response.'

'I'm not stupid, Ajay. One doesn't sell a business when it's doing badly. If you think you can buy me out on the cheap, think again.'

He raises an eyebrow and I feel like slapping his face.

'And besides,' I continue, 'the screw-up with BUYIT TV was because you rang them to swap over the machines. I suppose you did that on purpose to undermine me and to reduce our profitability so that you can buy my shares on the cheap. Well, it's not going to work!'

'Lydia, I did not make any phone call. I do not want this business to fail. In fact, quite the opposite.' He talks in a low, slow voice, his eyes narrowed. 'I want a fresh start. I'll give you a fair payout, and you can go and do whatever you want.'

'No,' I say, anger coursing through my veins. 'What about the new evidence that has come to light? The fact that someone saw your car leave our house on the night Adam died? You're still a person of interest to the police. You're probably a murderer.'

His eyes narrow and his lips tighten. Veins stand out on his neck and he clenches and unclenches his fists. Fury is pulsating off him in waves, and it is scaring me. As he takes a step forwards, I take another step backwards; now I'm up against the door. I reach behind my back and grasp the door handle. I know every word I utter is provocative, but I can't let this one go. It's like a mosquito bite that you just have to scratch, even though you know it might make it infected. 'And what about your conviction for GBH when you were in your early twenties. You conveniently forgot to mention that to me, didn't you?'

'What the fuck!' Ajay shouts. 'How do you know about

that?' But then he slumps back against the windowsill. His voice is quiet again, and I can't decide whether I'm more scared of his overt anger or his silent menace. 'Yes, you're right. I did glass someone in a pub. He attacked a friend, and I did it in self-defense. I paid my dues. It's in the past, and I didn't see any reason to tell you. Marianne has known about it for the past twenty years. But you're also wrong. The police have no proof that my car was at your house that night. If they did, don't you think I'd be locked up? Look, Lydia, have I ever given you reason to think I'm violent?' He stares at me intently.

I shake my head and whisper, 'No.' But that doesn't mean I'm not scared of him. I am. I don't know who the real Ajay is; I don't know if he is capable of murder or just angry that I've found him out.

'You should leave,' I say, opening the door. When he walks past me, I shrink as far back as possible. He turns.

'Think about what I said, Lydia. It's for the best.'

He goes then, walking straight past his office and out the front door.

I FIND it hard to concentrate, playing over and over in my mind what Ajay said. But the more I think about it, the more unjust it seems. Why should I sell this business? Cracking Crafts was my original concept. I don't need the money; I love working here. I know people will hate me for saying I don't need the money, but I, more than anyone, know that the saying *Money doesn't buy you happiness* is very true. Adam had all that money, but he died. It was Adam who wanted the trappings of wealth: the fancy cars, the big house, the latest media gizmos. I don't need any of that. What I need is the love I give to and receive from my family and my business. I love Cracking Crafts, and I feel so privileged that I'm doing work that brings me joy and fulfillment. And soon enough, the kids will have left home, and then I'll definitely need my work to keep me busy.

I call DC White, but he's not there, and before I can say *Please don't forward the call to DI Cornish*, he is on the line.

'Lydia, what can I do for you?'

'Did you know that Ajay Arya was convicted for GBH?' I ask.

'Yes, of course.'

'Is he still a person of interest?'

'Why are you asking, Lydia?'

'Um, it's just...' I don't want to get either DC White or Patrick's contact into trouble, so I can't admit knowing about the red car. 'Are you still investigating Adam's death?'

'Of course, although the investigation has been scaled back somewhat.'

'So Ajay isn't a suspect?'

'I can't comment on that, Lydia. We have talked about this before.'

'Are you saying that we may never know why Adam died?'

'That is a possibility, Lydia. I'm sorry.'

As soon as Patrick gets home, I tell him about Ajay's offer. His face lights up.

'But that's the ideal solution, isn't it?' he says, grinning at me.

'No. I don't want to sell.'

'But why not? You can take the money and live an easy life. Go on holidays, meet your friends for lunch, decorate our new home.'

'Is that how you see me, Patrick? As a lady who lunches?'

'No. I'm thinking about what's in your best interests. You have been increasingly stressed over the past few weeks. You haven't been sleeping well, and frankly, I don't think you're coping. This could be the answer to all of your problems.'

'What? So you can take my money and run off into the sunset?'

I regret the words as soon as I utter them. Patrick's face hardens and a pulse thrums in his forehead. 'I'm sorry,' I say, but I know the damage has already been done.

'Is that how you see me, Lydia? A freeloader?'

His face is bloodless. He turns, walks out of the kitchen, and slams the door behind him. I hurry after him, but he is already through the front door, which he also slams. I watch as he gets into his car and drives away at full pelt, little stones thrown up from the driveway, his rear lights fading too quickly.

'Oh shit, what have I done?' I murmur to myself as I sink onto the flagstone floor.

24

Patrick doesn't return for supper, so I tell the kids that he had to go and visit his poorly sister. I try calling him several times during the evening, but his phone goes to voicemail. Eventually, I go to bed, but I toss and turn listening out for his car, wondering where he is. At 1.30 a.m., even though I hate doing it when I'm alone in the house with the kids, I take half a sleeping pill. The alarm clock wakes me, and – to my total relief – Patrick is lying asleep next to me.

I know I was out of order last night. Just because I read an article in the papers about romance fraud doesn't mean that Patrick is a fraudster. He has done nothing but show love and affection to me. As I sit up in bed, my head spins and my throat feels totally raw. At first, I assume it's because I was so upset last night, but when I try to get out of bed, a bone-aching lethargy almost makes me tumble. I am freezing cold. I sit on the edge of the bed, shivering, my teeth rattling.

'What's the matter?' Patrick asks, levering himself up.

'I think I'm sick,' I say. 'And I'm really sorry about last night. I shouldn't have said those things.' My voice is croaky.

He rubs my back. 'And I shouldn't have walked out. At least

we've got our first really big fight out of the way.'

I lean back onto the bed, relieved that we appear to have weathered the storm. 'I don't feel well. I think I've got a fever.'

He puts his hand on my forehead. 'You're burning up. Get back into bed and I'll get you a jug of water and some paracetamol. I told you that you needed to take a step back and start looking after yourself.'

I don't rise to the bait. I don't have the energy, and right now I feel like crying tears of self-pity. Five minutes later, Patrick returns and I struggle to swallow two paracetamol.

'Can you take the kids to school this morning?' It hurts to talk.

He looks at his watch. 'It's going to be bloody tight. I've got to be in Guildford at 9.30 a.m. for a meeting with Began Fire Extinguishers.'

'Please, Patrick.'

His jaw tightens, and then he disappears to the bathroom.

Some time later, Oliver comes into the bedroom carrying a bowl of cereal and a cup of tea. I heave myself into a sitting position.

'Patrick said you're sick.'

'Yes, I've got some bug. Thank you, darling.'

He places them on my bedside table. 'You're going to be ok, aren't you?'

'Of course. At worst, it's the flu. At best, it's a heavy cold. Nothing for you to worry about.'

'If you're sure,' he says, hovering at the end of my bed.

'I promise you, Ollie. I'll be fine. You need to hurry, though; otherwise you'll be late for school.'

'Ok, Mum.'

Mia appears in the doorway, her coat on and her rucksack over her shoulder. Evidently, she responds better to Patrick's chivvying her along than me. She still thinks he's amazing. I suppose I should be pleased about that.

'Hope you feel better soon, Mum.' She throws me a weak smile.

'Come along, kids. We'll be late,' Patrick shouts up the stairs. 'You'll be ok, won't you, Lydia?'

I croak, 'Yes,' but I doubt he can hear me. I wave the kids away and listen to their thudding footsteps and the slamming of the front door. Then the house falls totally quiet and I feel very alone. I am rational enough to know I'm feeling down because I'm sick, but I had hoped Patrick might have come up to say goodbye, that he might have asked me if I needed a jug of juice or some food. But perhaps that's asking too much. Adam wouldn't have been any better.

After calling Nicky to tell her I won't be in the office today, I close my eyes and drift into a deep sleep.

I HATE DAYTIME SLEEPS. When I awake, it's light and I am totally disoriented. It's as if I'm being tugged from a dark abyss. Something has woken me. I strain my ears and then the sound comes again. It's the doorbell.

I pull myself out of bed and the room spins. I lean against the wall, and when the bedroom stops swirling, I reach for my dressing gown and wrap it around me. The doorbell sounds again. I grab my house keys from my handbag.

'I'm coming,' I croak, but I know whoever it is won't be able to hear me. My legs feel leaden as I stumble down the staircase. I glance at myself in the hall mirror. I look dreadful, with deep rings under my eyes, a red nose and pale, almost grey skin. I run my fingers through my bed hair and unlock the door, keeping the chain on as I open it. I expect it to be the postman delivering a package.

It's not.

'What are you doing here?'

'I have an offer for you for the business.' Ajay holds up a white envelope.

'I'm sick. Can you pass it to me?'

'No. We need to talk, Lydia. Properly talk about us and the future of Cracking Crafts.'

'Not now, Ajay. I'm feeling crap. Just leave me the letter.'

'Please, Lydia. Open the door and let me in. I'll make you a cup of tea, and we can talk for a few minutes. Nicky told me you were at home today.'

And suddenly I feel very, very vulnerable. I'm alone in the house and Ajay wants to come in. It would be easy enough for him to break the chain on the door. He is looking at me with a strange expression, his eyes questioning, his mouth slightly lopsided, almost as if he can read something from my expression that I'm not aware of myself.

'For God's sake, Lydia! We've known each other for half our lifetimes. All I want to do is have a civilised conversation with you.'

I shake my head. I think he can sense my fear. 'I don't want to sell.'

'You can make that decision when you know what my offer is.'

'Just give me the envelope,' I say, putting my hand out. I'm shivering now, partly through cold, but mainly because of the fever. My head feels fuzzy and my bones ache. 'I'm really not well.'

'I'm sorry you're not well, but Lydia, I've done nothing wrong! I didn't touch Adam. I'm sorry your husband died, but not for one moment have you considered that I'm also a victim here. My wife was cheating on me. And Adam was a friend of mine. Don't you think I feel betrayed too? It's horrible what we've all been through. But you and me, we were doing ok, managing the business, back on an equilibrium. That was until Patrick came along and started fueling your suspicions!'

'No, that's not true. Patrick has nothing to do with it. He's just looking out for me. It's because the police are suspicious of you, because I think you're undermining me and the business. And you have a criminal record, which you conveniently never told me about.'

'This is nonsense!' His voice is raised now and he starts pacing, his hands deep in his coat pockets. 'Let me in, Lydia.'

'No,' I say weakly. It feels as if my knees are going to give way. I haven't felt this ill in years. 'I'm going back to bed now.' I shut the front door on Ajay, but a moment later, he is banging on it. If it wasn't such a sturdy, ancient oak door, I would be scared he might break it down.

'Bloody let me in!' He thumps the door again.

'If you don't go away, Ajay, I'm going to call the police.'

I back away and walk into the kitchen to grab the phone. I remember Patrick telling me I must call the police if I'm scared of Ajay. I wait out of view. He bangs the door another couple of times, but then an envelope is slipped through the letter box and lands on the doormat. I tiptoe into the living room and peek around the side of the curtains. To my relief, I see Ajay getting into his Mercedes saloon. He drives away at speed.

After picking the envelope up, I feel totally drained, and it takes every ounce of my remaining strength to pull my weary, aching body up the stairs. I collapse into bed.

I am dozing when, an hour later, the phone rings.

'Hello,' I whisper. My voice is barely there.

'If you won't talk face to face, we'll talk on the phone,' Ajay says. 'Have you studied my offer?'

'No, not yet.'

'Right. I'm not taking no for an answer. I'm coming back and we are going to sort this mess out.'

'No–' I say, but he's hung up on me.

With trembling hands, I open the envelope. It's as I expected, valuing the company at about fifty percent less than I would have expected. I don't need an accountant to tell me that this is a lousy offer. I need Ajay to go away and stay away.

I call Patrick. His phone rings and rings and then his voice-mail kicks in. 'Can you call me, please? It's urgent,' I say, in a hoarse whisper. I need him now. Ajay is frightening me. And then the doorbell rings again. I can't deal with this. So I do what Patrick told me to do and I call DI Cornish for the second time in as many days.

A woman answers. 'I'm sorry, DI Cornish isn't available. Can I help?'

I explain who I am and how I'm concerned about Ajay's behaviour.

'And what exactly has he done to you that is threatening?'

'He was insisting on coming inside the house. I sent him away and now he's coming back again, and I'm scared.'

'Has he caused you any bodily harm?'

'No, no. He hasn't touched me.'

'And has he caused any damage to your property?'

'No,' I whisper. I know where this conversation is going.

'So other than ringing your doorbell, what exactly are you accusing Mr Arya of doing?'

'It doesn't matter,' I concede. Perhaps I'm overreacting because I'm feeling so ill. 'I'm sorry to have bothered you.' I hang up.

The doorbell chimes again, and I just can't stand it. I need Patrick. Now. He needs to come home and tell Ajay to leave me alone in peace. I try his mobile once again, but it still goes straight to voicemail. Where did Patrick say he was going today? I search my pounding, cotton-wool brain. Guildford. It was a fire extinguisher manufacturer, but I can't remember the name. I grab my phone and do an online search. It's the first on the list. Began Fire Extinguishers. I'm sure that's what he said. I hope he won't mind me disturbing him, but I have to do this.

'Hello, I understand you have a consultant visiting your

offices today. His name is Patrick Grant. I'm sorry to disturb you, but I need to speak to him urgently.'

'Ok.' The receptionist sounds dubious, but perhaps that's because my sore throat and hoarse voice make me sound bizarre. 'Please hold on for a moment.'

I listen to an electronic rendition of *Eine Kleine Nachtmusik* three times before she eventually comes back onto the line.

'I've spoken to all the directors and we don't have anyone of that name in our offices today. I'm sorry.'

'Are you sure? He might have left already.'

'I'm quite sure. We're only a small company, just ten people in this office, and we've had no visitors today.'

'He's a consultant. Works on systems and stuff.'

'As far as I'm aware, we haven't employed any consultants recently. I think you must have the wrong company.'

'Ok, thank you,' I say and drop the phone onto my duvet.

Where the hell is he? I need him. Why did he tell me he was going to see Began Fire Extinguishers if he wasn't? It doesn't make any sense. I am shivering again, feeling absolutely terrible. Everything aches, and even just turning my head is an effort. I force another couple of paracetamols down my burning sore throat, and then I burst into tears. When the sobs stop, I haul myself out of bed to check if Ajay's car is still here. It's not. Relieved that he's gone, I snooze for a short while until lunchtime, when I call Cassie.

'What's happened to your voice?'

'I'm sick.' I sniff. 'And I'm worried and a bit scared.' I tell her about Ajay and my concerns about Patrick.

'Lydia, calm down.' She says it in a kind way. Cassie is always the voice of reason. 'You've not nothing concrete to go on. Ajay hasn't threatened you with anything other than wanting to talk to you, and Patrick is probably in a meeting somewhere else. Honestly, I think you're blowing this out of proportion because you're feeling ill.'

'You're probably right,' I admit.

'Go back to sleep, and if Patrick hasn't surfaced by 5 p.m., call me back.'

'He has to. He needs to collect the kids from school.'

'I can always do that if necessary.'

'Thanks, Cass. I don't know what I'd do without you.'

I PEEK OUTSIDE AGAIN, and Ajay's car has gone. I make myself a hot lemon and honey and return to bed, and I sleep. When I wake up again, it's 4.30 p.m., and there are voices downstairs.

'Hello, love, how are you feeling?' Patrick is standing in the doorway, the hall light on behind him.

'Pretty lousy,' I say. My voice is totally gone now and all I can manage is a whisper. 'Did you get my messages?'

'What messages?' He pulls his phone out of his trouser pocket and looks through it. 'Oh sorry, Lydia. I missed them. I've had a hell of a day. Back-to-back meetings.'

'You weren't where you said you were going to be.'

'What?' He frowns. 'Yes, I was.'

'I tried calling you at Began Fire Extinguishers' Guildford offices and they had never heard of you.'

'Oh, Lydia.' He shakes his head, and his tone is patronising. 'I was at their Working office, not in Guildford; I don't know where you got Guildford from.'

'You definitely said Guildford.' My voice cracks on the final syllable. It's so sore, I wouldn't be surprised if my throat was bleeding.

'Why are you questioning me, anyway?' He runs his hands through his hair, turns his back to me and then swivels around to face me again. 'Look, love, you're sick and you're under a lot of pressure. I know things haven't been easy for you, but you've got to start trusting me. I'm not a liar like Adam.'

'Ajay was here today. That's why I wanted to speak to you.'

'He was?' Patrick's brows knit together and his jaw juts forwards. 'What did he want?'

'To come in. To talk to me. I told him to go away.' I realise from Patrick's expression that I need to play this down. I don't want Patrick storming over to Ajay's house and beating him up. The way he's glowering, nothing would surprise me. 'He made me an offer for the business.'

'And?'

'It's too low. There's no way I am accepting it. Could you make me a Lemsip? I can't talk anymore; my throat is too sore.'

He nods, and I think I see a flicker of irritation on his face, but he turns away and I hear his heavy footsteps descend the stairs.

Ten minutes or so later, Oliver knocks on my door.

'Come in, sweetheart,' I whisper.

'Oh, Mum, you've lost your voice.'

'Yes, and you'd better stay away. I don't want you catching it. Just leave the drink on the chest of drawers, sweetheart.'

I haven't got the energy to do anything except mull over the day's events, thinking about Ajay and Patrick. Is my new husband telling me the truth? I could have sworn he said Guildford this morning, but why would he lie about something like that? And why does he seem so sure that Ajay is Adam's murderer? I wonder if he knows something that he's not telling me.

At some point, he brings me a mug of soup and a piece of toast. I think it's vegetable stock, and I don't feel like drinking it. Later in the evening, Patrick comes into our room and collects some of his clothes.

'Where are you going?'

'Sleeping next door in the spare room. I don't want to catch your germs.'

I roll over onto my side. That annoys me. Whilst I understand he is being sensible, I don't want to be lying here all alone.

'Sleep well, Lydia. Hope you're feeling better in the morning.'

The next time I awake, the phone is ringing. I fumble in the dark to find it, as I don't suppose Patrick will hear it ringing from the spare room.

'Hello,' I whisper. Silence. I glance at my alarm clock. It's shortly before 1 a.m. I hang up. Not again, please not again.

But just as I've dropped back into another deep sleep, it happens all over again. This time I don't hang up, but hold the phone in my hand as I stumble through the bedroom, out into the hall, and ease open the closed door to the spare room.

'Patrick,' I whisper, 'can you wake up?'

'What is it?' He jerks awake, bolting upright in bed.

'I'm sorry to wake you, but we've had another silent call. Two, actually.' I hold up the phone.

He beckons me over and I pass it to him. He holds it to his ear. 'It's just a dial tone.'

'They must have hung up.'

'Ajay probably, pissed off because of what happened today, I suppose,' Patrick says.

'I'm scared, Patrick.'

He lies back down in bed.

'No reason to be. Just pull the socket out of the line so you're not disturbed. I'll leave my mobile phone on. Wake me up again if you're scared.'

'Okay, thank you,' I say and shuffle back to our bedroom. But I'm not appeased. It may be my illness, but I can't rid myself of that sense of impending doom that sends my heartbeat soaring and my nerve ends tingling. Before Adam died, I had no inkling that something bad was about to happen, but now, I've got the sense that worse may be just around the corner.

25

The next morning I struggle to open my eyes. I turn to look at Patrick and see the uncreased side of his bed. Then I remember. He slept next door – and we had those silent calls. Again. I am just trying to heave myself up to go to the bathroom when he walks into the room, dressed in a suit with a smart navy coat over the top. I don't think I've seen the overcoat before.

'How are you feeling?'

'Lousy.' I flop back onto my pillow.

'I've got to go to Manchester for the next two days. It's something I really can't get out of. Will you be ok by yourself?'

'I'll have to be,' I mutter.

'I've sent Cassie a text message asking if she can collect Mia and Oliver from school.'

'Ok.' I know Patrick must have had help from Cassie when organising my birthday party, but I wonder how often they are in contact with each other.

'I'm not happy about these silent calls.' He rubs his chin. 'Make sure you keep the doors locked and leave your mobile phone on all the time. And the slightest hint of any trouble from Ajay, call the police.'

I nod. I wish he wasn't going. I don't feel like spending the next forty-eight hours without him.

'Who's the client?' My voice definitely sounds less croaky than yesterday, and it isn't quite so painful to talk.

'An important one, from the States. Right, I need to get going now.'

'Take my car.'

He stops still and his face lights up. 'Are you sure?'

I know he prefers driving my Porsche Cayenne to his Golf, which he only got back from the garage recently. And I don't blame him. But the real reason I want him to take my car is that I'm nervous of him driving the kids in the Golf. If it was that severely damaged in the accident, is the chassis really safe? I know that all my thoughts are out of control at the moment, that I'm probably worrying about nothing, but even so...

'But I'll be leaving it overnight in the station car park. And won't you need it?'

'I'm not going anywhere, and if I have to, I'll take the Bentley.'

'Thanks, love. Get better soon, and I'll call you tonight.' He blows me a kiss and leaves. A moment later Mia and Oliver appear in the doorway.

'Have a good day, kids,' I say, trying to force a smile.

AFTER SEVERAL MORE HOURS OF sleep, I wake feeling marginally better. I have a shower and put on some old clothes. It's a relief that no one turns up at the house and the phone doesn't ring. By the time Cassie brings the children back from school, I have defrosted some fishcakes and, drugged up on Lemsip, am just about functioning.

Cassie offers to stay and help, but I send her on her way. I don't want her catching my lurgy.

Later on, after they have both done their homework, the three of us watch a catch-up episode of *The Apprentice* on television.

'They're so thick!' Mia exclaims. The candidates are running around Amsterdam like headless chickens, trying to find items at the lowest possible cost. They haven't got a clue what most of the products are.

'And aggressive. I can assure you it's not like that in the real world,' I chip in.

There's a crash.

From outside.

It sounds like the lid of a metal dustbin landing on tarmac. We don't have a metal dustbin.

'What was that?' Oliver sits bolt upright.

'I don't know.' I press the pause button on the television remote.

'Sounded like it came from outside,' Mia says.

'It's probably just a fox, or a branch that fell down.' I stand up and walk out of the room. I don't want the kids to see the look of sheer terror on my face. 'Carry on watching. I'll just go and investigate.'

'No, Mum!' Mia jumps up from the sofa.

'It's fine, darlings. Just stay here. I won't be two ticks.'

I stride to the hallway, but don't switch the light on. I have a good view of the driveway from the window next to the front door, but I stand back and hopefully can't be seen. My eyes take a few moments to adjust to the darkness, and then I see it. A dark figure creeping near the magnolia tree.

Or have I imagined it? Is it really a figure? It's windy outside, and the trees are swaying. I switch on the outside lights, flooding the front of the house with a pale-yellow glow. I stare wildly. Yes, the branches are moving, but I can't see a person. Perhaps it was a fox, or a deer, even. We have plenty of wildlife visiting our garden. But no. I was right the first time. There is a car, the slamming of a car door. I make a small involuntary whimper and immediately hate myself for my weakness. The rear lights of the car flicker on and it drives away at speed.

I know that car.

It's a maroon-red Mercedes.

The only person I know who drives a maroon-red Mercedes is Ajay. Not again.

I lean against the wall. Shit. He came back. What the hell is he trying to do?

'Is everything ok, Mum?' Mia says as she walks along the corridor towards me, her Ugg boots making a squelching sound on the flagstone floor.

'All fine,' I say as brightly as I can manage, bearing in mind my hoarse voice and the terror still coursing through my veins. 'Just a fox. I saw the damn thing slinking off into the bushes. It must have been trying to get into the rubbish bins.' Mia wrinkles her nose and walks back to the living room. When I have eased my breathing, I follow her.

But I can't concentrate. It is absolutely not acceptable for Ajay to turn up at my house at night and to slink around the outside. What if he put a firebomb through the letter box? And now I have to jump up and check the doormat at the back door.

I am being stupid.

There is nothing there.

As I try to control my racing heart, I remember my promise to Patrick. Call the police. This is harassment. I don't bother calling DI Cornish's team but ring 999. The officer is very gentle with me and promises that she will log everything I tell her. She explains that due to lack of resources it's unlikely anyone from the police will visit me tonight. I'm not surprised.

After Mia and Oliver have gone to their rooms, I call

Patrick. His phone goes straight to voicemail. That pisses me off. He knows I'm on edge, and that I'm not feeling well. I leave him a curt message, asking him to call me back as soon as possible.

I call Cassie instead.

'I'm coming over,' she says, when I explain what's happened.

'No, hon, don't. We're fine.'

'No arguments. I'm coming.'

And twenty minutes later, there she is. My best friend, who scoops me up whenever I have any problems.

'I've got something for you,' she says.

She hands me a strange-looking black can.

'What's this?'

'It's pepper spray.' She lowers her voice. 'It's illegal in the UK, so keep it hidden, but I want you to have it in your bag all the time, just in case.'

'God, Cassie. Where did you get it?' I hold the can as if it is dynamite about to explode.

'You don't need to know that. And better not tell Fiona! She might have me locked up!'

We laugh. 'Talking of Fiona, she mentioned that you're going on holiday together.' I'm shivering again, so I take a throw off the back of the sofa and wrap it around myself.

'Probably not. She suggested it; two single saddos off to some sunny resort, but I don't think the finances will be up to it. I can't see Fiona slumming it, can you?'

I'm relieved. I know it's not kind to say that I am jealous of Fiona's friendship with Cassie, but I am. Just a little bit.

'Would you like me to stay the night?' Cassie asks. 'I've bunged some overnight things in the car just in case.'

'You're a sweetheart, but it's really not necessary. I appreciate the offer, though. No, go home and make sure you don't pick up my germs.'

· · ·

WHEN CASSIE HAS LEFT, and I have checked that every door and window in the house is locked and bolted, wearily, I make my way to bed. It isn't until I'm slipping under the duvet that Patrick calls me. I'm angry with him. He promised he would leave his phone on.

'I'm sorry I couldn't call earlier. I was having dinner with colleagues and I had to have my phone off. Are you all right?' He sounds rather breathless.

'Ajay was here, creeping around the outside of the house!' I say curtly.

'What the hell! The bastard needs to stay away from us. Have you spoken to the police?'

'Yes, they've logged it. I've told them that he's stalking me.'

'And did you tell them about the silent calls?'

'Oh shit, no, I forgot about them.'

'Lydia!' he groans. 'I'm really worried about you. It's obvious that Ajay is unhinged, and I hate to think what he has got planned. You need to get the police onside.'

'I'm trying, Patrick. Really, I'm trying. I was given a police reference number, so I'll call them back in the morning.'

'Ok, darling. But if he scares you, call me, day or night. I'll leave my mobile on all night, and if necessary I'll come back from Manchester early. I've been giving some thought to security, and I think we should install a better security system with night-vision cameras.'

'That's an expensive thing to do when we're about to sell the house.'

'The kids and your safety is worth all the money in the world. Look into it. Promise me? And try not to worry too much. I doubt he'll be back tonight after you caught him creeping around the house earlier. Take a sleeping pill.'

But I won't. If something happens, I want to be alert and

able to deal with it. My priority is to make sure Mia and Oliver are safe. It makes me realise that Patrick will never truly understand me, because he doesn't have children, and he can't comprehend that I would lay my life down to save theirs.

'Sleep tight,' he says before hanging up.

But I don't sleep tight.

I think about Ajay and the business and why he is trying to scare me. What is Ajay's motive? It's evident he wants to acquire the business at a silly price, but is he really a bully? Is he really a violent man? A murderer even? If circumstances were different, I would reach out to Marianne. Perhaps she could give me an insight into her husband, an understanding of him that I currently don't have. But I am not going to get in touch with Marianne. I can't forgive her for her duplicity.

And then I start thinking about Patrick. I shouldn't have doubted him. It's obvious that he loves me. We have agreed to share everything for better or worse. I resolve that that's exactly what I will do. What is mine is his.

26

I wish I had been able to take a sleeping pill, because I don't sleep. I am on heightened alert all night, despite switching the burglar alarm on downstairs and triple-checking that all the doors and windows are locked. I still roam around the house by torchlight at 3 a.m. It takes me back to when the children were babies, and I awoke at the slightest creak or sniff.

I have to force myself to get up to take the children to school. My head feels as if it's going to split in two and my limbs are leaden. There's too much going on in my life to be ill right now, so whilst the children are eating breakfast, I make myself a doctor's appointment. The receptionist must take pity on me, with my barely-there voice, because she gives me an appointment for 10.30 this morning.

I put the pepper spray into the pocket of my anorak. I am glad that Cassie gave it to me, and even though I hope I'll never have to use it, it's like a comfort blanket. I ease the Bentley out of the garage very carefully. I hate driving this car. It's too big and ridiculously expensive. The merest touch of the accelerator, it feels as if the car is going to take off. Mia also hates the

Bentley. I have to park a street away from school so no one sees her and Oliver getting out of the car. I resolve to sell it. I'll buy Patrick a better car and put the leftover sum towards our new house purchase.

The doctor's practice is in a new purpose-built block in Horsham, housing three surgeries and a large chemist. I have never seen the same doctor twice and have no idea who my assigned GP might be. I take the lift to the second floor and put in my date of birth on the screen. I hate how I have to touch the same screen as all the other sick people who have been in before me, so I surreptitiously lather my hands with the antibacterial spray that I keep in my handbag. The waiting room is full, and I resign myself to a long wait. There are copies of women's magazines in a rack and today's edition of the *Daily Mail* on a small table. I help myself to it and take the last remaining chair near the back of the room. The man in a suit sitting to my left edges slightly further away. I suppose I look as ill as I feel, with a scarlet-tipped nose and dark rings in my pasty face.

My head pounds too much to read the newspaper properly, so I skip from headline to headline until I see the title *Stepmother in Feud To Take All*. The article describes the fight that is taking place between three adult children and their stepmother. Their mother had died when the children were young, and their father remarried. He then died without writing a new will, and all of his estate passed to his new wife, with nothing going to his children. The three children have taken their stepmother to court to force her to hand over three-quarters of their father's estate, which they say he would have wanted them to have. Apparently, under inheritance laws in England and Wales, if a married partner dies without leaving a will, all of their estate passes to their remaining spouse, not their children.

'Shit,' I mutter under my breath. The besuited man edges even further away. I realise that as it currently stands, if I should die, Patrick would get everything, and Mia and Oliver nothing. Whilst I doubt this dose of flu is going to kill me, it's imperative that I get my will sorted out. The thought of Adam thinking that all of his earthly goods would be given to Patrick makes me snort, a snort that turns into a rasping cough.

'Lydia Grant to room two, please.'

I fold the newspaper back together and drop it onto the table as I pass, walking through a set of double doors and following the signs to room two. I knock on the door and walk in.

Dr Stone is an attractive woman, probably mid-thirties, with apple cheekbones and tortoiseshell glasses that match her glossy shoulder-length hair.

'How can I help you?' She smiles as she swivels to face me. She has a compassionate but confident manner.

'I think I've got flu,' I say.

'There's a lot of it around at the moment. Let's have a look at your throat.'

She peers down my throat, feels my glands, takes my temperature, and then she checks my blood pressure. Her touch is gentle and efficient.

'It's definitely a virus, so not a lot we can do. You'll need plenty of rest and fluids. Is everything else all right?'

I don't know what it is about this woman, who must be a decade younger than me, but she sets something off. And I realise that no, everything isn't all right. My first husband died under suspicious circumstances, my business is in danger, I'm being threatened by my business partner, my new husband is lovely but somehow not as substantial as my first one, and my kids are suffering. As all of those thoughts flood my head like the rush of bathwater swirling through a drain when the plug is lifted, tears plop out of my eyes.

'Sorry,' I say, brusquely wiping them away.

'There is nothing to be sorry about. Would you like to share with me what's going on?'

So I do. I tell her that I'm not sleeping. That I'm consumed with fear. That the stress at work and sometimes at home is in danger of overwhelming me. And when I stop talking, it's as if I've opened the floodgates, and by dumping it all on this stranger, I feel a sense of levity.

'I think it would be a good idea if I refer you for a course of counselling,' she suggests. 'It will take a while to come through, so if you can afford to go privately, that would be more expeditious.'

'I can,' I admit, almost ashamedly. 'And I think my kids could do with counselling too.'

'That's very likely, considering the trauma your family has suffered.' She writes the name of a woman she recommends on a piece of paper. She then turns to her computer. 'I can see that you were prescribed a course of sleeping pills after your husband died. Do you have any left?'

'About two, I think.'

'I'll give you a course of sleeping pills for five days. Take them and come back to see me in a week's time. I'm sure you'll feel much better after decent sleep.'

She prints out a prescription, which she hands to me.

'Thank you.' I throw her a weak smile as I leave.

BACK AT HOME, I make myself another Lemsip and I call Fiona's mobile. I expect it to go to voicemail, but she answers.

'Lydia, how are you? I'm sorry I haven't been in touch for a while. Been snowed under with work. How are you doing?'

'Fine,' I say, my default response. 'Actually, not so fine. I've got flu. The reason for the call was, I was wondering where you're up to with rewriting my will?'

'I haven't started yet. We need to discuss your wishes in

detail.'

'Can we do it now, on the phone?'

'I suppose so, but what's the rush?'

'Nothing, it's just that I read an article about a man who died intestate, and his children got nothing because their step-mother was entitled to everything. As much as I love Patrick, it's essential that I leave as much as possible to Mia and Oliver.'

'There's not something you're holding back from me, is there?' Fiona's voice is edged with concern. 'You're not sick, are you? Really sick?'

'No!' I laugh. 'I've only got flu. It's nothing like that, but I want to get my will sorted. Can you let me know how I should go about setting things up so that Patrick is left enough for his life, but ultimately, everything goes to the children?'

There is a long silence. 'Are you still there?' I ask.

'Yes, yes. I'm sorry, I was just thinking about the best mechanics for setting this up. Do you have any particular sum that you wish to leave to Patrick?'

'Um, no. I haven't thought through the detail. What do you think?'

'It really isn't for me to comment. Why don't you have some further thoughts on that and let me know.'

'Ok. How soon can you draw something up?'

I hear her fingernails clicking on a keyboard and then she sighs. 'I am totally snowed under this week. I could probably get to it by the end of next week.'

I thank her and we say our goodbyes.

I SET my alarm for 3.30 p.m. and return to bed. It isn't my alarm that wakes me, but the slamming of a car door. I sit bolt upright in bed. And then I hear keys in the front door and the beep of the alarm being switched off. I throw on an old jumper and a pair of old jeans and hurry out onto the landing.

'Patrick?' I say.

Footsteps, and then he appears at the bottom of the stairs.

'Oh my God!' I exclaim, my hand rushing to my mouth. 'What's happened?' I rush downstairs, barefoot.

He looks as if he's been caught in a brawl. There is a cut on his forehead, and he has bruising down one cheek.

I reach up to touch his cheek, but he takes a step backwards. 'Sorry. It hurts,' he says, grimacing. 'It probably looks worse than it is.'

'What happened?'

'Had a car accident.'

My heart sinks. Patrick was driving my car.

'I'm sorry, love. It only just happened.' He leans back against the wall, his head resting on a framed antique map, his eyes briefly closed. 'I was driving back from the station.' He opens his eyes and turns away from me. 'I'd got an early train back especially to be here to look after you. Everything was fine, the trains were on time. The car seemed to be driving normally out of Horsham and on the A24, but when I got onto the back road – you know that really tight bend, just after the humpback bridge – well, I braked as normal and nothing fucking happened! The brakes failed. The car ploughed into the hedge.'

'My God,' I say. 'Was anyone else hurt?'

'Nope. Just me.' He turns to face me and takes a step closer. 'When was the car last serviced, Lydia?'

For a moment, I can't think. Is he implying that somehow this was my fault? That's what his tone of voice suggests. 'Um... February. No, it was June. That was the month we bought the car. The business bought it. It's still under warranty. There's no way the brakes would just fail, surely?'

He places his hands on my shoulders. 'That's exactly what I thought. It's a top-of-the-range, quality car. I hate to tell you this, but I think the brakes were tampered with.'

'What!' I shiver.

'It's the only explanation, Lydia. The car was parked by the station, left alone for over twenty-four hours. Anyone could have done something to it.'

'But you parked in the station car park, didn't you? There's bound to be CCTV there.'

He growls, runs his fingers through his hair, and then winces as he touches his sore head. 'That's the frustrating thing. The car park was full, so I had to park it a couple of streets away. I haven't been back to check, obviously, but I doubt there was CCTV.'

'What do the police say?'

'Nothing as of yet. They took a statement; they're organising for the car to be towed. They said they'll check the CCTV.'

'I'm so sorry, Lydia. Your car will be out of action for a while. I can't believe this has happened. Two accidents in such a short time. I've never had an accident before. Never!'

'Don't worry, it's only a car,' I say, grabbing his hand. 'The most important thing is that you're safe.'

'I am. The trouble is, I don't think you are.'

I freeze.

'I think the brakes were tampered with on purpose. Ajay quite probably followed me to the station or he saw the car per chance, and either he played around with the brakes, or he paid someone to do it. Would he be capable of such a thing?'

I shake my head. 'I don't know. He's very mechanically and electrically minded, so probably. But tamper with brakes! He'd be sent to jail for murder for doing something like that.'

'Come on, let's sit down.' Patrick gently pulls me towards the kitchen. 'I need a whiskey, and it looks like you could do with one, too. You're as pale as a sheet.'

'I can't. I need to collect the children from school, and besides, I'm dosed up on Lemsip.'

He pours himself one and makes me a cup of tea. When

we're both sitting at the table, he says, 'If Ajay was snooping around here last night as you suggested, he would have seen my car parked out the front and assumed it was me who was at home. Does your car have a tracker?'

'Yes.' And then it dawns on me. Ajay kept all the details of our company cars: his, mine and a couple of our other senior managers. It was only Adam's Bentley that was considered inappropriate and too expensive to be a company car. My car has a tracker, and of course Ajay has online access to the tracking company. 'He can easily find out where I've parked it.' I shiver again.

'That's what I feared.' Patrick shakes his head in disbelief. 'So he knows it's parked near the station. He knows that I'm safely ensconced here at home with the kids, so he has all night to tamper with the brakes.'

'I can't believe he would do something like that!' I say, but there is no longer any conviction in my voice. 'But why?'

'Darling, I really think that Ajay wants you out of the way. I think he wants you to die.'

'No!' I bury my face in my hands. I do not want to face up to this hypothesis, but the more Patrick moots it, the more probable it seems. If Ajay wants the business, then the easiest way to achieve it is by killing me off. 'What do the police say?' I ask in a whisper.

'Obviously, I've shared my suspicions. They took a statement, and I told them about how Ajay is forcing you to sell your share of the business; about how he's been stalking you. The silent calls and everything that's been happening. The policeman said he'd be liaising with DI Cornish. They'll need to run some tests on the car. I'm so sorry, Lydia,' he says, his head tilted to one side.

'No, I'm sorry,' I croak. 'Your life is in danger and it's all because of me. What the hell are we going to do?'

27

D I Cornish and DC White come to see me the next morning. Unannounced. Patrick has taken the kids to school, in his car of course, and then he had to go to some meeting or other, so I'm alone in the house, feeling just marginally better.

'Sorry, I've got flu,' I say, opening the door to let them in.

'We won't get too close, then.' DI Cornish laughs, but his eyes don't crease and his lips barely rise at the corners. 'Is Mr Grant here?'

'No, he's at work.'

They follow me into the kitchen, where I make them two cups of tea and ferret out a pack of ginger biscuits from the larder. We all sit down at the kitchen table.

'Your husband has suggested that the brakes might have been tampered with on your car.' He emphasises the word *husband*, drawing out the second syllable. I can guess what he's thinking. *Married the next one a bit quickly.*

'Yes. The car is regularly serviced, and what happened makes no sense.'

'Unless, of course, Mr Grant simply lost control on the

bend. It wouldn't be the first accident to happen there and no doubt won't be the last.'

'But he–'

'The advantage of a fancy car such as yours is its onboard computer. We'll know exactly what speed Mr Grant took that corner at as soon as the garage has downloaded all the information. It should also show whether the brakes were indeed tampered with. Mr Grant explained his concerns, but I would be grateful if you could talk me through once again what has led you to file reports of harassment by Mr Arya?'

I shift uncomfortably on the sofa. It feels as if my torso is coated in perspiration, even though it's quite cool in here. I wonder if the fever has come back. I tell them about the clattering noises outside the other night and how I saw Ajay's car driving off, and about the silent calls and how Ajay banged on my door and is trying to get me to sell my share of the business to him. They ask to see his offer letter. Reluctantly, I give it to them.

'You and Mr Grant seem very sure that Mr Arya is behind all of this, but is there anyone else who could hold a grudge against you, or indeed against your deceased husband?'

'No.' I sigh. It seems as if we're about to go over old ground, and it's frustrating me. 'I'm scared. For me and my children. What are you going to do to protect us?'

DC White raises his eyebrows and glances away. DC Cornish stares at me.

'We have allocated as many resources as possible to investigate both Mr Palmer's death and the accusations you have levied against Mr Arya. Perhaps there is some further information that you are withholding from us?'

'No, there isn't!' I say indignantly.

'Just out of interest, when did you and Mr Grant meet for the first time?'

I redden, even though I know I have nothing to hide and

have done absolutely nothing wrong. 'We met via
4everlove.com about three months after Adam died. Our relationship may seem hasty, but please remember that Adam and
I were in the process of divorcing.'

'Yes, so you have said on more than one occasion.'

'Mr Arya claims that Mr Grant is planting ideas in your
head; that he has some bizarre grudge against Mr Arya. What
do you think?'

'No! That's nonsense. Patrick is just trying to protect his
family.'

'Mmm.' DC Cornish doesn't sound convinced.

'So what's next? Have you interviewed Ajay again? When
are you going to arrest him for Adam's death?'

'We have interviewed Mr Arya and we will be doing so
again. Rest assured, we are taking this very seriously. In the
meantime, please call me if you have any further concerns.' He
stands up. DC White follows suit.

After they have left, I can't stop thinking about Ajay.
Whether or not he is guilty of everything we're accusing him of,
he is going to be livid, and that's only going to make our fight
over the business even more difficult. I simply can't see a solution and just pray that the police will get to the bottom of everything, quickly now.

I spend the rest of the morning cleaning the house, tidying
things away and trying to view my home through the eyes of a
stranger. On Saturday, Gail Smithers has organised an open
house. From 10 a.m. until 3 p.m., our home will throw its doors
open to strangers, and anyone who might be interested in
purchasing it has been invited to have a good snoop around. I
hate the concept and tried to persuade Gail that our unique
home was much better suited to individual viewings. She was
having none of it. In her polite but firm way, she told me that
she was the expert in selling expensive houses and that I

should allow her to get on with her job to the best of her abilities. Patrick agreed.

By 2 p.m. I am, once again, exhausted and spend the rest of the afternoon asleep. I'm awakened by Gail calling me.

'Just to let you know that we have had a great deal of interest in your house despite the downturn in the economy. I'm very optimistic for Saturday. My assistant and I will arrive at 9 a.m. to ensure everything is in order, and then I suggest that you and your family make yourselves scarce for the rest of the day.'

'What!' I say, trying to focus. 'Are you saying we've got to go out?'

'Absolutely. There is nothing worse than the owners of the house clipping the wings of prospective buyers. I've seen it time and time again. If for any reason the buyers don't like you, that will get in the way of their liking of the house. And unfortunately, Mrs Palmer, there is a whiff of notoriety about you and your circumstances, for which, of course, you have my deepest condolences, and I would hate to encourage voyeurs and the wrong type of person to the open house. As it stands, I don't see any reason why prospective buyers should know that you are the owner of the property.'

'I suppose that makes sense,' I say, faintly amused by her description of my 'whiff of notoriety'. I can just imagine that nosey parkers would love to have a snoop around my home.

'I suggest you remove any photographs of yourself and your immediate family. Let's have plenty of vases of fresh flowers, and we'll have coffee on the go in the kitchen, which will bring a lovely aroma to the place. Fingers crossed for a fine day.'

THE KIDS ARE unimpressed that they need to get up early on Saturday morning, but Patrick has the day planned out for them. One hundred percent his idea.

At 8 a.m., they are both hunched over their bowls of cereal, still in their dressing gowns.

'We're going to a racing track this morning, and you're both going to be driving a Lamborghini, and then a professional racing driver will take you on a high-speed circuit,' Patrick explains. 'When we're done there, we'll have lunch, and then you can go shopping. If you ask nicely, I'm sure your mum will give you some cash.'

I try not to bristle. Oliver literally bounces off his chair, his fists pumping the air. Mia glances up, a smile twitching at her mouth. I wondered if she would be interested in racing cars, but clearly she is. 'The bad news is, you need to be in our car and ready to go in forty-five minutes. Think you can make it?'

'Yes!' they say in harmony.

I am not so thrilled with the prospect. I am still under the weather, and even if I wasn't, hanging around a racetrack, my heart in my mouth as my kids are driven at high speed, is not my idea of a great day out. My voice sounds relatively normal, but my head feels as if it's stuffed with cardboard and my back aches. Nevertheless, by the time Gail arrives with two of her staff, the house looks as neat as it's ever going to look, and we're ready to leave her to it.

I can't stop thinking about Ajay. Have the police arrested him? What is happening? I've heard nothing from DI Cornish during the past forty-eight hours. I know the team will be doing the best they can, but I have to steel myself to be inundated with work when I return to Cracking Crafts on Monday. Without any of us three directors at work during the past week, I have no doubt that decisions won't have been made and payments withheld.

With my car in the garage or perhaps being examined by the police, I suggest that we take Adam's Bentley. I hand the keys to Patrick and his eyes light up. It's the first time he will have driven it.

'Take it easy,' I say, trying to keep my advice light. 'It's ridiculously powerful and quite hard to keep within the speed limits.' He rolls his eyes at me as he presses the button to open the electric garage door.

I slip into the passenger seat, pushing my basket of handicrafts and my laptop to one side. I don't go anywhere without my project-on-the-go. I keep a bag with my crafting projects in the car and another one in a bag by the back door next to the coat rack. I suppose crafting is as addictive to me as gaming is to Oliver. The kids climb into the back of the car, but Patrick is still in the garage. He bends down into his knees and looks underneath the car.

I open my car door. 'What are you doing?'

He beckons me with his finger and motions for me to get out of the car. 'Just checking there isn't a bomb or any device underneath the Bentley,' he whispers in a low voice.

'What!' I exclaim. And I thought I was paranoid. 'Really?'

'I'm not taking any chances, Lydia,' Patrick says, gently pushing me back towards the passenger door. 'All clear. Let's go.'

I spend most of the day in the car, listening to the radio, doing my knitting and catching up on emails.

About 2.30 p.m. Gail calls me.

'We've had lots of interest in the house, Lydia. Lots of interest. And bear in mind the market conditions are terrible, so I am very optimistic. There were two couples who have booked another viewing for this coming week. I really think that we could be seeing a quick sale.'

'That's great,' I say. 'Can we come home?'

'We'll be done here about 3 p.m. Will you be back in time, or should I lock up?'

'Please lock up and post the key back through the letter box.'

.   .   .

ON SUNDAY MORNING I have a sleep-in, and when I awake, I can tell straight away that the flu has dissipated from my body. It is such a relief. Patrick is in the shower, so I walk downstairs in my dressing gown and am surprised that Mia is already in the kitchen.

'Sleep well?' I ask, yawning.

'Yeah. It was fun yesterday.' She hovers next to the toaster. 'I can't wait to be old enough to drive.'

I open the doors to the big pantry unit and take out my jar of granola, the same breakfast cereal that I eat every morning: a mixture of nuts and oats and dried berries that I make myself. After tipping a decent portion into my bowl, I open the fridge and take out some milk and mixed berries. I make myself a mug of mint tea and sit at the table, switching on BBC News 24 to catch the headlines.

I know within seconds that something is wrong. My throat tightens up and my tongue begins to swell, as if it is much too big for my mouth. I try to stand up, but the dizziness forces me back down again and I miss the chair, collapsing onto the stone floor.

'Mum!' Mia screams, her face contorted with terror.

I try to speak, to tell her to get my EpiPen, but she knows what to do and she knows where we keep it. She rushes to the pull-out drawer to the left of the larder. As my breathing gets tighter, I watch her chuck the contents of the drawer onto the floor.

'Where is it?' she screeches, rifling manically. 'It's not here, Mum! Shit, it's not here!'

'My handbag,' I try to say, but the words don't come out.

'Patrick! Patrick!' Mia screams. 'Where the fuck!' She rushes out of the room and almost instantly returns with my handbag. I don't know how she does it so quickly. She tips the contents out onto the kitchen table. 'No! No!' she says. My world is starting to go black, and I know I need to hang on in there. I must be strong for my children.

'It's not here either,' she says. Her voice is ragged. And then she runs out of the room and I can hear her heavy footsteps. And then blackness and nothing.

'WAKE UP, MUM!' Mia is crouched over me, her face white as snow. 'Please, Mum.' She is crying.

'It's getting better.' I try to talk, but I'm not sure if the words come out properly.

'I couldn't find your EpiPen, Mum. I don't understand. It wasn't in the kitchen or in your handbag, and I thought you had several.'

'I do,' I say, reaching up to hold her. She lies down on the floor next to me, her wet cheek against mine.

'I thought you'd died, Mum. I thought I'd lost you too.' She is crying now, her body shaking with sobs.

'It's all right, darling, I'm all right.' I can feel the swelling reducing, normality returning to my aching body.

I hear footsteps.

'What the hell! Oh my God, Lydia. Mia? What's happened?' Patrick crouches down on the floor next to us.

'Mum had an allergic reaction,' Mia says, pulling away from me. 'I shouted for you, but you didn't come. Why?'

'Sorry, but I was in the shower. I didn't hear anything.'

'You were in the shower for a bloody long time,' she says, pushing herself off the ground. 'She'd have been dead if I hadn't been here.'

'Well, thank God for you, Mia,' Patrick says.

'I couldn't find any of her EpiPens. Not here in the kitchen or in her handbag or in her bedside table. Where the hell are they?'

Patrick raises his hands in a gesture of helplessness. 'So how did you save her, or did she come to by herself?'

'Are you really that bloody ignorant?' Mia snaps. 'She nearly died! It's only because I have an EpiPen that I saved her.'

'Thank goodness you did.' Patrick strokes my forehead. 'How are you feeling, love?'

'Shit, like I normally do after an anaphylactic shock,' I say.

Patrick stands up and reaches for the phone. 'I'm calling for an ambulance.'

'I don't need to–' I say.

'Yes, she does,' Mia interrupts. 'She could get a delayed anaphylactic reaction. The doctor told me about it.'

'We need an ambulance. My wife has had an allergic reaction to something.' He gives our address and confirms that I am able to breathe for now.

'They're sending an ambulance straight away. It's an emergency, apparently.'

'Of course it's a bloody emergency,' Mia says. Her eyes are streaming. 'If I hadn't had my own EpiPen, Mum would be dead!'

THE AMBULANCE ARRIVES within fifteen minutes, by which time I'm feeling almost normal. Even so, Patrick suggests I remain lying on the kitchen floor. He's found a blanket that he's wrapped me in and has made me sip a milky, sugary tea.

The paramedics check me over, but to my disappointment, they insist I go with them to the hospital for a full check-up. So I'm bundled into the back of the ambulance, strapped to various machines.

'I'll follow the ambulance in my car,' Patrick says.

'Can you ring Cassie, get her to look after the kids?' I suggest. And then the doors are slammed shut and we're away. I wish Mia was with me. The look of terror on her face is something I will never forget.

Three hours later, I'm lying on a hard, plastic bed in a small curtained cubicle in Worthing hospital. Patrick is sitting on a grey plastic chair, his foot bouncing up and down. Impatience is coming off him in waves. When a doctor enters, a young man who looks as if he's only a couple of years older than Mia, Patrick is off the chair like a rocket.

'Why does it take so long?' he asks.

'I'm sorry, sir, but we have to see patients in order of the severity of their symptoms.'

'It's fine,' I say.

'I understand you went into anaphylactic shock. Is that correct?'

'Yes, I have a severe peanut allergy.'

'And did you eat peanuts?'

'Not that I'm aware of. I just had my normal breakfast cereal. I make it myself. But I suppose–' I glance at Patrick. From the look on his face, he has already reached the conclusion I am coming to. Quite why it has taken me the best part of three and a half hours to work out what may have happened is beyond me. I normally pride myself on being a quick thinker. Perhaps it's a combination of the flu and the allergic reaction.

The young man gives me a thorough check over and declares me well.

'I assume you'll need a new EpiPen?' he asks.

'We couldn't find mine. They weren't in the places I normally keep them in. Fortunately, my daughter used to be allergic to peanuts, but she seems to have outgrown the allergy. I insist she keeps a pen anyway.'

'Very sensible,' he says. He issues me a prescription for a new EpiPen. And then I'm discharged.

When we've paid for the parking and Patrick is easing the car out of the car park, trying but rather failing to be patient as the elderly drivers in front of us drive at a speed slower than walking, I turn to him.

'Are you thinking what I'm thinking?'

His face looks pained. 'Yes. I think we're going to need to report this to the police. But let's see what's in your granola.'

'Do you think Ajay could have turned up yesterday as part of the open house and put peanuts in my granola?'

'I don't know, Lydia. But I fear that might be exactly what happened. Let's check it out when we get home. Or more like, I'll check it out. I don't want you anywhere near that granola.'

We drive home in silence.

I GO STRAIGHT UPSTAIRS to tell Mia and Oliver that I'm fine.

'Lydia,' Patrick shouts upstairs. I leave Mia's room and stand at the top of the stairs. 'You were right. I've just checked in the kitchen. There are some broken-up peanuts in the granola. I've put everything back into the jar, because we need to give it to the police.'

But when I'm in the bathroom, all alone, collecting my thoughts on the day when I nearly died, something hits me. Ajay might have had the opportunity to put peanuts in my granola jar. Ajay might have had the opportunity to take the EpiPen out of the drawer in the kitchen. But has the EpiPen in my handbag been missing for nearly two weeks? Because yesterday I had my bag with me at the racetrack, and prior to that, Ajay won't have had any access to my bag, as I've had it with me all the time, except two weeks ago, during our last run-in at the office. Has he been planning this all along, or has this been done by someone closer to home?

No. Surely not. Patrick loves me. He was as shocked as we were. It must have been Ajay. Premeditated murder.

28

D I Cornish isn't on duty this weekend, so another couple of detectives pop around. They take statements from both Patrick and me and they remove the jar of granola, putting it in a see-through evidence bag. They promise to be in touch with Worthing hospital to get my medical records.

As much as I haven't warmed to DI Cornish, I still wish he was on duty.

Sunday night, and once again I'm exhausted. We're both in bed. I'm struggling to keep my eyes open whilst Patrick is reading the weekend papers, the crackling noise as he turns each page jolting me awake and setting my teeth on edge. For a man who works with technology, he is surprisingly old-fashioned when it comes to his reading methods. No Kindle or iPad for him. And then suddenly the bedside lights flicker and we're plunged into darkness.

'What's happened?' I ask.

'Must have been a power cut.' I hear him drop the newspaper onto the floor. 'Oh well, let's make the most of it and go to sleep.' He shuffles down the bed and then reaches over for me, pulling me into his arms. I welcome the security of his steady heartbeat and the warmth of his body, and I melt into him. I'm just about drifting off to sleep when there is a massive crash.

'What was that?' I sit up in bed and automatically reach to switch on my light. Nothing happens. My breath is shallow and frantic.

'I don't know.' I hear Patrick fumbling around and then there's another noise. It sounds like something has been dropped on the stone floor. 'Perhaps it's one of the kids gone downstairs for a glass of water?' He switches on the torch on his phone.

'Did you put the alarm on?' I ask.

'No. You told me not to have the alarm on when we're all at home, in case Mia or Oliver go downstairs in the night and forget to switch it off.'

He's right; I did tell him that. He swings his legs out of bed and pulls on his boxer shorts and the shirt he was wearing today, the light from the phone jiggling up and down.

'I'm going down to have a look.'

'No!' I say, clutching the edge of the duvet. 'We need to check the children's rooms first.'

'You're not going anywhere. Stay in bed and I'll have a look in on them.'

I watch as he opens the door, the flickering light throwing ghostly shadows across the walls. My heart is thumping and I shiver underneath the duvet, listening for any more untoward sounds. A few moments later he returns.

'They're both in bed, fast asleep.'

'Oh God,' I murmur. If it wasn't one of the kids, there must be an intruder inside the house. 'I'm calling the police.' I reach for my phone, but I can't find it and knock my alarm clock off my bedside table.

'That's a bit premature, Lydia. Let me go and have a look. It might have been nothing.'

'No! Please don't go. I couldn't bear it if something happened to you.'

'Nothing is going to happen to me,' he says, turning on his heel.

'Please, Patrick! Remember what happened to Adam, and someone tried to kill me this morning!'

'Don't worry. I'm strong. I'll be back in a tick.'

I sit rigid on the bed, straining my ears to listen out for any more unexplained sounds, but I hear nothing. Not even Patrick's footsteps downstairs. I suppose he's walking barefoot. I make silent prayers to God. *Please look after Patrick. I know I was mistaken to suspect him of anything. I love this man. Please keep us all safe.*

A minute later the lights switch on, and the old house creaks back to life. And then Patrick pads back into the bedroom.

'Something must have fused,' he says. 'One of the fuses was switched down in the box, and there's no one in the house. I had a good look outside and I can't see anything. Must be just one of those things.'

'I can't take it,' I say, clutching my side.

He strips his shirt off and gets into bed. His freezing foot touches mine and I shiver melodramatically.

'Chill, Lydia. There's nothing to worry about. I've switched the alarm on downstairs just in case. Try to get some sleep now.'

'I think Ajay is going to kill me.'

'Hey,' he says, pulling me towards him. 'I'm here to look after you. We'll be moving house soon, and everything will be fine.'

I wish I could believe him. But Patrick never saw Adam's body; he never went through the horrors that the kids and I experienced. That terrible, shocking loss. The police should have Ajay in custody, and they should be patrolling outside our house. I want to call DI Cornish, to find out what they're doing about Ajay, but it's now shortly after midnight and I know he's not on duty until tomorrow.

'I'm scared, Patrick.'

'Have you checked out security systems yet?'

'No. I haven't felt up to it.'

'Just as well I have, then,' he says. My neck feels uncomfortable on his muscly arm, but I don't want to pull away. 'I've got a mate who can put a top-of-the-range system in, with night vision and alarm monitoring, top-notch sensors, backup to the cloud, and the whole malarkey, for around fifteen grand.'

'That's a lot of money.'

'Still worth it. We can't put a price on security and safety.'

'But we're likely to be moving soon.'

'Even so, I want to make sure you're safe. This is a big old house, and I'm still going to be away a lot. Sleep on it and let me know what you think tomorrow. We can't rely on the police to look out for us; we'll need to protect ourselves.'

'Ok,' I say reluctantly, shifting my neck so it's off his arm. 'I still can't believe that Ajay would do something so evil. I've known him for years, and I just can't fathom it.'

'People change. They get greedy.' He shifts onto his side away from me. 'What's Marianne like?'

'She used to be brassy, ballsy, a hoot. She married Ajay when she was twenty-three. Over the years she mellowed, became more sophisticated. It's like she reinvented herself, morphing from an unqualified hairdresser from the rough part of town into the posh wife of a successful businessman. I used to like her. She said it as it was, and I thought she was the perfect partner for Ajay.'

'Like you are for me.' Patrick grins.

'She was the homemaker who just let him get on with whatever work he needed to do. And he spoiled her. Over the years, her wardrobe changed from Etam and Dorothy Perkins to Net-A-Porter's finest. She liked to spend Ajay's money, that's for sure. I saw less of her as the years went by. Perhaps just two or three times a year at Cracking Craft's Christmas party, and again in the summer when they used to organise a BBQ for their friends. Occasionally, we'd have them over for dinner, but I think Marianne used to feel a bit left out. After all, she was the only one of us who didn't work in the business.'

'There must have been something alluring about her; otherwise Adam wouldn't have been having an affair with her.'

I harrumph.

'And their marriage, did you get any hint as to what it was like?'

'No. Ajay never said anything, and I didn't see Marianne by herself. I suppose she's the only person who really knows Ajay's state of mind.'

Patrick is silent for a moment, and then he turns on his side to face me. 'I think you should go and talk to her.'

'What! No. I don't want to lay eyes on her ever again.'

'Think about it, Lydia. You want to find out the truth about what Ajay has been up to and what he's planning. Marianne is the only person who'll be able to tell you.'

'I can't talk to her. She was sleeping with Adam.'

'I know. But things have moved on since then.'

'She's hardly going to say, yes, I think my husband killed my lover, is she?'

'Perhaps not, but you will definitely get an insight into her relationship and find out about Ajay's state of mind. She's the only person who might be able to resolve things.'

After a short while, Patrick's breathing slows down, but for me, sleep seems far away.

The more I think about it, the more I realise that Patrick might be right. Marianne is the only one who can help us sort out this mess. She's the very last person I want to see, but it will be worth it if we can get some sort of resolution. And she owes me. Back at Adam's funeral, she was begging me for forgiveness.

Unsurprisingly, once again, I can't sleep. I take a sleeping pill, but two hours later I am wide awake.

'll do it,' I say to Patrick, as I'm wearily clearing away the breakfast things.

He peers at me over the top of the newspaper. 'Really? You'll meet up with Marianne?'

I nod.

'Good decision,' he says. 'The police have come up with nothing. We've waited quite long enough.'

'I think you're right. I've been so angry with her for having an affair with Adam, I've never listened to her side of the story. Adam was no saint, and Marianne wasn't his first affair. But if they really loved each other, then I guess she's hurting, too. She'll know in her heart of hearts if her husband killed her lover. I'm going to look her in the eye and ask her if Ajay killed Adam.'

'She's hardly going to admit it, Lydia. I think that's naïve. You need to come up with some good questions you can ask her.'

'We've got to get a resolution. This situation doesn't just affect me – us!' I wave my hands around. 'It affects everyone who works for me. I'm not sleeping, and it's making me ill. My business is going down the drain, and if that happens, my staff will lose their jobs and we'll lose all of this. This wealth and high standard of living, which you seem to enjoy ever so much!'

I know that last sentence was totally uncalled for; I regret it the moment the words slip from my lips. This is all getting too much for me and I'm taking it out on the people I love the most.

Patrick slams his mug onto the table, and coffee slurps out of it onto the pale blue tablecloth. 'Do not make this about me! I am trying to protect you, Lydia!'

'I'm sorry.' I squeeze my eyes closed.

'Look,' Patrick says. 'I'll help you. I'll take you to the Aryas' house and make sure you're safe. If Ajay is as violent and volatile as we think he is, he could kill you if you step foot in his home. Does he go out anywhere on a regular basis?'

'I'm not sure.' I run my fingers through my hair as I think. 'Actually, yes. He's a member of the local photography club, and they meet up every Tuesday evening. He always had to leave work on time on a Tuesday.'

'Fine. We'll do something tomorrow night and I'm going to help you. I'm not letting you go by yourself. I'll give it some thought, and we can discuss our plans this evening.'

'Thank you,' I say. I walk towards him to give him a kiss on the cheek, but he steps to the side and leaves the room. I hear him shut the front door, and then his car starts up. Patrick has left home without saying goodbye.

IT'S TUESDAY, early evening. We eat supper at 6 p.m., not that I have the appetite to consume chicken breasts, rice and vegetables. Instinctively, I feel that it's the right thing to visit Marianne, but I'm nervous. Twenty years ago, I could probably have anticipated her reaction, but these days, I don't know her. I just hope she will agree to talk to me.

'I'll drive, ok?' Patrick asks. He dangles the Bentley's key in front of me. I've noticed how much he enjoys driving the Bentley, and it makes me smile.

'Ok,' I say as I put on my anorak.

I am zipping up my coat when the telephone rings.

'You get it. I'll start the car,' Patrick says.

I hurry towards the kitchen, knowing there's not a chance of either of the kids answering the landline.

'Hello,' I say, slightly breathless.

'Lydia, it's Fiona. I'm sorry I've been out of touch for a while. Work has been crazy.' From her echoey voice and the fluctuating white noise, I assume she's calling me from the car. 'Anyway, just wanted to let you know that I've got the first draft of your will done. It's an outline, as we haven't discussed the detail, but I was wondering if I could pop over to show it to you?'

'Sure. When were you thinking?'

'In five minutes or so.'

'Um, we're just about to go out.'

'Oh, that's annoying. I'm literally passing your front door in about five minutes. My diary is so jammed I'm not sure I'll be able to see you for another fortnight at least. Are you going to be out for long?'

'About an hour, I suppose.' It will only take us fifteen minutes to get to Marianne and Ajay's house, and I can't imagine I'll spend more than half an hour talking to her. Of course, she might send me packing immediately, which will mean we'll be back within half an hour. 'Why don't you come over anyway,' I suggest. 'The kids are both at home and there's a bottle of wine in the fridge. Help yourself to the television in the living room. I'll tell Mia to let you in.'

'Thanks. I've got work to catch up on, so I won't need the telly. I'll be there shortly and see you soon.' She hangs up before I have time to say any more.

I run upstairs and barge into Mia's room. She looks up from

her laptop and sighs, but she doesn't reprimand me for entering without knocking.

'My friend Fiona is coming around in a few minutes. I'll leave a bottle of wine and a glass in the kitchen for her. Tell her to help herself.'

'What, are you worried I'm going to drink it?'

I don't grant her a response. 'We won't be long. Just finish your work, please.'

I run downstairs, grab a three-quarters-full bottle of white wine from the fridge, and place it next to an empty glass on the kitchen table. I find a packet of crisps and place them next to it. Then I hurry to the front door and close it behind me. It's getting dark outside, and I can see Patrick in the driving seat of the Bentley, his fingers tapping impatiently on the wheel.

'Sorry,' I say as I get into the car, pushing my craft bag to the side of the footwell and placing my handbag on top of it. 'Fiona just rang. She's on her way over, as she's working on a legal document for me.' I bite my lip. That sounds very suspicious, but Patrick doesn't question it. It will be awkward if I admit to him that I am changing my will and leaving the bulk of my estate to my children.

Patrick is driving slowly with both hands gripped tightly around the steering wheel, his forehead creased. He turns left out of our drive onto the dark country lane. We're both quiet for a couple of minutes as he navigates the narrow roads. My heart is beating fast. I'm really unsure about confronting Marianne.

'Right, let's go over exactly what you're going to do,' Patrick says. 'I'll stay in the car out of sight whilst you check if Ajay's car is there. If it isn't, ring on the doorbell. If Ajay answers, run. If Marianne answers, then ask her if Ajay is there. Once you've established that he isn't at home, send me a text message.'

I lean down and rummage in my handbag for my phone. It will be better if I have it in my coat pocket.

'Shit,' I say quietly.

'What's the matter?'

'My phone, it's not in my bag.'

'For God's sake, Lydia! Why the hell haven't you got your phone with you?' He thumps the steering wheel.

'I'm sorry. I thought it was in my bag.' I have another feel around. No. It's definitely not there. How frustrating. I was sure I had left it in my handbag.

'It's so irresponsible not having your phone. You know that Ajay is dangerous. He's tried to poison you, cut the brakes on your car, threatened you at home, undermined you at work by exchanging the Knit It Qwik machine for the NitNakNok–'

I inhale. Loudly.

How the hell does Patrick know the names of the machines? I certainly never told him that detail. But what if...?

I turn my head very quickly to stare at him. Patrick looks away, out of the side window, but his jaw is tight, a nerve pinging, and despite the low light I can see he is abnormally pale. It strikes me, making me breathless. It was Patrick. My husband exchanged the machines. But why? I look at his fingers, which now are gripped so tightly around the steering wheel, they are white.

'What did you do?' I whisper.

He swerves the car to the left, onto a grass verge, underneath a row of beech trees, their bare branches hanging low over the roof. Patrick kills the engine. We both sit for a couple of moments in silence. My heart is beating so hard, it feels like it is going to fly out of my chest. And then the internal car lights go off and we're plunged into darkness. But a car goes past and it catches his face. His pupils are large black orifices and I can sense myself being pulled into them.

'What?' I ask again, but the hoarseness I have only recently lost reappears, making the word sound unintelligible. 'What have you done, Patrick?'

30

I stare at this man who is my husband, who I thought I knew, who declared his love for me over and over.

'Did you pretend to be Ajay? Did you swap the knitting machines over to make me fail?'

It seems ridiculous, petty even. Why would Patrick do that? I pray that he will deny it. That he will laugh and say that my imagination is working overtime, that I am crazy. But he doesn't. Patrick sits there in the darkness, so silently it's as if he isn't breathing.

'Patrick, what's going on?'

And still he doesn't answer, doesn't move a muscle.

'Patrick, what have you done?' This doesn't make any sense. Are Ajay and Patrick working together to undermine me? Did Patrick know Ajay from before? Are they linked somehow?

And then I think about everything else. The car accidents. The silent calls. The noises outside the house. And the peanuts in the granola. Have I been accusing the wrong man all along? Is that why Patrick has been so keen to paint Ajay as the murderer? Is that why the police haven't arrested Ajay: they simply don't have enough solid evidence against him?

'The peanuts in the granola. Was that you?' I ask, utterly horrified, thinking how it was Mia who saved me, how she struggled to find my EpiPen. Does Patrick want me to die? Am I in danger now, not from Marianne or Ajay, but my own husband? The man I have committed to; the man whom I have been sharing a bed with. The man whom I really don't know very well at all.

He turns then, and despite the low light I can make out his face. The hard edges, the narrow eyes and the small, sharp teeth, and despite the familiarity, I don't recognise him. How is that possible? I shift in my seat, edging towards the passenger door, slowly moving my hand to the door handle.

'Say something, Patrick!' My hoarse voice quivers.

I need to get out of the car. Now. None of this makes any sense. Patrick is terrifying me with his silence. I pull down the door handle and throw the door open, hurling myself out of the car.

'Lydia!' he shouts.

I stumble and fall on the grass verge. The internal car light illuminates a patch of earth covered in rotting leaves and the puddles of rainwater from an earlier downpour. A coarse hedge runs alongside the road, and I know what's behind it. Trees. A small copse. There are no houses here. No one will hear me, and the only sound is my scrabbling and panting.

What has Patrick done? Has he set up Ajay, made him the fall guy? But why? My hand comes away muddy and slimy from where I slipped and put my hand down to halt my tumble. I haul myself upright, but I'm wearing leather ankle boots that slip and slide on the sodden earth.

'Wait!'

Patrick is out of the car now. He slams the driver's door closed. I glance over my shoulder. He's striding towards me.

'Patrick, tell me that I've got this all wrong. That you love me. That you didn't do anything bad.'

'Don't move,' he says. His voice is low and menacing. I step backwards and grab the side of the car to get my balance.

I can hear a vehicle approaching now; its headlights bounce through the branches and then it lights up the whole of the car.

'Stop!' I scream. It comes faster and faster towards us, oblivious to my terror. Patrick is just one stride away from me, but the headlights of the approaching car pick up something in Patrick's hand. It glints and shimmers as he holds it out in front of him.

A knife.

And then the car has gone and the light disappears, leaving us again in the dank, cold darkness. I shove my hand into my pocket, my fingers gripping the small can. I pull it out just as Patrick takes another step.

'Please don't hurt me!'

I can only see two things. The gleam of his eyes and the flash of the blade.

'No!' I shout as I press my index finger down hard on the nozzle of the can, spraying it straight into Patrick's face.

He screams in pain as he staggers, bent over, unseeing. He's moving towards me, but I dart out of his way.

'Patrick!'

'I'm going to kill you!' he roars. But he trips, and it's obvious that he's blinded and disoriented. The pain must be unimaginable, but even so, it's as if there's a magnet between us, guiding him towards me. 'You're as miserly as your bastard husband!'

What the hell is Patrick talking about? Did he know Adam? My stomach spasms as the thought hits me.

Did Patrick kill Adam?

I dart to the other side of the car and pull the driver's door open, hurling myself inside and slamming the door shut. I press the central door-locking button and feel a sense of relief as I hear the click. He's left the key fob in the central console, but the car seat is much too far back for me to reach the pedals, so I have to fumble with the seat memory button to bring it forwards. The car shakes as Patrick throws his bulk against it.

My finger slips as I start the car. *Come on! Come on!* This is such an expensive car, it must start. It always starts. I can see his shadow on the driver's side of the car.

There's a massive crash. The whole car shakes, and then there's the sound of splintered glass and I freeze, waiting to be speared by sharp fragments of glass. But no. The front driver's window has imploded just millimeters from me, but the glass doesn't cut. I thought the windows of a car like this were unbreakable.

No!

Patrick's head is through the hole of the window, his eyes raw red and tears pouring down his cheeks. He is lunging towards me.

'Go away!' I cry. 'Why? Why are you doing this?'

This man who is supposed to love me is an animal. He's going to kill me unless I kill him first. I lean over as far as I can, towards the passenger footwell, and grab one of the knitting needles poking out of the top of my craft bag.

'You don't deserve any of it. None of you do!'

His words make no sense to me, but in that split second, I know what I have to do. I swing my arm towards him with the sharp end of the knitting needle pointing towards him and plunge it straight into his left eye.

Patrick screams. A noise that I have never heard before. A primal scream of such agony and horror I know that if I survive this, I will hear it in my head for the rest of my life. He tumbles away from the car, blood pouring from his eye, dark crimson all over his hands, and with another roar, he disappears from view. I reach out of the broken window for him, this man who just minutes ago was my husband, the person I thought I loved, but my hands are just covered in slippery redness.

I have to go. I have to leave him.

I release the handbrake and put my foot hard down on the accelerator. The car spins slightly as it pulls away from the muddy bank at speed. There's a turning just here on the left, but not to a house. It's just a track into a field, used by the local farmer. I swing the car around and manage to get it back onto the road without doing a three-point turn. The car is beeping at me, telling me to put on my seatbelt. But I haven't got time. I'm two, perhaps three, minutes from home. I need to go home. Call the police. Get help. I pass Patrick, a heap on the ground. My husband.

Was all of this planned? I can't make sense of it, and for a moment I wonder if I have it all wrong. Did I just attack my husband for no reason? Will I be going to prison for grievous bodily harm, or murder? Oh my God! Have I just killed Patrick? I need to call an ambulance and the police.

And then I remember his words. *I'm going to kill you!* And I know that it was him or me. How is it possible to have so many thoughts rush through my head in such a short time? Patrick, the man who I thought loved me, has done all of this. Created this terror, this horror. But why? How could I have got it all so wrong?

The headlights are on and I press my right foot hard onto the accelerator. I am shaking so much, the world outside is bouncing up and down. All I can think of is Mia and Oliver. They need me. I can't die. My job is to protect my babies. I've got to get home now.

I'm not sure that I have ever driven so fast, not on these small, narrow, winding country roads.

And as I throw the wheel to the right, the tyres screeching as I skid into our driveway, I have never been so relieved to hear the little splinters of gravel throw up against the sides of the car. Home. I'm home.

The lights are all on upstairs and downstairs.

And thank God! Fiona is here. I slam the brakes on, throw

the car door open and run like I've never run before to the front door.

'Call the police!' I shout as I hammer the door with the palms of my hands. I stare at the marks I'm leaving on the wooden door. Blood prints. I look down at my front, and the light from the porch shows my navy anorak gleaming with a viscous fluid, and I think I'm going to throw up. Is that my blood or Patrick's? Have I just left my husband to die at the side of the road?

'Open up!' I scream.

And then I sob. How can I let Mia and Oliver see me like this? It is too much for them to bear; I thank heavens that Fiona is here. Sensible Fiona will know exactly what to do.

31

The front door flings open.

She stands there totally frozen, her eyes so wide, her mouth a perfect O. I watch as the blood drains from her face, and, as if in slow motion, her hand moves from hanging at her side to covering her mouth. The look of shock on Fiona's face is so profound, it would be comedic if these were different circumstances.

'What's happened?' she whispers.

'He tried to kill me.'

'Who?'

'Patrick. My husband! He tried to kill me. He wants me dead and I don't know why!' I start sobbing now.

Fiona continues to stand in my doorway as if she's glued to the floor, unable to move. Why isn't she saying anything? I am shaking like a leaf, but Fiona is a statue.

'We need to call the police. An ambulance, too. I think I killed him. I stabbed him in the eye.' My voice cracks. I look at my hands, stained with blood. And still Fiona doesn't move.

'What?' she gasps.

'We need to call the police!' I squeeze past her and hurry towards the kitchen, my feet leaving muddy footprints behind me. She follows then, with heavy footsteps. I look at my beautiful designer kitchen, so picture-book perfect. How can so much horror have happened in this house? To me? To us? It simply doesn't make sense. I reach the phone, pick it up.

'No!' Fiona screams.

I swivel to stare at her.

'L-let me do it!' she stammers, grabbing the phone from my shaking hand. 'Sit down. Now!'

'Why?' She isn't making sense. We need help now.

I put my arm out to take the phone back off her, but she turns to face me, her lips thin and tight. 'Just do it! I need time to think!'

'You? Why do you need to think? We have to call the police! Now!'

Fiona is shaking her head vigorously, as if she's trying to shake off an insistent fly. 'I know what I'm doing,' she says. Her voice is deeper than normal, but it's the look in her eyes that frightens me. As if she knows something that I don't. As if the horror that has just unfolded is her horror, not mine.

'You're bleeding,' she says, pointing at my hand.

Fiona is right. My hand is cut, yet I don't know how that happened. I don't feel any pain. The agony is in my heart.

'I'm going to tend to your wounds, and then we'll call an ambulance. The police.'

With the phone firmly clutched in her right hand, she grabs one of my kitchen chairs.

'Sit,' she says.

'But we need to call them now.' My voice cracks, and the sheer terror of what has just happened makes my knees give way. I crumple onto the chair she pulls out for me. Her eyes are darting backwards and forwards, as if the danger is here.

'He's dead,' I say again quietly. 'Or if he's not dead, he must be blind.'

'No!' Fiona's voice pierces my head. She swivels quickly, and, chucking the phone onto the granite workshop, she lunges for a knife.

And then it hits me. Fiona isn't taking the knife to protect us, she's going to use it. On me. Why do we keep knife blocks out on kitchen surfaces? It's as if we're saying to strangers, *Come and help yourself. Take one of my knives. Kill me with it. It's fine, I'll make it easy for you.*

'What are you doing?' I cower away from her.

She takes a step towards me. I don't recognise this woman. Her eyes are pale, icy blue and her teeth are bared. 'All of this money. This obscene wealth. It isn't yours! It belongs to Patrick, you bitch!'

'What?'

The carving knife is just centimetres from my face now.

'Everything belongs to Patrick. He is Adam's brother! I can't believe you never worked that out.'

She laughs then, a bitter, cruel-edged laugh more like the cackle of a hyena. 'We wondered if you'd ever notice the similarities between Adam and Patrick. But you didn't, did you? Too self-absorbed.' She waves the knife again, just millimetres from my face. 'They say people go for the same type, and you fell hook, line and sinker. You made it so easy for us, Lydia. Your desperation for a bit of attention; flattery from a good-looking man.'

'I don't understand,' I say.

'Patrick is Adam's half-brother.'

'But Adam didn't have any siblings.'

'Patrick and Adam have the same father. The bastard of a man who cast Patrick and his mother aside. The result of an affair that ruined the poor woman's life. He refused to recognise

Patrick during his lifetime, but Patrick thought that when he died, his father would leave him half of his estate. But no. Patrick got nothing. It all went to Adam, and you. Patrick asked Adam to share his inheritance, but Adam told him to go to hell. And you. We tried to come up with ways to avoid you having to die, but you're just as greedy and entitled as Adam, flouncing around in your fancy cars, living it up in this mansion, screwing people over in business. What do you know about poverty and deprivation? We quickly realised that you have to die, too.'

My brain seems to have slowed down, and I'm finding it hard to follow what she's saying. Is it really possible that Patrick was Adam's half-brother? Then I think of those strange letters I found that Adam wrote to his father, and it's beginning to make sense. But I must keep her talking. The longer she talks, the more likely I am to distract her and to make it out of here alive.

'What have you got to do with Patrick?' I don't understand how Fiona knows all of this. Was she the solicitor to one or all of them? And why does she want to harm me?

'Patrick is the love of my life.' Her voice softens as she says this. She glances away and I wonder if now is my moment. If I can jump up and wrestle the knife from her hand. But that fleeting millisecond is already over.

'Did you really think he loved you?' she mocks. 'He used you, Lydia. Patrick and I are lovers. Soulmates. We have been for years.'

'He targeted me for my money?' My voice is small. 'He went to all of this just for money? Are you saying he never loved me?' My throat feels as if it's closing up, just as it did when I went into anaphylactic shock, and I wonder if it's happening all over again. 'But why didn't Patrick just ask me for the money? I would have given it to him if I knew he was Adam's brother.'

'No, you wouldn't,' Fiona sneers. 'You are just like Adam. You would never have handed over half your wealth to a stranger. We know your type. And then, when you started going on about changing your will, we knew we had to act quickly. You were about to cut Patrick out, just as Adam and their father did.'

'My will,' I murmur. 'But you were going to change it for me.'

Fiona smiles and my stomach clenches. I realise then that it was all a charade. 'You're not really a solicitor, are you?'

'Clever, clever girl,' she mocks, waving the knife again. 'You should have died from the peanut allergy. But lucky Lydia got away with it again. You have a lot to thank your daughter for.'

'My children! What have you done to Mia and Oliver?' Blood roars through my head. Has this evil woman hurt my kids?

'You don't need to worry about them. They're safely upstairs. I'm sure pathetic Cassie will look after them when you're gone. All the same, it's a pity that they'll be orphaned at such a young age.'

'Did Patrick kill Adam?' I need to know. I need to know before I die, so that I can make a silent apology to Ajay.

'Of course he did. Adam deserved to die. He was so heartless towards Patrick. And he made it easy for us. Ajay was our perfect fall guy. How wonderful that his wife was sleeping with your husband. Everything was set up so it looked as if Ajay was to blame. The cut brakes on your car; a similar car to his on your driveway; the silent calls. The fear you had of Ajay was laughable. You really are so very easy to manipulate, Lydia.'

'But the police will work out that you and Patrick killed Adam and then killed me.'

'No, they won't. We had it all planned out. You and Patrick were on your way to Ajay's house and I was here as Patrick's alibi.' And then she moans. 'What have you done, Lydia? You've killed the love of my life!'

Fiona sobs now, as if the realisation that her plan has failed has at last sunk in. But rather than crumbling, she seems more resolved. Anger makes her nostrils flare and her eyes narrow.

She stands above me, her legs planted wide, and lifts the knife high into the air.

'You've stolen my love. I want revenge. Lydia Palmer, I want you dead!'

32

I refuse to die. I refuse to let this woman leave my children as orphans. What Patrick and Fiona have plotted is unfathomable, and there are so many strands that don't make any sense to me, but right now, I can concentrate on just one thing.

Survival.

I make a slight movement as if I'm going to stand up, but she comes closer, the blade of the knife nicking the skin on the side of my neck.

'You'll be jailed for life, Fiona. This is crazy. Let's talk it through.'

'Shut up! Put your hands on top of your head.'

I do as she says. The pupils in her eyes are little pinpricks. She's holding the knife's handle with both hands, and to my dismay, it's not even wavering.

'Please don't kill me here,' I beg. 'Please don't let the children find me here in their kitchen. They've already lost their father. Please!'

She laughs again. That spine-chilling cackle. And then the most horrific thought hits me. Was she lying when she said the children were upstairs? Are they even alive? Has she butchered them?

She pushes the tip of the blade a little further into my neck and I gasp. It stings and I can feel droplets of blood dripping down my neck.

'Get up!' I do as she says, slowly.

'Take one step forwards and keep your hands on top of your head.'

She kicks the chair away and now I can feel the blade in the back of my neck. 'Walk forwards, slowly. The slightest move out of line, I will stab this knife into your jugular and leave you to bleed out on your kitchen floor. Understood?'

'Yes,' I say under my breath. I walk very slowly, one gentle step at a time. Where is she taking me? I try to glance from side to side, looking at my kitchen, the navy-blue painted island unit, the cream cupboards, the warm oak beams. This house that I thought would protect my little family. I pray. *Please God, look after Mia and Oliver. Protect them. Please.*

'Stand still,' she says when I am one step away from the back door.

I think of all of those crime programmes on television. *Keep them talking. Keep them talking.* But my brain is empty. What the hell should I say?

'Did your husband really die?' I ask, after what seems like a chasm of time.

'The only man who will ever be my husband is Patrick.'

'And his sister, Sandra.'

'There is no sister!'

'But he repaid me the money!'

'This was all planned, Lydia. We gained your trust, and you believed what you wanted to believe. The ring on your finger.'

'What about it?'

'It's cubic zirconia. You don't think we'd waste good money on a bloody diamond, do you? The same for those earrings. But he shouldn't have taken you to Le Goût de L'époque. That was our special restaurant.'

'The wedding?'

'A sham. It was legal all right. It had to be; otherwise Patrick can't inherit your obscene wealth, the money that should have been his.'

'And Graham, the witness at our wedding?'

'A not-very-good actor, from what I heard.'

'But Patrick took me to his flat. There was nothing there to suggest you live together.'

'That's not our flat! If only. It was an Airbnb. Patrick and I live together in Crawley. We have done for years. You have no idea how much I have sacrificed to allow him to gain what is rightfully his. I did that because I love him.' Her voice is choked with emotion, and for one ridiculous second I feel pity for her. How difficult it must have been for her to watch me with Patrick.

'Can you imagine what it's like to know that your soulmate is sharing a bed with someone you hate? I knew he was sacrificing himself for us both, pretending to find you attractive.'

'No!' I say. 'You can't fake that. You can't!'

I am not sure who is shaking more. Me or her. Although I can accept it was largely an act, there was undoubtedly an attraction between Patrick and me. Surely that's something you just can't pretend? But now I feel a stomach-curdling disgust. I have been used and abused in the basest way.

She pushes me, her hand hard on my back, and I stumble forwards, my right knee slamming into our pale limestone floor. I know that she is going to plunge the knife into my back now that I am on the ground. Despite the searing pain in my knee, I need to haul myself back up. But there is an almighty crashing sound.

Someone else is here.

A scream. Not me.

Fiona collapses onto the stone floor next to me, her skull making a cracking noise as her head bounces backwards. The knife flies out of her hand and clatters, skidding under the table.

'Mum!' Mia screams, over and over again. 'Mum! Mum!'

She is holding my Le Creuset saucepan, the cast-iron blue one with a long handle that I left on the hob after supper.

'It's ok, Mia. It's ok!' My voice trembles as I scramble under the table and grab the knife. Ignoring the pain in my knee, I race to the back door, bolting it shut just in case Patrick comes back.

Mia is sobbing and shaking violently. I need to take control. I lift the heavy saucepan out of her hands and place it on the counter.

'Darling, are you all right?' I grasp her, but she is staring at the blood on my hands and down my front.

'What's happened?' she stutters.

'Oliver. Is he ok?'

'I think he's in his room.'

She looks so young and fragile, my daughter, shivering, her arms hanging loosely by her sides, her fringe almost hiding her eyes. I want to scoop her up, apologise for being such a terrible mother, for failing to protect her. But we need help. Now.

I seize the phone.

And then there is the most terrifying bang, followed by a roar. It sounds as if a grizzly bear has slammed through the front door, sending everything in its path flying, and is now getting nearer and nearer. Mia freezes. I grab her and pull her behind me.

I grasp the phone in my left hand and snatch the knife from the counter where I placed it. I hold both behind my back.

Footsteps thud along the hallway. The internal kitchen door is kicked wide open and Patrick crashes in.

'Where are you, bitch!' Patrick screams. He staggers towards me, blood pouring down his cheek, wildly waving a knife so much larger and more vicious than my kitchen knife. He must have pulled the knitting needle out, because little remains of his eye. My stomach lurches as I look at his disfigured face.

I shove the phone into Mia's hands. She needs to get out of here and call the police. We are standing between the stove and the island unit. If Mia runs the long way around the island, she can dodge Patrick, who is moving closer and closer to me.

'Run, Mia!' I say. 'Run upstairs and lock the door!'

'No, Mum!'

'Go! Go now!' I shout at her, and the terror in my voice spurs her to move, skidding around the side of the island unit and darting behind Patrick just as he turns to face her. As her footsteps thump up the stairs, he turns back towards me.

'Where is Fiona?' Patrick is waving the knife from side to side. His shoulders are hunched forwards, and his chin juts out.

I don't answer. She is crumpled on the floor just a metre behind me. He might be blind in his left eye, but surely he will see her with his right eye. I need to talk to him, to distract him. It goes against every instinct, but I take a step towards Patrick, holding the knife behind my back.

'Did you love me, even just a little bit?' I ask. I have to know.

'What has love got to do with it? I'm only taking what is rightfully mine.'

He lunges towards me, shoving the knife forwards, but I am quicker than him and dart to the left, sticking out my right leg. He topples towards me, and with both hands, I hold the kitchen knife out in front of me, plunging it with all my strength into his stomach as he lurches forwards. I'm shocked how easily it goes in. He collapses to the floor, right next to Fiona. For a moment, I stand there, utterly horrified at what I have done. And then, unthinking, I lean down and pull the knife out again. Patrick lets out a guttural, terrible howl. Blood is seeping through his shirt and puddling underneath him.

'Help me!' he whispers. But it is as if I am frozen. All I can do is stand there and watch in horror as the blood pours from his body, creating an ever-increasing pool of sticky redness on the kitchen floor.

I hear the sirens, as if they are coming from a place far away. When the blue flashing lights strobe through the kitchen windows, I still feel as if I'm detached, watching a horror movie unfurl in my home.

They surround me then, these unfamiliar faces, crowding our home once again.

They take me to the living room. Oliver is there, still in his school uniform, his face the colour of our white walls. And Mia, my brave girl, has her arms around her brother, her childhood dissipated in the space of the last thirty minutes.

We sob all together. Then DI Cornish arrives and confirms what I intuitively already know. Patrick is dead. Fiona is still alive and has been rushed to hospital with a major head injury.

33

FOUR MONTHS LATER

This time last year, Mia talked about having a big sixteenth birthday party. Adam promised her a disco with the best DJ in town, a marquee in the garden, a night to remember.

But that was last year.

Instead Mia, Oliver, Cassie and I go to Brighton and eat fish and chips in newspaper, and big whirls of candy floss, and when it rains, we hold our faces up to embrace the heavy droplets and dance along the promenade. We take a ride up the tall observation tower, and although we thought we'd see nothing, the clouds part and the sun rays shine through, glittering on the choppy, grey English Channel.

Cassie buys Mia a leather bag with tassels from a little shop in The Lanes and then whispers something in her ear. Mia turns to me and asks if she could have her hair cut short like Cassie's, and coloured perhaps? And I can't say no.

Now we're back at home, knee-deep in packing boxes. Everything is labelled and ready. It's our last night here. Tomorrow, we're moving to a new house in Guildford. It's smaller and modern; an easy house, within walking distance of the town.

Mia and Oliver are going to another school despite the fact that Mia is midway through her GCSEs. We are all having a fresh start.

I don't think Ajay will ever entirely forgive me, and why should he? I sold my shares in the business to him. It seemed like the right thing to do. He upped the share price and offered for me to stay on as a non-executive director. I declined the offer. The kids and I have more than enough money; I never need work again. But I will. I've got plans to give a lot of it away.

'Right, I think we're done,' Mia says, interrupting my thoughts. She's scraping bits of sellotape off the knees of her skinny jeans. A popping noise makes me jump. Blood is sucked from my face, and I have to grab onto the pile of boxes to stop myself from fainting.

Cassie walks into the living room, holding a bottle of champagne.

'It's ok, Mum,' Mia says, squeezing my hand.

Cassie notices my pale face. 'Sorry,' she says. 'Didn't mean to frighten you. I kept this out and four glasses. I know they're too young to drink, but still...'

I take several slow deep breaths and smile. Mia, Oliver and I are all seeing a therapist; individually for now, and perhaps all together a few months down the line. It's helping. Every day, I think a little bit less about what happened: how clever Fiona was in befriending Cassie first and then me; how my desperate need for love made me a sitting duck for a man as devious as Patrick; how easy it was to set up innocent Ajay as the fall guy; and how Adam's father set all of this in action by denying the existence of his illegitimate son.

And then there's me. I don't think I'll ever date again, not seriously, anyway. Having been taken in by such consummate actors, I doubt I will ever truly trust again. But I have the children. I have Cassie. I have a new future ahead, and that should be enough.

'Oliver, come and join us,' I shout upstairs.

He clatters down the stairs. Cassie pours a finger measure of champagne into a glass and hands it to him. She pours a bit more into a glass for Mia. She and I have such full glasses, we have to sip from the rims.

'A toast,' she says, holding up her glass. 'To a much happier future and joy in your new home!'

We all take a sip.

'Ergh,' Oliver says, holding his glass out in front of him as if it's contaminated. 'It's gross.'

'More for me, then.' Mia grabs it and pours the remaining champagne into her own glass.

We sit on the floor, our backs against the bare walls.

'How are the plans for the charity coming along?' Cassie asks.

'Good. I've pulled together a brochure, and I've found us a small office in Guildford. I think it's on my bed, if you want to see it.'

'Yes, I would,' Cassie says.

'I'll get it for you, Mum.' Mia leaps up. All of her adolescent sulkiness has dissipated. It breaks my heart that she's had to grow up so quickly.

'Can I go and finish packing?' Oliver asks.

I smile. His room was finished hours ago, with the exception of his iPad. I don't mind him going off to play games.

'Have you decided yet?' Cassie asks in a low voice when she's sure both the kids are out of hearing distance.

'Yes. I'm not going to do it.'

She nods. 'The right decision.'

It was DI Cornish's idea. 'We could organise DNA testing on a biological sample from Patrick Grant that is being held by the coroner. It will let us know whether Patrick really was Adam's half-brother. What do you think?' he asked.

I told him I would mull it over. And I have. I don't need to know. Patrick was an evil man, whether or not he was related to Adam. I'm not sure that anyone would want to know that one of their relatives was a murderer, and I can't see how knowing whether Patrick was a real relative, by blood or not, would make any difference to my children's lives. I need them to heal, to restore their faith in humanity. And I have no desire to give Fiona any reason to justify the horrific actions she and Patrick took. Sometimes, I think that I want her to rot in prison for the rest of her life; other times, I feel pity for her.

For my part, I have set up a charity for the victims of internet and dating fraud. We've only been going for two months and already have had exposure in the national press. Dating fraudsters come in many different guises, and I want to be there both to educate people and to pick up the pieces for those who get conned. I know I'm one of the lucky ones. I don't need to worry where the next meal is going to come from or how to pay the heating bill, but I want to be there to support people who have been ripped off for everything they own.

Cassie walks slowly into the room. She's reading my brochure. She has tears in her eyes.

'I didn't think you'd make it so personal.'

'It's my story, Cass. It'll resonate with other people.'

She reads it out loud:

I expect you're like me. You think that it will never happen to you. You might be older or younger, richer or poorer; it doesn't make any difference. You could be male or female or gender neutral. None of that matters in the slightest. You probably think that you're sensible, cynical maybe, that you would spot a fraudster a mile away. Who in their right mind would ever lend or give money without financial guarantees in place? Not you. Not me.

But you see, I was like you. I was looking for love, for another chance. To see out the rest of my years in quiet companionship. I had a heart and I wanted to share it. And that's all it took. Once you become a target, once they unearth your vulnerability, your ability to love, they attach themselves to you with limpet ferocity. They will never quit taking what is yours. Not until they bleed you dry.

And how do you stop them? I don't know. I want to believe the world is full of good people, but there are some bad ones, and they contaminate our earth with their evil. I don't want you to become cynical, to be looking over your shoulder for the rest of your life. I want you to open your heart to love without fear. But to open your heart is to take the risk it will be broken. Please take that risk. Be careful but not cynical. And if in the unlikely event things go wrong, we are here for you.

With love,
Lydia

——————————————

If you enjoyed *Roses Are Red*, then Miranda's bestselling psychological thriller *You Are Mine* is right up your street, a chilling and intense story about love and obsession.

GET IT HERE!

A LETTER FROM MIRANDA

Dear Reader,

A huge thanks for reading *Roses Are Red*.

I'm dedicating this book to my mother. She will never read these words because she only likes happy books (her view is that there are enough scary things in the world without having to read about them in fiction!). She is the linchpin of our family, the most caring and strongest person I know. Thirty years ago, she told me I should be a writer. It's frustrating but true when they say your mother is always right! I wonder if our daughter agrees...

Thank you to Cyril Mills, Becca McCauley and my father for their specialist advice. All mistakes are mine alone. And huge thanks to Brian Lynch, Garret Ryan and the team at Inkubator Books. I am truly lucky to be published by such a forward thinking and supportive publisher.

Lastly but most importantly, thank *you* for reading my books. Without you and the reviews left on Amazon and GoodReads, I wouldn't be living my dream life as a full-time author. For that I can't thank you enough. Reviews help other people discover my novels, so if you could spend a moment writing an honest review, no matter how short it is, I would be massively grateful.

With thanks and warmest wishes,

Miranda

Leave a Review

www.mirandarijks.com

ALSO BY MIRANDA RIJKS

I WANT YOU GONE

(A Psychological Thriller)

DESERVE TO DIE

(A Psychological Thriller)

YOU ARE MINE

(A Psychological Thriller)

FATAL FORTUNE

(Book 1 in the Dr Pippa Durrant Mystery Series)

FATAL FLOWERS

(Book 2 in the Dr Pippa Durrant Mystery Series)

FATAL FINALE

(Book 3 in the Dr Pippa Durrant Mystery Series)

Published by Inkubator Books
www.inkubatorbooks.com

Printed by Amazon Italia Logistica S.r.l.
Torrazza Piemonte (TO), Italy